LIGHT
YEARS

Also by Tom McDonough
Virgin with Child

LIGHT
YEARS

Tom McDonough

Grove Press · *New York*

Published by Grove Press, Inc.
920 Broadway
New York, N.Y. 10010

"Tender Is the Light" (in shorter form), "Gunga Duke and the Temple of Zoom" (in shorter form), "The Wolfman Falls in Love" (under the title "Dancing in the Dark") and "Dem Ol' Talkin' Cinematography Blues" (in different form) previously appeared in *American Film*. "The Gentlest Object Imaginable" (in shorter form) previously appeared in *The Movies*.

Grateful acknowledgement is made to Farrar, Straus and Giroux, Inc. for permission to reprint the following copyrighted material: excerpts from *A Man with a Camera* by Nestor Almendros, English translation © 1984 by Farrar, Straus and Giroux, Inc.; and excerpts from *An Outside Chance* by Thomas McGuane, © 1980 by Thomas McGuane.

Grateful acknowledgement is made to the University of California Press for permission to reprint copyrighted material from *Masters of Light* by Dennis Schaefer and Larry Salvato, © 1986 by Dennis Schaefer and Larry Salvato.

The author thanks the National Endowment for the Arts for its support.

Library of Congress Cataloging-in-Publication Data

McDonough, Tom.
Light years.

1. McDonough, Tom. 2.Cinematographers—United States—Biography. 3.Cinematography. I.Title.
TR849.M393A3   1987   778.5'3'0924   [B]   87-17677
ISBN 0-8021-0014-7

Designed by Paul Chevannes

Manufactured in the United States of America

First Edition 1987

10   9   8   7   6   5   4   3   2   1

For Wendy Ewald, Art Feiner,
and Lynn Schnurnberger,
who mean what they see.

Contents

Lens Job,
an Introduction

Your body is an instrument, an organ or a drum . . . Moooompitcher yaah!

—Nathanael West, *The Dream Life of Balso Snell*

Some years ago, while shooting a commercial in L.A., I made a pilgrimage to F. Scott Fitzgerald's last apartment on North Hayworth. The stucco was nostalgically peeling. The current occupant was too busy conducting a lawn sale to show me around, but from what I could see, Fitzgerald had a splendid view of the Hollywood hills.

It was here that he played out his last years, awed and humiliated by the manufacture of American fun. To the end, cranking out unsuccessful screenplays, he cultivated an attitude of great expectations and romantic disgruntlement toward the industry. "It was like visiting a great turbulent family," he wrote of the film crew that appears briefly in

Tender Is the Night. "They were a people of bravery and industry; they were risen to a position of prominence in a nation that for a decade had wanted only to be entertained."

It's still dumfounding, this triumph of California craft over High Seriousness. What movies mainly do is warp the shape and time of things-in-the-world. Since they do this in a way that we regard as realistic—photo-representationally, narratively—we are soothed by the distortion. The movie's most profound power is their power to make us feel ecstatically smaller than what we see, to share in their bigness so that we feel heroically adjusted to our place in the scale of things. It's a religious effect—what the good sisters used to call "pagan awe." Cinematography, the actual making of moving images, is the basic tool of this magic. As with other forms of idolatry, the point most often fudged is mortality.

Gregg Toland, who shot *Citizen Kane,* knew all about the voodoo of his trade. And because he also knew that when you're talking technique you're probably not communicating, he assured Orson Welles that anyone could be taught the mechanics of cinematography in a few hours. This is rhetorically true: you can learn to drive a car by studying a motor vehicle bureau manual. The issue of course is not how cameras work, but how Gregg Toland works.

Happily, movie workers tend to be a garrulous lot, like ballplayers. Between takes, they are the sharpest, most judicious spectators I know—instinctive Deconstructionalists. With the help of my friend and fellow cameraman Ted Churchill, I've been able to spend time on big-budget film sets without the handicap of being branded a writer. Writers working on celebrity profiles have to negotiate their way past the many *monsignori* clustered around the Pope. With Teddy, I was just "Duke," one of the guys hanging around the grip truck. In my old neighborhood, the nickname Duke was used as a tip of the hat, a pat on the back, now and then a sly twist of the arm, as in "How 'bout taking out the garbage once in a while, Duke?" The cameraman's instinct is to watch, to serve, to come in an expert second. Duke seems an appropriate *nom de camera*.

The character of Teddy in this book is neither Ted Churchill nor me, but a third entity—a composite character, the way Duke is a character. Ted himself, the genuine article, remains the techiest of technicians and unabashedly human. His persistence in searching for the soul of his machines inspired this book.

Me, I grew up in the medieval fifties: First I wanted to be St. Francis Xavier, then I wanted to be Walt Disney, then Carl Furillo, then Fats Domino, then Scott Fitzgerald, then François Truffaut. As it turned out, my "career" in camerawork has mostly been like playing stickball and getting paid for it. Perhaps "Irish cameraman," like "Italian warrior," while not entirely a contradiction in terms, falls short of a state-of-the-art definition of the trade. Like the Italian soldier who loves gold braid but whose notion of the heroic does not, sensibly, include getting shot at, I'd most times rather be doing something else—something marginally useful and monkishly detached, like gardening or fishing or manuscript illumination. Or writing. The kind of movies I like to shoot are extremely small potatoes, more like writing than mainline cinematography.

I suspect that everybody who works in movies, from the stars to the grips to the go-fers to borderline cases like me, goes into the business because we *must* get our fingerprints up there on the screen. Movies touch us; we have to touch them back. Many times, in this stardom-by-association, it's hard to take being human seriously. We feel like accessories, bit players in somebody else's dream. As in a dream, it's unclear who or what is actually in control. You wake, forgetful and frantic for more dream-employment. You realize that very little of what you go through to make a picture gets on the screen. You've erased some of yourself. Waiting for the phone to ring, there comes a moment when your ambitious camera goes blind and the world, with its warty, roughcut density, feels unpicturably private. Because moviemaking is not a dream, it's work, a boogie-down type of thing. And there is very little privacy in it. Privacy, though, remains part of us—even, or especially, in the case of technicians and conjurers.

My subject is not behind-the-scenes peekaboo, but interior life. Rather than thinking of literary models in arranging these stories (writing about movies tends to be teacherly or hysterical), I thought instead about the crucial something that cinematographers call "contrast ratio"—the relative intensity of the brightest and darkest images on the screen. How cleverly a cameraman works this range is the first measure of his artistry.

There are two, maybe three contrasting kinds of stories here. I don't have categories for them; in any case, I've tried to vary the ratios of light to dark, of surface to interior, from one topic to the next, from shooting in India to flyfishing in Maine to doping in the Andes to groping my way through darkest Hollywood. Some are quick cuts, some contemplative. Mostly they're about the way that incessant watching-for-pay shapes the man: the strangest thing is that every facet of everything the cinematographer sees, like lines of poetry read on a plane descending unsteadily toward LAX, looks alive on purpose.

This book is a "reader": See Teddy Shoot, See Duke Run. Everyone except John Milton, who reportedly could read classical Greek at the age of four, seems to have done a certain amount of living before learning to read. Since TV, we learn precociously to watch before we see. With the effort of living, we become rich, broke, exalted, exhausted, loved and unloved. We may be small, and life is certainly large. But as a wise old gaffer once said, we're here to see everything there is to see and beg our living from a world we'll never quite know by heart.

Fitzgerald's apartment, of course, has long since been condoed. Pix to follow.

LIGHT
YEARS

The Wolfman Falls in Love

"Oh yeah, I just got back from L.A., too, Duke. Met these Steadicam operators at a convention. Aviator glasses. Thighs as thick as my waist. Animals. This one guy must do seventy-five miles an hour getting out of bed without coffee. He looks like a member of the Dallas Police Department. My nightmare is the Steadicam Olympics and I'm going out of the gate against this guy. But what do they think when they look at me? Skinny guy, kind of arty. The issue is charisma, Duke. Sure. In the end, we all know it's brute strength, humping this thing around."

Grand Central Station, lower level. Tonight Teddy Churchill was working on *Falling in Love*, starring Meryl Streep and Robert De Niro.

Down in the bowels of Track 115, we crossed a ladder-bridge, *Raiders of the Lost Ark* style, over discarded snacks and pails of rat poison. You didn't want to look too hard at those tracks. On the platform: hampers stuffed with cables, scrims, tripods, light stands—heavy hardware folded two-dimensionally waiting to create the effect of a third. Grand Central Station, the most eloquent and romantic crowd container in American architecture, makes a great set.

The assistant directors waved 150 extras into the train. "Some of you people know each other," a bullhorn barked. "Strike up a conversation with the person next to you. Not too many smiles." A calico tomcat skulked along the tracks, ogling the intruders with wild eyes.

The prop department started the smoke machines. There was no reason for smoke in a contemporary railroad station, but the effect, inherited from sentimental departure scenes from days gone by, remains a staple of the cinematic vocabulary. Peter Suchitsky, the director of photography, arranged for a banner of red light across the top of the train; otherwise the shot would look black-and-white. Peter was careful and cosmetically sophisticated about his work. He wore a silk scarf at all times, inside or out, an insignia of stylish insouciance.

Streep and De Niro materialized like exotic birds. The shot called for them to make eye contact in the midst of commuter chaos. Teddy walked in front of them with his Steadicam as they got off the train, backed up the stairs, glided through a level spot, up more stairs, snaked around a column, through a doorway, and out into the hall. De Niro played it up, strutting like a star. Teddy panted.

The crew decamped to the next location, outside Rizzoli's bookstore on 57th Street. It was nearly summer, but the scene was supposed to take place at Christmastime, so the leaves of tubbed trees were bandaged in black. There was a tropical balminess in the twilight.

I perused a pink copy of the daily call sheet, the shopping list of personnel and material needed for each scene. Here were a few of the items required to shoot two blocks of midtown Manhattan:

Atmosphere & stand-ins: 300 background—report @ 8 P.M.
Winter wardrobe, all with shopping bags, 50 with cars.
Special Equipment: 1—40′ scissor lift, 1—70′ cherry picker,
1—100′ cherry picker, 1—Titan Crane.

The Titan Crane, a giant seesaw used to boom the camera
to a height of four stories, came with a driver big enough to
clear most barrooms.

"Who's on the crane tonight?" Teddy asked. "Genghis? Is
that Genghis Fabulous?"

Genghis Fabulous looked genetically engineered to operate
a Titan Crane. In his off hours, he was a regular on a late-night
cable show in which he played a gorilla named Flash Pan.
Genghis's only complaint was that his low-budget gorilla
costume got hot under the lights, causing him to sweat
through its eyeholes. "Lovely evening," he said gently.

Teddy introduced me to another burly man by the camera. "This is my friend Duke."

"Douche?" Horsehead said. Horsehead was the only applicant ever to ace the electrician's test which, according to
him, consisted of razoring perfectly straight lines of cocaine,
instead of the wiggly ones other crafts permit. He looked
like a badly eroded Elvis.

The International Alliance of Theatrical and Stage Engi-
neers is the oldest and heavy-dutiest film union, and it has
perfected the neighborhood schoolyard style, a cigar-strewn
working-class consciousness. Still lots of fathers and sons in
the membership. Not nepotism exactly, but clannishness, a
higher cronyism, with its observances of code and its expertise with equipment that tends to be intimidating because it
is bulky, like its jockeys, and forever on the verge of ob-
solescence, also like them. They were the kind of guys who
played gladiatorial softball well into their fifties, who knew
how to lean on the fender of a '49 Ford, and knew how to
spit rhetorically, which Horsehead did now, narrowly missing a chubby go-fer.

The crew lit Streep's stand-in in Rizzoli's (doubles save the stars' bones in stunts; stand-ins save their time during long lighting setups). Outside, Teddy, Genghis, and I perched on the stoop along with Horsehead, who was trying to recall the names of all Seven Dwarfs. "Sleepy, Grumpy, Dopey, Happy . . . what two are missing? Bashful and Doc! I didn't say Bashful and Doc, did I?"

Genghis propped his feet on a camp chair labeled "Special Guest" and reminisced about *The Cotton Club,* one of the longest jobs he'd done. "Well, it had a few submachine guns, but not enough for a gangster movie. It had a little dancing, but not enough for a musical. It had a little love, but not enough for a sex movie." Genghis attributed the decline in Coppola's work to a syndrome he called "Dago Monumentalism."

"Yeah, the Commies got us by the balls," Horsehead agreed. "They're the ones that's pushing the coke." He annotated this non sequitur by honking and looking around for something to slime.

"He's focused on infinity," Teddy whispered.

De Niro and Streep rehearsed a scene in which their Christmas presents get mixed up. Streep flirted luminously. De Niro, hair slicked back, did Cary Grant turns with the shopping bags. For eight takes, their smiles were die-press identical. In the midst of all the machinery, the stars radiated a modest, practiced humanity—precisely the right pitch for film acting, a craft which, rather like short-story writing, calls for keeping your gestures more refined than your surroundings.

Midnight lunch break. Genghis glared at the chicken gumbo: "What the fuck is this—Alpo?" A hundred and fifty crew members and extras jamming the sidewalk and the catering service just ran out of forks. "I don't get a fork," Horsehead advised a go-fer, "I don't eat. I don't eat, I'm on double time." Two hundred forks flew in.

We carried cups of egg drop soup back to the camera truck. The night chilled. Teddy changed into his long johns.

"Talk about hardware!" Genghis said.

"I want them to see what they're paying for. I just wish the producer had as much respect for me as I have for Velcro; I'm an artist."

Miner's headlamp strapped to his brow, Teddy began to fuss with his wireless transmitter; he had it in pieces on the table in the back of the truck and was going through the ritual of mechanical crisis and high-pressure repair, voltmeter wiggling, soldering iron aglow. "Let's see, everything must be grounded to this thing—right? This is a full duplex headset; you know, like a weightless walkie-talkie. Nice idea, only it's a total piece of shit. Okay, so let's plug it in. Then watch for the blue flash, as I fudge my shorts." He spit on the soldering iron and hummed in tune to its sizzling. "The thing is, I never wanted to be this kind of guy. My father used to solder his ham set. One day I went down to the basement. I knew the iron was hot, but I had to touch it. Burned the shit out of myself. So I'm a little shy."

Teddy seized my arm. "But oh, the machines, Duke! The machines!" He gestured at the racks crammed with lenses and accessories. "Gosh, wouldn't you like to own some of this stuff for yourself?"

"Sure would," Horsehead said. He showed Teddy some new tricks: how to throw the Panahead (a geared camera mount) into neutral so you could fling it through a fast arc in order to track, say, a speeding car. There was an intelligence visible in the sheen of the mute machines, the kind of thing you notice in collectors' shotguns or in certain sculpture.

Between a cameraman and his camera there develops a Roy Rogers-and-Trigger relationship. Cameras, like other machines that shoot, are simpleminded; it's the refinements and elegance of design that are coveted, jealously guarded.

"Panaflex, Panaglide, Panafade, Panastar . . . Pana-this, Pana-that," Horsehead was saying. "Panavision is thinking of suing Panama. Did I tell you about the Panaflex that got stolen from General Camera? They found it in an icebox in the Meadowlands with a dead canary in the lens port."

Teddy snapped a Polaroid of Horsehead wearing the barney (a sort of camera cozy) on his head. He labeled it "Pana-Conehead." Then me. "Closer, Duke. Lower your head. Lean on something and relax. Good. Now you look like Voltaire."

Horsehead's brother Ponyhead arrived on the set. Pony-head asked Horsehead how many hours overtime he'd logged tonight. With his right foot, Horsehead tapped three times on the snack table.

Against the lights, black and patternlike on his battle horse, loomed the gigantic figure of Genghis Fabulous.

Tender Is the Light

My Aaton is so quiet, I can shoot in a confessional booth.

—Albert Maysles, testimonial for
Aaton cameras.

We used to call it "altarboying." For many boys in my neighborhood, it was our first job. It didn't pay anything, but it was a job. It took training, discipline, a knack for mumbo-jumbo, a certain amount of style, the coy sort of exhibitionism favored by working-class kids, the ability to take pleasure in numbing rituals and a fascination with exotic equipment whose origins and functions were often obscure.

When I got a little older, I became a cameraman. How is a cameraman like an altarboy? He knows the ritual responses, he knows how to carry heavy candles that weep light, he knows how to pay attention; he knows he's there to add to the look of things. And he acquires an inside knowledge of how the sacred is staged.

LESSON ONE:

Lighting

First thing, turn out all the lights in the room. Go sit in front of the mirror. Take your flashlight. Hold it at heart-level, aim it straight up, toward your face. Switch it on. What movie are you in?

Frankenstein, right. Or *Bride of Frankenstein*.

Now take your flashlight and hold it directly over your head, aimed down. What movie are you in?

The Godfather. Very good.

Light a cigarette, blow a lot of smoke around. Hold the flashlight behind your head, aimed forward. (This is kind of a stretch; you may need an assistant.) What movie are you in now?

Casablanca, *Close Encounters of the Third Kind*, or *Alien*. Excellent.

Hold the flashlight at arm's length, aim in at your eyes. Don't blink.

You got it. The evening news. Or *Dallas*.

LESSON TWO:

Fictioneering and Film Envy:
the Pete Zavras Principle

Then, somewhat older but unalterably an altar boy, I became a writer. How is a cameraman like a writer?

One of the mysteries, forever to be unsolved, in F. Scott

Fitzgerald's unfinished Hollywood novel, *The Last Tycoon*, is a character named Pete Zavras. Zavras is a studio cameraman whose rivals have spread the slander that he is going blind, with the result that he hasn't worked in a year. In despair he tries to kill himself by jumping off the balcony of a studio building, but succeeds only in breaking his arm. Monroe Stahr, Fitzgerald's protagonist and the studio chief, hears about this, and arranges for a doctor to certify Zavras's eyesight. In his notes for the *The Last Tycoon*, Fitzgerald suggests that a grateful Pete Zavras will come to the rescue of Monroe Stahr, betrayed in the end by false love, labor goons, and treacherous business associates.

I'm not enough of a Fitzgerald scholar to know which real-life cameraman Pete Zavras might have been modeled on, the way Monroe Stahr was drawn from Irving Thalberg. But as to how Zavras felt when he tossed himself off the balcony, that's not so mysterious. He felt, I think, something like Fitzgerald himself toward the end of his Hollywood days—wounded by fame and gossip, fretful about making a living, helpless and half serious about ending it all. (It was only a second-story balcony Zavras jumped from.) Still, in what Fitzgerald left of his book, Pete Zavras is his hero's only loyal friend. The cameraman was Fitzgerald's last fictional hope. Odd choice.

The mystery about cameramen is, quite simply, what do they do? Why does Meryl Streep go out of her way to thank Nestor Almendros, her cinematographer in *Sophie's Choice* and *Heartburn,* so profusely? Does Streep need help looking gorgeous? What is the magic angle? Why is Pete Zavras the only reliable soul in Fitzgerald's Hollywood?

The mystery about photography, and especially cinematography, is whodunit—the cameraman or the camera? Or the subject? The answer is elusive not just because movies have always been a congenial home for the collaborative imagination, but because they have absconded with rational discourse, not to mention narrative, and cinematography is implicated in the crime.

In an early draft of *Tender Is the Night,* Fitzgerald concocted Francis Melarky, an expatriate cinematographer who happened, like his creator, to be idling on the Riviera:

> More than anything in the world he wanted to make pictures. He knew exactly what it was like to carry a picture in his head as a director did and it seemed to him infinitely romantic. Watching, he felt simply enormous promise, an unrolling of infinite possibilities in himself.

Fitzgerald, a celebrated man of letters marooned in the movies, sensed the mystique of cinematography. It was Zavras/Melarky, he came to suspect, who controlled the green light at the end of Daisy's dock.

One gropes for comparisons to demystify the title "Director of Photography." Captain? Maître d'? Bird colonel?

If Fitzgerald spent any time on the sound stages, he must have observed that in the combination war game, orgy, traveling commodities exchange and storm-tossed ship of fools that is a major motion picture in production, the cameraman is the captain. He doesn't own the ship, he doesn't decide its destination, but his word is law.

Each film craft has its own MO. Temperaments range from gracious Mr. Goodwrench to cigar-chomping, mud-wrestling fetishists whose most articulate utterance is the scuffing of their knuckles on the ground as they scamper toward the catering truck. Sound men tend to be high school science nerds triumphant; assistant directors are head waiters, rude and tender by turns; script clerks, frantically keeping track of takes and continuity, are solemn standup comics whose shtick is solid geometry; wardrobe mistresses are fluttery bridesmaids, their veils hysterically speckled with cigarette ashes. Editors are temperamental chefs, slaving over a hot Steenbeck, whipping ingredients around.

And the cameraman*—in this generic Central Casting sense—the cameraman is a cowboy with a self-image somewhere between Shane, Evel Knievel, and Lord Jim: around the world seven and a half times by the time he's thirty, flaunting his traveler's sense of privileged purpose; a roman candle conversationalist, his anecdotes having acquired a high glaze in the course of camping alongside camels and Eskimos; a motel prankster fond of hazardous jokes and equipment flexing, palsy-walsy with the production assistant who's marketing Drano-grade cocaine; a barroom buddy in scallop-toed boots, earringed like a pirate, vested like a bandito; a devout abuser of his own body, addicted to risk, equipped with the self-adjusting recklessness of chronic boyhood . . .

A scholar of drunken diagrams on Holiday Inn tablecloths, a fatigue ecstatic, hair sweat-pasted to his scalp, twenty straight hours on his feet at triple time, ever the nimble minister to excitable machinery; a bored mercenary, veteran of glamorous escapes, stomach quilted with shrapnel scars from the Beirut Hilton bombing, multiple marriages calamatied by incessant travel and deserts of idleness and unexpected squalls of extra money squandered on conspicuous perishables; he is an individualist, yet heir to Hollywood's Brass Age of Moron Romanticism—showboat Yids, throbbing Wops, crooning Micks, shuffling Spades, squinty Chinks, curly-daggered Wogs of all descriptions—the New World of immigrant dreams all done up in the color of nightclub kisses. What a guy.

Cameraman psychology may be slightly northeast of nor-

---

* The word is still, with very few exceptions, camera*man*. Sandy Sissel, a top camerawoman, happened one day to be shooting a news story with a black male correspondent. A cop ordered the correspondent to "get that broad with the camera" out of the way. "You don't call him a nigger," said Sandy, holding her ground. "How come you call me a broad?"

mal. Still, whose dreams are in good taste? And years from
now, when our standards of disgrace are revised . . .

> The trouble is, I want things to be inter-
> esting.
>
> —Teddy Churchill

Teddy Churchill, cameraman and author of the riotously
candid *Steadicam Manual of Style,* lives alone with an im-
pressive inventory of media equipment he's constantly
customizing—a flange here, a lens shade there—a collection
sacred to him but to civilians perhaps a little absurd, like
rare stamps.

We were driving uptown to the Panavision-sponsored film
tech seminar. A blue rubber shark jiggled on the dashboard.
We munched bagels.

"Remember in *The Seventh Seal?*" Teddy asked. "The
Magician says to Death, 'Nothing escapes you,' and Death
says, 'No *one* escapes me.'" Teddy is a connoisseur of morbid breakfast conversation.

He was scheduled to demonstrate his Steadicam—a camera stabilizing device—at the seminar, and he was in a snit
because the new data-base program he'd just bought for his
IBM personal computer was not compatible with the old
version, or at least he couldn't figure it out. "Plus I just
woke up out of a sex dream," he said, skittering between
stage fright and luscious memory.

Teddy and I started out together as documentary cameramen who brought our rookie expectations to the film
business in the sixties, when hand-held cameras were as
much in vogue as acoustic guitars and stood for the same
things: spontaneity, blue-eyed soul. Teddy was one of the
cameramen on *Woodstock.* He and the film business em-
braced Steadicam at about the same time; he became one of
half a dozen or so cameramen in the world able to exploit

the machine's potential for camera moves of balletic intri-
cacy. He went from aging flower child to specialist in the
Big Time. In the past five years he's worked on dozens of
features and countless commercials.

We unloaded the Steadicam equipment at the Holiday Inn
on 57th Street. The heaviest piece was Teddy's bag of pro-
motional brochures. He dumped his equipment backstage,
loose change and spare parts clinking in his personal bag.

The corridors smelled of anonymous motel sweat. Backstage, the equipment to be discussed at the seminar was
spread out like an enormous model train layout: Loumacrane, Optimax, Tyler Mounts, Hustlers, PeeWees, Panastar,
Panaflex, Panafade . . . hero products all, triggering toy
memories of steam locomotives chugging into small town
stations, the Industrial Revolution raw and incarnate, chugging itself to smithereens—only smoothly now, shim-
meringly, hinting of the joystick future.

A middle-aged man named Carl, from Dennison, Iowa, was
keeping an eye on Panavision's hardware. Of the French
Loumacrane, which came in six carryable cases and rigged out
to the dimensions of a whaler's mast, he commented, "A
couple of farm boys with a junk pile could do just as fine."

Teddy turned pop-eyed to a troublesome connector cable.
"This thing is definitely going to be history. Actually I'm
surprised I'm still enthusiastic about it. But I've been into
fantasies all my life. Adventure and money—you can't argue
with that."

His battery chargers hummed, his enthusiasm accelerated.
He lifted a Panaflex out of its case. The camera body sat in
notched foam rubber, but the way he cradled it, altar-
boyishly, it might have been a liturgical instrument accustomed to nesting in red velvet.

"A real cream job," he said. "Machined by the best mechanics on the globe. Next to fighter aircraft, let me tell you,
Duke—supersmooth. Look at this milling. They're not

really complicated machines, movie cameras—just gears, pull-down claws—but they have to do what they do right every time, or you're in deep shit."

"Hi, I'm Harry Matthias. You see arrayed around you a quantity of technology." Harry, bearded and crisply tailored in a double-breasted suit, is a cameraman who lectures and writes about the latest tech. He skipped to the blackboard with the merriness of a man who'd just invented bubbles.

"Hi-speed cameras," he began. "In the 120 frames-per-second-and-under category, the Arriflex. Photosonic instrumentation cameras run to 3,000 fps. 120 fps is not fast enough for a *Bonnie and Clyde* type explosion. What frame rate you use for a running panther depends on the lens and the size of the animal in the frame. Panthers in captivity are flabby; ripples of fat are not appealing. The last panther I shot looked good at 120 fps. Coins falling in closeup, you go higher."

Harry had them now.

"There's been a subtle change. Remote control led to everything. A large part of the cameraman's expertise these days is fine-tuning cameras. Like helicopter pilots wonder if the rotor blades are balanced right before taking off. With the Loumacrane and the Skycam, the cameraman can achieve positions and attitudes in space where the human body could not be. . . ."

The seminar turned to Tyler mounts and the hazards of helicopter shooting. I recalled a night eight years ago in Pismo Beach, long before the *Twilight Zone* chopper crash. Eighteen passes over the moonless dunes, the gung-ho pilot backing into treacherous tailwinds . . .

"It's a dirty trick kind of race," said Teddy. "A rubber underwear kind of deal."

A helicopter cameraman, on crutches, pulled himself to his feet. "I've buried a lot of my friends," he testified.

Harry gnawed his lips and sighed. "You can't be too careful."

Teddy, wearing a Steadicam vest that made him look like an extra in *Spartacus*, walked on. His glasses frames were red. His pipestem was mended with red masking tape.

"Steadicam . . ." Harry narrated. ". . . figuring the focus on the fly . . ."

Teddy swooped between the first two rows of spectators, did his Wolfman walk, illustrating the assaultive school of cinematography.

"We assume that the discovery is the machine," Harry was saying. "But we have to invent ways to operate it. Thank you, Teddy."

LESSON THREE:

The Unspeakable Desire to See

Ah, the cameraman—prince of the inscrutable alchemic clan. What tales he could tell if only he could speak!

In nearly a century of film history, less than a handful of cameramen have written books with an autobiographical cast. One is Nestor Almendros. Another is Billy Bitzer, D. W. Griffith's cameraman and, for all practical purposes, the first director of photography. It is almost as if, in addition to the vow of invisibility cinematographers share with Thomas Pynchon, they must take, along with J. D. Salinger, a vow of silence. There will probably never be a Montaigne of cinematography; it is too frenzied a profession.

There are many fine books by non-writers: baseball players, opera singers, perhaps too many by fly-fishermen. In the realm of cinematography, there is Leonard Maltin's *The Art of the Cinematographer* (1971), a compilation of interviews, mostly with old masters like Hal Mohr and Lucien Ballard. The tone is folkloric, curmudgeonly. And there have been, to be sure, several how-to books by cameramen; Freddy Young's *The Work of the Motion Picture Cameraman* (1972) is the most comprehensive, though somewhat outdated. Aside from a picture of himself shaking hands with the Queen of England and some stern advice about keeping in shape and being careful not to catch colds, Young offers nothing at all about what he might have been feeling during fifty years of shooting major films.

It's easier, of course, to talk about the mechanics of the piano than about the music. And what kind of opinion, after all, is one supposed to have about eight zillion bucks? There's something about lots of money and machines that silences grown men, then incites them to play. The technical chauvinism of the entertainment industry—that and the secret stage mother in all of us—keeps us from saying anything smart about the machinery.

You're mute, of course, when the camera's rolling, and strangely deaf: concentrating so intensely on the image, in that connect-the-dots way, drains your ability to hear. You are literally seeing the world through a glass, darkly. It doesn't much matter what the actors are saying; you have too many other things to pay attention to—how many degrees of arc is that hat from the clock, will the nagging cramp in your thumb (arthritis at such a tender age?) cripple the smoothness of your zoom?

Shooting a movie is like . . . is like . . . well, try watching TV standing up. Put on some comfortable clothes and the snazziest running shoes you can buy; turn the TV on, stand there and watch it. For six to eight hours. You may smoke if you like or sip coffee or chat with a friend, but you can't sit down and you can't take your eyes off the screen. The concentration is ferocious; you have abdicated a good part of your consciousness—your human sense of things, perhaps not all that serene under the best of circumstances—to the machine. Where things are and what they look like—but *exactly,* to the millimeter, to less than a blink's worth of light—that's all you care about. What these things mean is somebody else's headache. What you know is the nausea of professionalism, the dutiful alertness. If you think entropy is just another one of God's remote gags, try it.

> He wanted actually to live *inside* the light
> that captured his eye.
>
> —Mark Helprin, *Winter's Tale*

By 1940, nearly twenty years had passed since Billy Bitzer had worked as a director of photography. Intimidated by changing film technology and disheartened by the mess a busy career had made of his family life, he semi-retired, living off his investments and puttering in the film archives of the Museum of Modern Art, where he restored antique cameras and began to write, in block letters on lined paper, the story of his life in the movies. Bitzer's death in 1944, like Griffith's four years later, was scarcely noticed by the film community.

Even allowing for the superior vitality of old-time heroes, *Billy Bitzer, His Story,* now out of print, reads like *Ragtime,* stunning in its simplicity and biblical forthrightness. Here is his straight-faced description of an epically complicated shot in *Intolerance*:

> The reason we had to have the camera dolly was that the balloon, which we tried first, did not work. I had to get the entire set in view—a real bird's-eye view—from the air, then zoom downward gradually to the dancing Virgins of the Sacred Fires on the steps, then zoom into the big banquet hall, for many yards, and finally pinpoint a little toy chariot, drawn by two white turtledoves, as it moved across the floor with a love letter from Belshazzar to the Princess Beloved.

As for Bitzer's sense of himself as an artist:

> I have heard many things about my work which are flattering, but which I was unaware of until I read them in print. When

they said of my early photography, "Bitzer was an artist, he followed no accepted school of lighting, neither the German nor French, yet his effects were remarkable," or something along that line, I hied myself to the Metropolitan Museum and asked one of the doormen to direct me to the French school. He finally understood me, even if I didn't know much about art. Of course I did know that the paintings with faces coming out of deep shadows were Rembrandts.

Perhaps because he never imagined he would see his book in print, Bitzer allowed himself some personal touches:

> Although I had my work and all the money I needed, I was past forty and childless, except for the pathetic woman I called wife, who was worse off than me. What I had filled my life with was endless hours of concentrated work. All I thought of really was my camera. How fondly I regarded it can only be realized by some other camera-fiend. I kept it in the pink of condition at all times, never retiring for a night without running my fingers lovingly over it, looking for some real or imagined defect. My sole concern was that lovable/ugly camera, the Pathé. To take it from me would have hastened my demise.

In the early twenties, when the darkly authoritative Bell & Howell camera appeared along with German cinematographers and their cunning Expressionist shadows, Bitzer came to be ashamed of showing up on the set with his frowsy old Pathé, and drifted away from shooting.

> I have always tried to avoid the folklore of
> my profession.
>   —Nestor Almendros

The most emblematic thing about Nestor Almendros's life is how frequently he's gone into exile. Born in 1930, he grew up in Spain and Cuba and studied cinematography in Italy, countries accustomed to major military interruptions. He smuggled an experimental film out of Cuba and its agit-prop film bureaucracy. He moved to Paris, where he lived down and out till he was adopted by the *nouvelle vague*. He lived in New York during the early sixties and made friends with experimental filmmakers. He washed dishes in Hollywood, taught Spanish at Vassar.

What line of work best suits a superbly talented film exile? Nestor Almendros became our most cosmopolitan cameraman, literate in movies, art history, and print. He became the cinematographer of choice for Eric Rohmer and François Truffaut. He shot *Days of Heaven,* that splendid coffee table movie, and won an Academy Award. Today he is one of the handful of cameramen able to choose the scripts he shoots. He jets from a megabuck *Still of the Night* to an underbudgeted *Pauline at the Beach.*

Since the late fifties, when Almendros wrote film criticism for a revolutionary Cuban newspaper, he has been consistently generous to interviewers and professional journals. His book, *Man with a Camera,* in fact, grew out of his responses to queries about his technique on certain films.

Almendros's message, refined by his knowledge of art and film history, is clarity, simplicity, elegance—a less-is-more philosophy counter to the intuitions of his hard-boiled contemporaries, shocking even.

In my opinion the main qualities a director of photography needs are a plastic sensitivity and a solid cultural background. So-called "cinematographic technique" is only of secondary importance, and depends above all on one's assistants. Many cinematographers take refuge in technique. Once a few basic rules have been learned, the job is not very complicated. . . .

When it comes to lighting, one of my basic principles is that the light source must be justified. . . . I try to make sure that my light is logical rather than aesthetic. . . . In a studio set I

imagine that the sun is shining from a certain point outside,
and I decide how the light would come through the windows. The rest is easy.

Easy for *you*, Señor. In an industry dominated by exhibi-
tionist bullies whose products are hewn mostly with blunt
instruments, Almendros's light is *tender*.

Almendros does not, despite Truffaut's high priest introduction to *Man with a Camera*, set out to forge on the smithy of
his soul the uncreated conscience of cinematography. For the
most part, his book is straightforward testimony about famous
stuff, written in the lucid, spartan style that is the hallmark of
the author's lighting. His account of shooting *The Valley* (for
Barbet Schroeder in 1971) is plaintively impersonal.

> The camerawork was nothing more than being there to record
> it. . . . For three and a half months we lived in huts of palm
> and bamboo, sharing the natives' lives. It was without a doubt
> one of the most exciting and enriching adventures of my career.

End of chapter. Next case.

Most times, it seems, the cameraman must be passive and
self-effacing to the point of emotional extinction. But there
remains, for the cameraman as for the audience, the thrill of
escape into romance with a sexy accomplice. "It is a grateful
medium," Almendros reminds us. "Everything tends to seem
prettier through the lens."

Although photography refuses to be put in its place, movies
still shuffle their feet in the presence of prose—of literature,
if you will. One needs money, the other respect. More than
once, they have managed to find the whore in one another.

It is tempting to measure Almendros's *Sophie* against
Styron's, but it is beside the point. What can be compared is
their rhetoric, their "voice." Styron writes that Yetta Zimmerman's boardinghouse was ". . . unrelievedly pink . . . from

the tender *rosé* of fresh lox to a more aggressive bubblegum coral, but everywhere there was pink, pink admitting rivalry from no other color. . . ." Styron's pink starts on a black-and-white page and insinuates itself in the mind through allusion: bubblegum, babies, Barricini candy boxes. Taste-o-vision.

Fortunately for Meryl Streep's complexion, Mrs. Zimmerman did not paint her house blue, or worse, green. Pink light, like Styron's prose, is lush, sweet, forgiving; it fills in the wrinkles. The blue-green end of the spectrum casts a clinical pallor and does grim things to your zits. In the concentration camp sequences of *Sophie's Choice*, Almendros favors the blue side of the spectrum, rendering Streep as close to ghastly as a madonna can get.

Sophie's Choice, the movie, displaces Stingo's adoring narrative voice with Almendros's *Mona Lisa* medium close-ups of Meryl Streep. It's a film about the problems of a face. For much of the movie, Streep is a talking head, though not disembodied; that's the trick. Light, as Roland Barthes has observed, is a carnal medium, a skin you share with anyone whose picture has ever been taken. Subtract Almendros's cinematography and you have a mere madonna, reluctantly corporeal, basking in the movie star's absentee narcissism. Yet Streep never loses her angelic edge, her radiance. We sense the house around her like an aura. How can you but adore a madonna so pinkly pictured?

LESSON FOUR:

The Quest for a Truthful Car Shot

> We worked very hard to make it look very simple.
> —Gordon Willis, of *Zelig*

In *Sophie's Choice*, cinematography and middlebrow prose wrestle to a draw—though the film, to Almendros's and

Pakula's credit, is less cluttered with Stingo/Styron's American fascination with "facts." Almendros's *Sophie* is superior best-seller cinematography, perfectly synchronous with the learnedly horny, diffuse, and essentially simplistic spirit of the book.

But somewhere there ought to be, I'd like to think, along with Fitzgerald in his younger and more vulnerable days, a cinematographer whose skill—whose style and narrative sense—is a match for Ernest Hemingway's. Here is Papa's description of Jake Barnes and Lady Brett Ashley going for a taxi ride through the streets of Paris at night:

> The taxi went up the hill, passed the lighted square, then on into the dark, still climbing, then levelled out onto a dark street behind St. Etienne du Mont, went smoothly down the asphalt, passed the trees and the standing bus at the Place de la Contrescarpe, then turned onto the cobbles of the Rue Mouffetard. There were lighted bars and late open shops on each side of the street. We were sitting apart and we jolted close together going down the old street. Brett's hat was off. Her head was back. I saw her face in the lights from the open shops, then it was dark, then I saw her face clearly as we came out on the Avenue des Gobelins. The street was torn up and men were working on the car-tracks by the light of acetylene flares. Brett's face was white and the long line of her neck showed in the bright light of the flares. The street was dark again and I kissed her.

Hemingway gets his effect in 177 words, inscribed with a cameraman's ultrakeen sense of the obvious.

Cinematographically, the scene is a nighttime two-shot in the back of a traveling cab. It would probably cost, exclusive of actors' salaries, at least $5,000. This shot is something you see all the time in movies. For cinematographers it is a set piece, as the Virgin with Child was for fifteenth-century painters. Its parameters are commonly understood in the profession, like "the Kiss" in a closeup or "the Wave

Goodbye" in a wideshot. It is a shot of almost punishing banality, a shot that tests the cinematographer's ingenuity and commitment to verisimilitude.

The odd thing about this shot is that it is almost never done realistically. Cars and movies are about the same age, and nighttime is older. You'd think cinematographers would have doped it all out by now. We arrive instead at an instructive impasse in American naturalism.

The simplest way to light the scene is to rig a low-wattage light on the dashboard or the hood and aim in at the actors. The trouble with this is then you have actors lit with a steady light from a direction where the light has no business coming from. What's going on? Are they being miraculously illuminated by the glow of a St. Christopher medal?

The most convincing night car two-shot I know of appears in *Pennies from Heaven,* a veritable anthology of lighting virtuosity unsurpassed in its tinkering with the limits of motion picture emulsion. It was photographed by Gordon Willis, the supreme maestro, the Prince of Darkness. With *End of the Road, Klute,* and the *Godfather* films, Willis's work changed cinematography, set radical new standards of honesty, the way Hemingway changed American prose. Well, almost.

Willis's shot looks like it was made in a studio, or, if outside, under exquisitely controlled conditions. Steve Martin and Bernadette Peters are intermittently lit by the headlights of passing cars, and these lights, never seen directly, are authentically random in frequency, intensity, speed, and distance. There are moments when the actors are totally in the dark. Willis is meticulous about this sort of thing. His reputation is such that he can get away with keeping light off stars' faces when it has no business being there.

According to its advertising campaign, *Pennies from Heaven* was a comedy. Did Willis's somber cinematography cause the film to flop at the box office? There *is* something sour about it. Willis's shots not only copy Edward Hopper's paintings picture for picture, they capture his emotional tone, his stark, staring puritanism. It's a clinically accurate light, the style is like Hemingway's. Comedy lighting is supposed to be flat. In movies, shadows equal Sad. Or Bad.

Hopper is the American painter most commonly consulted by cinematographers. The relationship between conceptualization, technique, and execution in Hopper are close to the cinematographer's approach. Despite his snapshot sense of composition, Hopper's paintings are supremely *premeditated*. Professional photography teaches the same lesson: there is no such thing as the beautiful light that just happens to be there.

We are creeping up here on speaking about cinematography as fine art, something that would put Pete Zavras out of work a lot faster than rumors of retinitis pigmentosa. Nevertheless, when Gordon Willis composes shots in *Pennies from Heaven* as *hommages* to Edward Hopper, insiders gasp knowingly. Though this may be "artistic" cinematography, it is not the reason why Willis is the James Wong Howe of his generation.

You cannot dwell on a movie frame the way you can on a canvas or a printed page. Movies—hybrids of light and time—tow us along in something like real time. But they have always had an uncertain connection with narrative. They were born as spectacle: See the Elephant Walk, See the Train Pull into the Station. Shock. *Ro*-mance. A little one-note suspense. It seemed necessary with the advent of feature-length films to install narrative or plot; writers were patched into the process. This lasted until directors weaned on television and educated in film schools started making movies, returning them to pure spectacle, with a light-show twist: See the Shark Eat the Man, See the Tall Building Burn Down, See the Spaceship Hover. Shock. *Ro*-mance. Special effects.

Willis and Almendros are the great illustrators of film's narrative interlude, and perhaps the last. Willis, so far as I know, has never made a shot untrue to the subtext of the narrative, not since his beginnings as a commercial cameraman. Even early in his career he was willing to risk technically "bad" shots—the overexposed homemovie-ish wedding sequence in *Godfather I,* for example—in order to reinforce a subtle story point. He uses his virtuosity to think about the narrative relevance, the emotional mortising, of his shots. (In *Windows,* the only film Willis has directed to date, he lapsed into static tableaux—hypnotized, I think, by the tour de force of photographing the Brooklyn Bridge in all kinds of light. The film is narratively inert.)

World-class professionals all know pretty much the same tricks. As much as the medium tends to overwhelm the message, the point is not the style. The point is the plot, the emotional trajectory of the story, the palpable intelligence, the human presence made transparent. And of all feature cameramen, only Gordon Willis has managed consistently to make this the province of cinematography.

Cameramen are most often called on not to be "real"—to reproduce reality, whatever that may be—but to execute a certain style or "look," a pleasing, faint reminder of a remote original—to tractor-mow, in short, the art-historical graveyard. Most of what they do boils down to shrewd. Leave a journeyman cinematographer to his own devices and he will fall back on taking the prettiest picture possible. Which is what Almendros fell into in *Days of Heaven.* Some pictures are more picturesque than others.

By this standard, the hard-bitten professional is kin to the saintly obscurantist of the avant-garde, Hollywood's gaumless nephew who conducts séances in the garage, communing via excruciating cinematic meditations on chairs, walls, windows, naked girlfriends—delivering sermons on photography's talent for bestowing souls on things. The difference is that the professional is a pitchman; he does not wait to let us discover the radiances of banality for ourselves. He dresses things up in light, revolves them, Christmas-trees them.

In this prestidigitatory spirit, cinematography is the heart and soul of commercial illustration. Take a frame, most any frame of a Hollywood film, and you will be looking at a species of fashion photography, relentlessly glamorous. Remember the swirling smoke and the flashlight in back of your head? It looks more Hollywood if you happen to be a blond with glossy lips.

To get an angle on what great cameramen do, and why Willis and Almendros have approached *auteur* prominence, consider the twin realistic traditions in "serious" American illustration: Thomas Eakins and Winslow Homer. They feed into cinematography via their contemporary, Eadward Muybridge, the inventor-photographer who came within a perforation of inventing a practical motion picture machine. Willis follows the Eakins tradition of looking hard at what's there, using as little light and movement as possible to make us examine the world of real people and ordinary things and marvel, the way he and Hemingway can't help doing, at the intense simplicity of it—the *story* of it.

In the sixties, Willis in America and Almendros in Europe took up James Wong Howe's struggle to wrest cinematography from the "high-key" glamor sensibilities of the Technicolor Corporation and its calendar art sense of what the world ought to look like. The development of a world-class cameraman's lighting is comparable to the progress of brushwork in a great painter. Murky, unflattering shadows were the reason for the decline in Rembrandt's portrait commissions. Willis became Woody Allen's court painter but it took him twenty years merely to be nominated for an Academy Award.

The other masters—Nykvist, Storaro, Coutard, Rotunno, Wexler, Zsigmond—all seem to follow Winslow Homer, who, before newspapers found a way to reproduce photographs, made his living drawing the daily news. Homer had a weakness for windblown effects, and his lighting was indifferent, but he was an unsurpassed draftsman whose renderings of motion seem poised to hop across the canvas. Almendros adds more than a dash of Flaubert, eighteenth-century French neoclassicism, and Italian neorealism.

Late in his life, Edward Hopper said that all he ever really cared about was the light on the side of a building. There is something teasingly melancholy about serious photography, as there is about *haiku*—at once bright and dark and savagely formal, like the desert under moonlight. Photography has everything: verisimilitude, good looks, wit, spiritual immanence. Everything but life.

Willem deKooning says that painting is merely a "glimpse" —an admission that, applied to film, would poorly serve the producer who feels that if he can't see his stars all the time, he's not getting his money's worth. It's an argument not without merit.

Pete Zavras, like Fitzgerald in Hollywood, was that peculiarly American mechanic, the hobbled artist for hire. And in the end, the best cinematography, even the thoughtful shooting of the sublime Gordy, is more *haiku* than Hemingway.

LESSON FIVE:

Inscrutable Secrets of Chopstick Lighting Revealed!

James Wong Howe, the legendary cinematographer who died in 1974, battled throughout his career for verisimilitude in film lighting. The story goes that during an employment drought caused by his fastidiousness about shadows, he opened a restaurant—Chinese, naturally. He was interested in getting publicity for his new place, so he called a friend at the *Los Angeles Times,* who dispatched a photographer to shoot some stills. Wong Howe, in his chef's apron, suggested to the photographer that if he stood a little further back and used a 24-mm lens instead of a 50-mm, he'd get a better shot. "Look," the photographer snapped, "you just cook the noodles, I'll take the pictures."

LESSON SIX:

Cinéma Voracité, or the Zapruder Principle

It was William Zapruder's fuzzy-lensed home movie camera that happened to shoot the ultimate snuff film: the assassination of President Kennedy. The Zapruder Principle: if it's real, it's shaky and blurred, just like life's nervous secrets.

Technology tends to make folks nervous. Movies and cars (Fitzgerald's last car was a convertible) are seductive, user-friendly ways of confronting technology. As opposed, presumably, to user-hostile ways—like high school, terrorism, or the fiction of Don DeLillo.

You'd think movies, because they record details so effortlessly—so . . . so photographically—would be the most realistic form. That's why writers find movies exasperating and intimidating. The camera seems to accomplish meretriciously what writers must do with ink-stained devotion to detail. The novelist may find consolation in his faith that the written word is wiser, more definitive: prose fiction, he believes, is the true *cinéma vérité;* the novel is best at conveying the experience of walking around in the world. The attentive novelist is still able to skip around the sensorium more adroitly, more evocatively than the cameraman. There are times when the merest preposition is slicker than zooming in. But movies are bigger. Not to mention more fun.

It's hard to remember what a hot, fecund, cross-pollinated idea *cinéma vérité* was in the sixties: Time-Life photojournalism, Drew Associates, portable photo technology, Cassavetes, Leacock and Pennebacker, *Woodstock, Salesman,* Robert Frank's radical snapshot ethic, Kerouac's "automatic writing," Mailer and Capote and the New Journalism, the elegiac commonplace. . . . *Cinéma vérité* made *auteurs* of mere scamps. Disaffected English majors toted 16-mm cameras around the way folksingers carried harmonicas. You listened with your toes, ready to jump in any direction. And away you went, happily, toward the next coincidence—every shot another blind date, the ultimate Once, the White Rabbit phosphorescing in the headlights: *cinéma voracité, cinéma vérité.*

Hard to remember—as hard as translating those two French words. The Maysles called it "direct cinema." Whatever the translation, it promised a "true story." It was American film's neorealism, an aesthetic built on technical limitations, postwar shortages, combat newsreels' deglamorization of Hollywood, and post-assassination media mop-ups.

For a few brief years, *cinéma vérité* returned the cameraman to the basics of Billy Bitzer's pre-Griffith days, when the intrepid cinematographer was pretty much the whole show, something like a novelist. But as film technology, with its unerring feel for fashion, turns the audience's attention from spontaneity to high-tech, the *cinéma vérité auteur,* again like the novelist, don't get no respect.

> The DP's AC says the POV with 28 F3.2, 85N3 & LC3 at 4.5 push 2 at ASA 125 is NG with the HMI, 2Ks & the 20-by-20. Besides, at 4 ft. the 35BL is 42 db with the 18 T1.3 which is only OK if it's MOS.
>
> —Teddy Churchill, *Steadicam Operator's Manual of Style*

There were a couple of late afternoon bottlenecks on the BQE but in less than an hour I was on Rockaway Boulevard, just a mile or so from the location of the McDonald's commercial. To the right stretched the eastern runways of

JFK. The service road was patched in long, wavy, roller-coastering swaths of asphalt which, at forty mph, set up sympathetic vibrations in the suspension so that my Malibu Classic *boing-boinged* down the road. Two blocks later I was driving through a suburb of mock Tudor homes on quarter-acre lots, tidily landscaped. I spotted the caravan of film trucks at the end of the street.

Teddy Churchill was calibrating his Steadicam in the driveway. He wore an apricot-colored mesh shirt, his pipe was chugging earnestly. Intermittent ground connections, unshielded power cables, sparking motor brushes—whatever the problem was, Teddy was getting so much interference his Steadicam monitor looked stranger than a '47 Dumont.

A jet zoomed directly overhead, low enough so we could look in the windows. This close, it seemed a model dangling in the sky.

Teddy had brought along his new briefcase computer. He'd painted over its original hobbyist gray with matte black, getting down in between the keys with a thin model airplane brush, and he'd placed color-coded bits of masking tape on the keyboard. He set it on the snack table, turned it on and punched up some phone numbers. He was using it as a $900 address-book. With a dark stare, he mentioned that Wendy, the rosy Canadian anthropologist who occasionally worked as his assistant, had just broken up with her cameraman boyfriend. "They had problems. Too intense. It's the same old story."

The commercial's storyboard called for little kids in Halloween costumes to knock on the door of the house. The nice blond housewife would open the door, give the kids some McDonald's Trick-or-Treats and the kids would run off down the street shrieking with delight. To create Halloween on this summer night, the prop department was scattering orange acrylic leaves on the lawn while three grips were squirting smoke-fog from bee guns and trying to get it to slither spookily along the picket fence. Art "Rhino" Feiner, the bulky best boy (electrician's assistant), was running down his repertoire of beautiful bird calls; the woman watching over the kid actors giggled appreciatively. The set had the ambience of an American Legion picnic winding down. Pot bellies cantilevered over card tables. Takeoffs tore up the sky every four minutes. It was an uninspiring scene somewhere between workaday inattentiveness and rigor mortis.

Teddy, sensing my boredom, reported on his recent trip to Detroit to shoot a linoleum commercial.

"I got the whole crew whipped up into a ten-minute frisbee game at lunch. It took them an hour and a half to focus on the job, they were so wasted. The shooting was cool. Had to make a sharp right-hand turn in a narrow hall-way, had to take my eyes off the monitor, could have trashed the whole Steadicam. But it was beautiful. We all had dinner in a great seafood place. I ordered the most won-derful mussels in garlic sauce. I was talking to this nice lady, she was a production assistant, and we went for a walk in the twilight. She was smart. I'd been kidding her all day; she knew I thought she was hot stuff. This was summer solstice, so it didn't get dark till nine-thirty or ten. We held hands and we were getting sincere. There we were in the twilight, kissing. When we went back inside the restaurant, everyone said, *Oooh! Where were you?* So that was nice."

As the daylight died, Teddy strapped on a battery-powered miner's headlamp so he'd have enough illumina-tion to continue fiddling with the interference problem. The front door was opening and closing, the kids were shrieking "Trick or treat!" the housewife was suburbanly beaming.

"The thing is," Teddy said, "I don't want to be some kind of arty pack mule all the rest of my life. I can't keep up with the computers. The Steadicam keeps breaking. I don't know." He flinched and looked at his sneakers; he was stuck in one of those Hitchcock wrong-man-with-a-blond

dilemmas. Maybe it was only the wistful pride and seriousness of a man in control of his machine. Or maybe he
was Billy Bitzer, trying to refurbish his fate with the hard-
earned innocence of an artist.

What is rare and charming about Teddy is that his heart is
unashamedly in his work, all of it. This is how he makes it look
easy. There was that night a nobility in his determination. In
the midst of the old guard's practiced cynicism, he kept his
energy up, demanded respect for his technical dedication. He
was deferred to as a valuable specialist, an eccentric; stories
were told about him with amusement and awe. Hypertech
Teddy, they said, the biggest act this side of Barnum. He was
lovable and he did beautiful work. Teddy the Tin Man.

At ten o'clock, he was called on to do five quick takes. As
soon as he emerged from the house, I shook his hand and
bid him goodbye.

"Sorry, Duke. It was a loser scene."

I turned my back on the island of illumination that was
the film set and walked to the parking lot by the railroad
station, the trees along the way swallowing me shadow by
shadow. On the way home, the malls were empty—stores
still lit, though, with the hollow light of late evening, like
TV sets tuned to off-the-air channels that had put everyone
to sleep but remained themselves alert, raw *Poltergeist* electricity, the dazzling ghost of cathedral darkness.

A mile down Rockaway Boulevard, not far from where
Fitzgerald's dark fields of the republic once rolled on under
the night, a dozen citizens had pulled their cars to the side of
the road so they could marvel at the jets screeching less than
a hundred feet directly overhead. I craned my neck toward
the hovering jumbo jet and gawked, perishing of occupa-
tional vertigo.

The adventure, the lust to penetrate the next minute, or at
least the relentless TV of the present, to follow Edison's and
Bitzer's and Griffith's and Spielberg's gadget-happy lead into

the electronic light where the gremlins dwell, the struggle to
retrieve this buzzing world in pictures and save it for the
future—the job schooled Teddy in emotional discontinuity,
the wisdom of abruptness. For me, movies were the muse I'd
flirted with for years, made it with once or twice, but didn't
respect in the morning. Cameramen don't have memories
exactly, but something like a recoverable light. We look for
love in the light and settle for the light. Blink and you're
someplace else, that's the movies. The jet thunked down,
tires smoking.

LESSON SEVEN:

Special Effects and Camera Movement

> Colui che mai non vide cosa nova produsse
> esto visible parlare novello a noi perché non
> si trova.
>   There's no surprising God; He's the one
> who invented talking pictures to startle us.
>
>   —Purgatorio, X: 94–96

Okay, now make sure all the lights are out. Take your flashlight, check the batteries, make sure the bulb is real bright.
Put the flashlight in your mouth and switch it on and off as
fast as you can. Your cheeks are blinking. What movie are
you in?

Deep Star Wars—very good.

Now take your skateboard and your kaleidoscope and go
to the top of the hill. . . .

Deep Wrist

I remembered, when watching movies as a child, how the theater seat—everything— would vanish, leaving me floating disembodied before the images on the screen. And it was this sort of possession you looked for when angling: to watch the river flowing, the insects landing and hatching, the places where trout hold; and to insinuate the supple, binding movement of tapered line until, when the combination is right, the line becomes quite rigid and many of its motions are conceived at the other end. When the initiative changes hands, the trout is soon in the net, without an idea in his head until you release him. Then you see him going off, looking for a spot, and thinking. We had this only briefly; our trip was over.

—Thomas McGuane, "Angling Versus Acts of God," *Outside Chance*.

On the porch there's a camp table with birch branch legs. Wasps strum the screen door. In the cabin there are crocheted rugs over linoleum, a rocking chair and a sepia lampshade stenciled with New England nautical motifs. The bathroom doorstop is fashioned from the thighbone of a moose painted red, white, and blue. And I'm tranced by those ruffled white curtains.

I first came to Maine twenty years ago in pursuit of land-locked salmon. At a lakeside lodge, I fell in love with Veronica, who was a painter. One morning, by a path soft with pine needles, an old guide hailed me as "young feller" as he lowered himself stiffly, stiffly, stiffly into his canoe.

Recently widowed, Arthur was delighted to have the company of a young couple he could instruct in fishing and in his patient remedies for solitude. He taught us how to flycast, took us fishing three cold mornings in a row and stayed with us till we caught our first salmon. When we came ashore, he poured tumblers of cheap bourbon that burned like kerosene. The issue of our engagement settled, Arthur recommended going north to a lodge run by his son. He sipped, an old widower savoring the treasure of his only honeymoon. North, he said, that's where the real salmon were.

Today the cabin's ruffled curtains are the scraps of our old nest, Veronica's and mine, fallen from its tree ten years ago—a lifetime, or long enough, at least, for life's direction to be decided. I was a cameraman, not a woodsman. So when Veronica began to get serious about farming and having children, I reinstalled myself in the city. She remarried, moved west, and gave birth to triplets. Ten years after our divorce, I've come back to Maine as a specialized refugee, honeymooning alone.

Leaving New York at 5 A.M., I kiss Sunny. She opens her

eyes and reaches out without touching me. "Why are you going?"

"I'm going fishing." But women are such detectives; she's not fooled. It's the third marriage for me, the second for Sunny. We take separate vacations.

Fishing is good for old grief, soothes the singlemindedness of it. Do unto fish as you would do unto women: dream them, study them, woo them, wonder at their wiles, rage at their refusals, chase them, trick them, bait them, hook them, kill them, gut them, garnish them, fry them, eat them, love them and miss them when they get away. Fishing in this mood is an utterly masculine trance. Fishing, a man cannot be lonely. Frustrated, perhaps, but satisfaction is something to be settled between nature and his skill. The negotiated pleasures of marriage are nothing compared to spending a day and a night in an open boat.

"Yep, it was a long summer for Pop," Gerry says. Arthur, his father, died one warm afternoon last fall.

Gerry's Cessna wiggles on its pontoons. He's getting ready to fly a honeymoon couple to a remote lake north of the Allagash. The boy is rigging a bobber. The girl stuffs her freshman Spanish text in the tackle box.

While filling the gas tank, Gerry introduces me to Amanda, his four-year-old daughter, who's wearing sequined sunglasses. "She thinks she's a movie star," he says. "That's good. She can support me when I get old."

"Why do they want to go there anyway?" Amanda complains, not wanting her father to fly away. "It's just a big dumb lake."

"Maybe that's all there is." Gerry winks in my direction.

Amanda ties her hair back with a ribbon and applauds as the pontoons lift from the water—the right one a little before the left, the plane banking to the east.

*   *   *

The first night is silver. Veronica is in the air. I dream all night. At first light, a mockingbird with an incredible vocabulary sings.

Out on the lake before dawn. Tufts of seagull down, the litter of their nocturnal groomings, float in the cove. My audience is a bull moose, legs spindly, seaweed dribbling on his antlers. He snuffles and gazes at me with eyes so blank I feel obscenely observed.

Drifting across the cove, I get a memory-glimpse of Veronica's easy smile. The whooshing of my fly line becomes Veronica's voice. It comes back to me, casting over the shoals, the way old Arthur used to lilt her name.

My first strike is a four-pounder who dives stubbornly. He plunges behind a boulder and saws the leader. I sit down with a thud of disappointment.

What is it about fishing? It's got refined equipment, it's got record keeping and contests, it's got traditionally sanctioned aggression, it's got mystique. And loss. Don't say mere rejection. Epic grief—a conspiracy involving all of nature.

The moose exits across the shallows, hooves suction-cupping in the slime, and crashes at last into the woods.

Fishermen, such dreamers on shore, must be truthful in the boat. The truth, I want to shout after him, is that men are multi-orgasmic in their wrists. The thrill of the struggling life force is transmitted to the wrist, most especially in fly fishing. And a cameraman's timing to move and snap the shutter happens in his wrist. A pitcher imparts a curve to the ball with a snap of his wrist; the golfer's and the batter's swing is centered in this most sensual hinge. The wrist and the wand. I will learn not to galumph around the boat, I will catch a respectable fish, I will forget Veronica. I flick a

yellow spider off the outboard throttle. Why do I keep remembering her? She was a memorable woman.

The Sullivans fly an American flag from the porch of the
neighboring cabin, something Arthur always did on holi-
days.

Retired on his army pension—Jim was a sergeant, Marge
a nurse—they've fished all over the world. Marge has severe
arthritis. "The osteo kind," she explains, gripping her knee.
It is quite an expedition for her to walk down the path and
step into the boat, though Jim has installed a handrail and
an antiskid mat on the dock.

"It's hard. Yes, oh yes. Jim doesn't like to go out alone.
Sometimes it's rough when he gets a fish on, he can't handle
the boat and the rod by himself." She wags her head in
girlish rue.

Jim invites me inside to see a picture of the four-pound
salmon he caught last week. He could have brought it out
on the porch, but he wanted to get away from Marge for a
moment. He'd become the nurse, she the wounded soldier.
He fetched a color print of himself happily displaying the
fish, shiny as a slab of aluminum.

Back on the porch, there's the stench of a hurriedly extinguished cigarette. Marge has her ceremonial escapes, too.
She recalls the raccoon—Betty, her name was—who used to
prowl the garbage cans summer after summer, a real old
timer. Sometimes she'd sit on the other side of the screen
door, nose-to-nose with their cat. But one of the city people
up for a few weeks shot her. City people don't know about
animals. They're afraid of them, afraid they'll hurt their
kids. Once Jim freed a loon that was snared in a fishing line.
Got good 8mm-movies of it, too.

Marge asks what I think of the new disk cameras; *she*
thinks they're swell. When Jim says he likes them too,

Marge corrects him by saying of course I probably have a big camera, a Canon or something. She gives me a copy of yesterday's Bangor *Times* with the crossword puzzle cut out. Well, I say, I'm going to tie three more Mickey Finns, give those salmon another chance.

The morning of the third day, I'm rocking on my porch, listening to the birds sing and the bees buzz and a woodpecker's knock echoing in the woods and waiting for Veronica to come again. I've been going to bed early, about 9:00, while there's still a little light in the sky. My sleep has been voluptuous with dreams. But dreams have yet to make a wise man out of me. No man is himself, Melville says, unless his eyes are closed. I'm on a cameraman's vacation: photography was invented while the young Herman Melville was off a-whaling.

I wake with the dawn, before five, and rehearse my city worries about little money, feeble career and the unfairness of all this to Veronica, who wanted so much to save me, who wanted me to pull myself together and love her.

I make a long cast toward the spawning beds and the magic ripples up my arm. The bass jumps once, towing the boat toward him. He is about three pounds, strong and scrappy. I net him quickly rather than risk losing the irreplaceable pride of capture. I feel satisfied, though still hectic and clumsy. Behind me, far out on the lake, a salmon leaps clear of the water, just frisking.

I clean the bass on the dock. I fry it with potatoes and open *The Portable Hemingway* at random and come across the scene in which Jake Barnes effortlessly catches eight trout and pronounces them "good fish."

The purist's form of angling is "catch and release": the prey, once landed, is returned to the water. The moment is captured without killing it, as in good camerawork. Writing, by comparison, seems a contemplative blood sport.

Amanda applauds the return of her father's plane.

The honeymooners, quite sunburned now, gaze confidentially at each other, the two of them a complete planetary system. He's teaching her to flycast. If she humors him, all will go well. He will teach her, she will keep him.

The drive back is misty through Maine and New Hampshire, foul-smoggy south of Boston.

My fire escape garden, particularly the hollyhock in the glazed tub, has shot up. Japanese beetles are chewing the blackberry bush. Sunny says she's sick with cystitis, and I've got a good idea what this means: she is somnambulistically wretched. A month later she moves out and in with another guy, the oncologist. Catch and release.

Gunga Duke and the Temple of Zoom

Surely in no other craft as in that of the sea
do the hearts of those already launched to
sink or swim go out so much to the youth
on the brink, looking with shining eyes
upon that glitter of the vast surface which is
only a reflection of his own glances full of
fire. There is such magnificent vagueness in
the expectations that had driven each of us
to sea, such a glorious indefiniteness, such a
beautiful greed of adventures that are their
own and only reward! What we get—well,
we won't talk of that; but can one of us
restrain a smile? In no other kind of life is
the illusion more wide of reality—in no
other is the beginning *all* illusion.

—Joseph Conrad, *Lord Jim*

In the spring of 1974, my life having become a series of idle threats against myself and my friends, I decided I had to travel. Not just to Maine for fishing or to Europe for *amour,* but far away, deep into a different culture where I would be a stranger and everything would be strange to me.

At a film party in darkest SoHo, I ran into Yvonne Hannemann, grazing on the baba gannouj. She wore her ashblond hair long, and she dressed simply, ascetically almost, in warm, solid colors. I kidded her about looking like a centerfold for the *Whole Earth Catalogue;* she winked amiably.

The United Nations, she said, had declared 1974 "World Population Year." Accordingly, the UN film unit was making plans for a media extravaganza: multiscreens, picturephones, video loops, slides, cycloramas, touchy-feely exhibits, sixteen-track sound spectaculars—all designed to make the delegates *experience* the problems of overpopulated countries rather than just nod out over the usual statistics.

The producer assigned to execute these schemes was an elegant young Indian named Rajeef Sethi, whose European education had wired him into McLuhan and Fuller. At eighteen, he'd spent a summer in Pierre Cardin's Paris workshop producing ties and handkerchiefs from Xeroxed footprints. Yvonne cautioned me diplomatically that while Rajeef's mind was westernized, his hands kept a Brahminical distance from physical labor.

The UN had given him an office on a high floor, a very large office, about thirty feet square, with a map of the world stretched across one wall and a real-life panorama of midtown Manhattan glistening through the windows of another. The map was sprinkled with pushpins. To each pin was attached a flag and on every flag was a date signifying the arrival of the crew, which, including Rajeef, would amount to six souls.

Rajeef materialized, backlit, in a sleekly cut suit of white linen. We checked out the dates on the flags: a fishing village near Oslo on the fifteenth, a slum in Rome on the seventeenth, Vienna on the nineteenth, Rio on the twenty-third, Recife on the twenty-fifth, and so on. At the party, Yvonne had mentioned a budget of $2 million.

The $2-million media junket was promptly cut back to two short films: a documentary on family planning and another on agriculture in India, and as long as we were going to be in the neighborhood, a third, perhaps, on the status of women in Sri Lanka. Yvonne would direct, I would shoot, and because of the delays in planning, we would have to do these things during May and June, the hottest months of the year in one of the hottest places on the planet. When I asked her about the possibility of first-class accommodations or other goodies left over from the original $2 million, she just smiled. "Not this trip, Duke."

As a matter of policy, Yvonne had been successful early. Apprenticeship with Charles Eames, photographs in *Vogue,* expensive vacations, exotic boyfriends—all in all, a precocious career woman. During a two-year Fulbright in Sri Lanka, she underwent a change, the full explanation of which she withheld, perhaps because of some feminine instinct for mystification, perhaps because she was as much a mystery to herself as to anyone else. "I realized on my last trip to Sikkim that I wanted to make films, but it wasn't going to be my source of joy. I was making films, I was in love, I had to pay the rent and all that, but the real journey for me was going to be a spiritual one."

She left two weeks ahead of me in order to cover a harvest festival in the Punjab. She said, "Meet me at the Imperial Hotel in Delhi on May first."

The Imperial Hotel . . . Delhi . . . May first. I envisioned slowly revolving fans, bearers in Philip Morris suits, and wicker chairs stuffed with gin-sodden colonialists, all played by Sidney Greenstreet. At last, a location where my bush jacket would not seem an affectation.

I spent the next few days testing equipment, getting an armful of inoculations, shooting a commercial, writing calculatingly indifferent notes to my girlfriend and avoiding farewell scenes for fear of making any promises. Better to keep everyone on a low flame.

On the runway of Delhi International, a starved dog whimpered and gnawed his fleas. The air was spicy, liquid. Two nomadic English matrons were directed toward the security frisk. "What?" one of them asked. "Those chaps with the turbans over there?" At six in the morning, the temperature was ninety-six.

There was no phone; at least the customs officer who detained me wouldn't let me use his, which rang incessantly, unanswered. I sat on my camera case, draining bottle after bottle of Fanta and panting like a spaniel. A clerk appeared with some papers for the officer to sign. The clerk had two thumbs on his right hand, one on top of the other, and he clasped the papers in the notch between them.

The officer, tiring of me, decided to impound my equipment. Bright green birds chuckled.

The Delhi bus arrived an hour and a half late, crammed with young vagabonds doing the dope tour. The temperature was now 103 degrees and accelerating. From my perch by the rear window, I leaned away from the angry oven heat, borne on a breeze that blew spittle from the corners of my mouth. There was no water. There was no coolness. Not even their memories. Only movie posters with axes and purple Krishna faces.

Sure enough, just as in my predeparture fantasy, the Imperial's main entrance was flanked by bearers in Philip

Morris suits. But there was no Miss Hannemann, no reservations. I leaned against a stuccoed column, scalding my shoulder blades. I decided to walk back down the Janpath Road and check into the first hotel that would have me.

Cinematography had taught me that in order to film something you had to understand its geometry, where it stood with respect to other things and yourself. In this India, the angles were obscure, if they could be made out at all. The heat and the strangeness hobbled the will to make compositional sense of things. You simply submitted and hoped to survive by accepting some position in the stream. I perceived very little—only a glimpse of the hotel in the upper right corner of my field of view. If I could just keep that fix, I'd be all right.

Then, lower, to the left, there was suddenly a man pushing a wheelbarrow, and in the wheelbarrow, yes, there was a human figure, swathed in black, sopping up the force of the hanging sun. Something in its eyes seemed to leap out and touch mine. It was not possible to be alive and suffer so, but the eyes were alive. My first leper.

At the hotel, the clerk said, "Yes, we have a Miss Hannemann registered."

Yvonne looked like she'd lost weight. Our conversation over drinks was disillusioningly practical.

"I'm not sure how to raise this point, Duke, but, uh, be sure not to, uh, let yourself get, you know, constipated. With all the rice we'll be eating and, uh, soybeans, it can be, uh, very painful."

I assured her I was in little danger of constipation. I was already experiencing a certain, uh, looseness.

The evening of the next day, Rajeef Sethi, the UN producer, took us to a concert of Indian folk music. In the middle of a dusty field scented with sandalwood smoke, a

theater troupe from Madya Pradesh was assembling to sing
the "MahaBarata," the ancient saga of a warrior who prevailed on a holy man to show him his future, then laid waste
much of his kingdom to prove the predictions wrong.

As the musicians tuned up, Rajeef spoke eagerly of his
applications of the theories of Buckminister Fuller. He was
interested, he said in his boarding-school British, "in the
positive and negative forces of the universe—something like
Tantra, you know. You know Tantra?" I nodded tentatively.

Kerosene lamps were hung to replace the fading sun. We
hunkered down in the dust as the leader of the troupe began
to sing. In one hand he held a staff and in the other a short
stick with tiny cymbals at the end. As the saga unfolded, he
manipulated the staff to represent at times a sword, a lover,
a bow, or a spear. Rajeef translated the verses and simulta-
neously continued the explanation of his career. "I am the
first person on earth to design a completely integrated solar
house."

The house, however, was not about to be built. Rajeef
was more interested in philosophical overviews than in applied technology. "Indian culture cannot use technology,"
he said. I was curious to know if India could change her
culture the way China had changed hers. "India has certainly been exploitable," he said, "by foreign businessmen
and native elites. But changeable—no. This culture"—he
gestured toward the musicians and the trees beyond—
"won't change. This culture is as well adapted as those trees
that live through cycles of monsoon and drought. India is
dust, very old dust. This is a very old and well established
neighborhood of hell."

The singer was shaking his head as he sang the refrain—
wagging it, really, in the peculiarly Eastern way that Westerners confuse at first with nodding "no."

Rajeef's ideas, he knew as well as anyone, were futile,
though his silvery English put us at ease.

*   *   *

In the morning Yvonne and I took a cycle-cab to UN head-quarters to get some advice about clearing my equipment out of customs. When the driver took a second wrong turn, Yvonne punched him in the shoulder and screamed at him. "This is my last trip," she said, "I've had enough." She wanted to go home, settle down, and get married.

We fell into talking about money. Neither of us had very much in those days and when I asked if she'd ever had all the money she could use, she said yes, when she was twenty-three, she had a good job—she ate at the best restaurants and vacationed in Greece. But now, when she was at a party and there was "a scene going down," she felt she'd done it all before.

We discussed the feasibility of filming a demonstration by striking railworkers. Since virtually all of India's food and fertilizer move by rail, the situation was roughly equivalent to a rail *and* truck strike in the States, and then some. Labor problems are an important reason why Indians don't eat regularly, so the sequence would be vital to our film. Only two days into the strike, the union leaders were all in jail, and one was dead of a "heart attack" suffered while he was being arrested at four in the morning. Rajeef cautioned us that it would be unwise for Westerners to be seen in the streets of Delhi, and suicidal to film a demonstration. We would most likely be shot or torn apart by strikers, police, or both.

In the morning, slumped as inconspicuously as possible in the back of a UN car, we cruised Delhi for a demonstration. On the Rajpath, a boulevard built by the British as an approach to the Parliament buildings, we found one. About six thousand workers were half a mile ahead of us, marching toward Parliament.

On either side of the boulevard were lovely broad lawns. I saw no police, no long curly daggers. I got out of the car and took a long-lens shot, compressing the perspectives of the workers and the buildings, which floated mirage-like in the heat shimmering off the pavement.

A cameraman is in a uniquely favorable position to feel the electricity of crowds, to plug into it, to analyze its currents, to distinguish, for example, the elevated energy of a concert from the raw and potentially lethal power of a soccer match or a political demonstration, which is always on the brink of going berserk. The mob in a political demonstration, unlike a concert crowd, has no center, and can shift at any time into a looting orgy, capable of breaking bodies, cars, or glass as easily as a bull flips a matador on his horns.

The chants of the demonstrators drowned out our whispers (what the hell were we whispering for?). Yvonne hopped out of the car and we fell in step with the marchers.

There is something about having a machine eye on your shoulder in the middle of all the excitement, a thrill of being at once the gunner and the target, a feeling of invulnerability—immortality, even—that comes from watching mayhem on a ground glass. The man with a camera assumes he can live through any experience if he enters it with the purpose of taking its picture. It's an illusion of separateness and control. Like the phenomenon of "retention of vision" which allows the human eye to see as a seamless sequence the alternating frames of image and darkness projected at twenty-four frames a second, it is an illusion built into all of us. In a crowd, the cameraman becomes a cowboy tossing his rope from a moving saddle, a pirate scampering up the riggings, a dancer in a magic dance whose steps only the initiated know—improvising every move, yet feeling it in advance. There are times when you know it's good, when the camera and your moves are meshing, and when compositions simply fall into place, as if with the complicity of the subjects.

So it was with the demonstrators. When I panned right, they followed. When I panned left, the march tapered in that direction, shaping a forceful diagonal in the frame. The workers seemed to flow by in classic poses, like figures in a revolutionary frieze of the thirties.

I caught a glimpse of Yvonne across the road at the opposite end of a row of marchers, aiming her microphone at the middle of the noise, her eyes wide with excitement as she half walked, half ran backward with the strikers. She tossed me a wink.

I ran ahead of the march and knelt down to get a low-angle shot of some protesters with a banner. They funneled around me with only an occasional sly look at the lens, shouting—God's truth—"Coca-Cola! Coca-Cola! Coca-Cola!"

We were working at last and it felt wonderful.

We flew that afternoon to the Punjab, where, in May, the hot wind blows. The Sikhs, who live with it, must have a name for this awesome moving sky that forces you to crouch in your jeep, shielding your eyes and camera from the dust which sails relentlessly at right angles to the trunks of beaten trees, while you squint longingly through crusted lids toward the frosty foothills of the Himalayas, far to the northeast.

Even when the wind drooped, there was dust, visible only as a deceptive whitish blur, which the novice eye might mistake for haze, just above the horizon. But there was not enough moisture in the Punjabi air to make haze, and too few industries for smog. So it was always dust and it insinuated itself into everything like a silky powder. Despite the precaution of wrapping our equipment in plastic garbage bags, gears soon began to grind. The dust caked our hair, stopped our nostrils, and on our tongues it turned to gritty slime. By the end of the day we looked like a couple of desperadoes out of a spaghetti western.

In the cafeteria of the university at Ludhiana, we met an agronomy student from Iran who said he'd be happy to show us around town. At dusk, Yvonne and I washed under the faucets in our separate rooms, shared sections of oranges as a predinner cocktail, and joined the Iranian downstairs.

It took him several kicks and stomps to start his motorcycle. I told Yvonne to get on, ladies first, but she declined and climbed on behind me. We chugged off.

Down the main street, where small foundries glowered and clanged, adding sooty density to the dust broth, we eddied through hundreds of bicycles, their bells clinging and clacking like crickets. The occasional truck chugged softly, like all Indian motor vehicles, its ignition tuned to idle just this side of stalling. At stops, the engines were turned off entirely to save gas, which had just jumped to two dollars a gallon.

The Iranian said something about having gone too far into the center of town, and as he started to turn, the motorcycle dipped dangerously. Yvonne grabbed my waist and said with effort, "It's all right," and we sailed along, suspended in the soot.

The restaurant was nearly empty, as the expensive ones were inclined to be at this time of the year. I ordered the most expensive thing on the menu. I don't remember its name, only my surprise at its oily sweetness.

"This is it," the Iranian said, indicating the empty tables. "This is the whole show."

"I guess the heat . . ." Yvonne began.

"This is nothing." Indian heat was a tale he'd told many times, a predictable complaint, and he was anxious to get through it. "Sometimes it goes to fifty, fifty-five degrees centigrade. And there's no electricity. So no radios, no fans."

"What about, uh, social life?" Yvonne asked. "Social life" had become our euphemism for sex.

"Social life? With chaperones? Even with chaperones, it's hard to get the girls to come here."

He excused himself, saying he had to return to the campus for a dance. I washed down my dinner with two bottles of beer and we returned in a bicycle-taxi, the ride this time more silent and somber, but just as sooty. It was two miles up a slight hill and the veins on the boy driver's legs looked ready to burst, his back soaked with sweat, so we told him to drop us at the campus gates. We walked past rose bushes. Colorless in the moonlight and without scent, their attraction was to the touch. They felt soft and finely woven.

We had arranged for rooms in the university dormitory. We dragged mattresses out on our adjoining balconies and lay down under the stars. Keeping up with the equipment problems caused by the dust was creating a strain between Yvonne and me. After shooting under the sun all day, we had to spread every piece of equipment out on the floor of my room—all thirteen cases of it—take everything apart, regrease it, and put it all back together again with sweaty fingers. With Ludhiana's supply of electricity rationed to an erratic four hours a day, the overhead fan wobbled, never really spinning, and the chargers for my camera batteries kept fusing out because of voltage fluctuations. At this rate, it would cost a couple thousand dollars and a month in the repair shop to put my equipment back in shape. I asked Yvonne to cable the UN for assurance that they would pay for repairs when we returned to the States. She balked, saying she didn't want to jeopardize the mission by suggesting to her superiors that we were having a hard time. The equipment, she insisted, was *my* problem, since I was renting it to the production.

I tried to sleep. I studied the starry night through the

screen, where a luna moth with a wingspan as wide as my palm was thumping itself to death. Outside, the purring of froggy bells and the plupping of water. Peepers were breeding in the holding tank. I rolled over and looked at the flickering red lamp of my battery charger, which I'd hazardously managed to fuse with a strand of copper wire.

Yvonne called over to ask if the mosquitoes were dive-bombing me too. No, I lied. Yvonne called again: had I taken my malaria pills? No, I said, lying again. I was annoyed, but then, I could force myself not to care. It wouldn't be *my* problem if the whole production, as well as the equipment, broke down. If she wanted to play that way, all right. She'd just have to row her own oar in this lifeboat.

Then I did something that every cameraman—and, I guess, everyone who hires out his hands—has to do once in a while: I stopped caring. I slapped a mosquito, rolled over and, privately, I quit.

I couldn't make out the red charging light on the battery. The power was gone again.

Yvonne had scouted a colossal irrigation project at the end of a canal some thirty miles north of Ludhiana. Late the next afternoon, we set out in a jeep, stopping frequently at milk bars for another hit of lhassi, or to make a shot of the wheat harvest. As we turned up the road by the side of the canal, we found the way blocked by a column of military vehicles.

The Indian army, generally pretty nimble when it comes to raping Pakistanis, was having a tough time figuring out how to convoy their trucks two abreast down a path barely wide enough for a bullock cart. We sat there steaming and sulking as the light died. Missing this irrigation project was a very bad break. It meant having to go another day to another canal in another desert—to the canal in Rajasthan, in fact, in the middle of India's hottest desert.

Yvonne hopped out of the jeep and paced beside an armored rocket launcher. "Stupid soldiers," she snapped at the dust, loud enough for the soldiers to hear. "Stupid soldiers. Stupid, stupid, *stupid* soldiers." She turned on her heels. "Stupid, they're all so stupid—all over the world, stupid soldiers. Don't they have walkie-talkies?" She kicked the dust. "What do they think they're doing? Who *are* these bums? Stupid, stupid—it's all so *stupid*."

A dozen privates who'd been smoking under a tree stared at her in astonishment.

Since there was nothing to be done for it, I stripped to my shorts, slipped over buffalo dung on the bank and dove into the muddy canal. The current was surprisingly strong, a liquid wind. Our driver, a Sherpa proud and protective of his crazy white masters, ran along the bank pointing me out to the soldiers, whom he encouraged to clap and cheer as I flopped in the rushing brown water.

Yvonne sat down on the bank. "Oh, it looks beautiful," she said, smiling as tears pushed the dust down her cheeks. I swam over and grabbed her ankle. "No," she said. "It looks delicious, but I can't. No. Oh, it looks so wonderful, I wish I could, but I couldn't swim in front of all these men."

Back in Delhi the next day, we were joined by Sam, a UN staff soundman, who'd come out late because of delays on a film in Sweden. Though he looked game enough—he had a boxer's biceps—and though, being Jamaican, he had to know something about working in the tropics, I couldn't help wondering how long he'd last in his black pants and black Italian shirt.

Sam introduced a disquieting note. He wanted to work only in capital cities, furnished with steaks and social life. He mumbled something about packing up and going home.

We packed—Sam and all—and flew the next day to Hyderabad in central India.

The Hyderabad Ritz, originally built as a castle by the last Maharajah for one of his favorite sons, looked exactly like a Hollywood set designer's idea of the Hyderabad Ritz. "It's so Indian," Yvonne said. "So gardenias-and-shit."

We took our meals in a deserted nightclub under low-key lighting. Our table was next to a revolving stage which had been stationary for some time. Sam, our dark force of indifference, droned on about the fare: the meat and fish were tasteless, often of questionable origin, tenderized and curried beyond recognition. It was not that there was no good Indian cuisine: there were just no fresh ingredients—they'd all been exported.

"What is this supposed to be?" Sam asked. "Water?"

It *was* water, Yvonne explained, but it had been treated with halazone tablets, which accounted for its swimming pool bouquet. "Why don't you try the beer?"

The local beer, to which brewers added glycerine as a preservative, tasted like Tide. I tried to cushion Sam's revulsion by saying that once we got to Bombay, the beer might be fresher.

Yvonne, a strict vegetarian of eight years standing, suddenly caved in over her vegetable patty and lunged for my plate of prawns.

She was smiling at the prawn on the tip of her fork when Sam said, "I'm going home."

Yvonne went ahead with arrangements to film a family of Tribals, country people who had migrated to the city to live off begging and prostitution when the food and work in their area ran out. Our driver advised us that such people were given to stoning cars with UNESCO or Family Planning insignias. We rented an unmarked car.

The Tribal family—about eighteen or twenty kids, cousins, aunts, uncles, and parents, as well as several dogs, a bullock, and two fly-blown sheep—made their home under a tree on the outskirts of town. There, they cooked, ate, bathed, slept, and multiplied—under that tree. There are bigger trees in Central Park. Five hundred million Indians live in villages such as these Tribals left. They are not, strictly speaking, agricultural people; they are nomads. They wander, like millions and millions before them, following their cattle toward centers of water and food and essential services.

Sam, who was biding his time to see what accommodations might come his way as a result of his ultimatum, slung the sound recorder over his shoulder. Yvonne, with the help of our driver, was bargaining with the men of the family about how many sacks of grain the shooting would cost.

The light under the tree, filtered through the branches and diffused by the smoke of a hissing fire, was very pretty. I shot some closeups of the women's jewelry, trying to follow-focus on the earrings and rings and wrist ornaments of an old woman who was pounding a wheatcake, her bracelets clinking and glittering magically in and out of the smoke. She was very dark, jet-black almost. Her eyes flashed, reflecting the fire, and through the snaking smoke, stalks of sun touched her now with gold, now with silver. So pretty. I tried to relax and track the movements of her head and hands.

Sam pulled me to my feet. I stiffened and spun toward him, ready to scold him for spoiling my shot. I'd send him home all right. I'd drop-kick him clear back to New York.

Our driver edged next to me. "They want money," he said, indicating that I should make Madame understand.

The men were circling Yvonne. With one hand, she hoisted a sack of grain that must have weighed twelve pounds and thrust it into the stomach of the man closest to her. It was only the energy of her movements and her shouts of "No, no" in Hindi that kept the men from rushing her.

Sam pushed me inside the car. The start of the engine was smothered by rising shouts. The car began to roll slowly through the crowd. Then, with eery formality, the men and the little boys bowed like jackknives—a droll, swift effect—and when they straightened up they all had stones in their hands. So this was how it was done.

I rolled up the window on my side, worried this might be a fatal signal of fear, and leaned over, poised to open the door for Yvonne. The car crept closer. She backed away from the men and climbed in, still shouting *"Ne, ne!"* She lowered the window and punched the sack of grain one of the Tribals was holding. The car crawled past faces whose eyes, like the eyes of my leper, glistened with the pain of the damned, anticipating only more pain. Sam and Yvonne exchanged glances. The line of his mouth was tight.

"What was I supposed to do?" Yvonne said, finishing her question with a look back at the tree. "The men would just take the money and spend it on liquor and get drunk and the kids would go hungry and the women would have to sell themselves. What was I supposed to do?"

"There's nothing you can do," Sam said cordially.

"You did okay," I said.

Yvonne flinched. Then we were clear of it.

According to conventional wisdom, "primitive" people are often camera shy because they fear the camera will steal their souls. The anthropologist Edmund Carpenter has amended this myth to say that a Polaroid picture will endow the New Guinea tribesman with a piece of the global electronic soul. For six years I'd worked as a cameraman, developing the pinball wizard skills and cowboy stoicism that was supposed to go with the craft. Still, I used to wonder about the photographers who took pictures of Vietnamese monks incinerating themselves to protest the war. How could anyone keep cool enough to operate a picture-taking machine in the midst of premeditated violence?

There is some sort of magical relationship between photographer and subject, some kind of energy transfer. I can vouch for it. Professional alienation—"just doing your job" in the midst of human misery—is something that happens, unnoticed perhaps but inevitable all the same, like aging. It is an instinct photographers share, this drive to take pictures when something extraordinary is happening, no matter what.

I found out about it one day in South Carolina when, in the course of making a documentary about the malnourished and worm-infested blacks of Beaufort County, I photographed an old man dying on the table of a country doctor's surgery. As the man's last breaths croaked from his throat, I turned to the sound man and said, "Did you get that?"

That particular movie, it turned out, was never finished, but my innocence was. It's true, the camera does steal souls.

We had the afternoon off, so Yvonne and I went shopping in the bazaar at the center of Hyderabad. My eyes and nose began to run from the spicy dust kicked up in the stalls by the crowds of people, cows and cars. Bullocks squatted, children squatted. We squirmed, tumbled, and tossed, not quite able to keep track of each other and our surroundings at the same time. Flies, cows, heat, dust, people, sun, stalls, spices, spilled grain—each sensation a separate presence, pushing in on us like so many henbirds diving and flapping and scratching to defend their nests. I wiped my eyes and tried to steer myself.

It was too interesting not to shoot. We went back to the car and fetched the equipment. I tried at first to walk a dolly shot through the stalls, but no matter what feints I used, people kept poking the lens and bumping into me. Had this been a Muslim area, everyone would have dodged me instead of bobbing in front of the lens. As it was, I fell prey to the International Small Boy Conspiracy. All photographers are acquainted with this cult—small boys between the ages of four and eleven who appear in great numbers, no one knows how, whenever a camera is set up. They have taken an oath, each and every member of the cult, to leave their noseprint on your lens. Additionally, the International Small Boy makes a lot of noise, so even if you manage to fake him out of the frame, the soundtrack of an otherwise serene landscape is cluttered with incongruous chuckles and shouts. Small Girls are invisible.

With one Small Boy clinging to my leg and two or three tugging at my shirt, I heard the thumping and bleating and tootling of a street band: clarinets, cornets, tubas, trombones, fifes, drums, crazed off-key kazoos . . . The wedding party filed shyly past as I filmed them.

Standing in the middle of the band, I shot a 360-degree pan, ending on the conductor, who was pounding a big drum with weighted balls strapped to the end of a thong which he clenched between his teeth. As I stepped closer, he gave me a big finish, doubling the tempo and rolling his head.

The bridegroom's father introduced himself in elaborate English and guided me to the courtyard of the reception hall. This was a flashy affair, a rich and gaudy Marwadi wedding, and since the arrival of strangers was considered auspicious, I was escorted to a position of honor next to a priest who was blessing the gifts, goblets of beaten brass and bright red silk saris embroidered with gold and silver threads. There was a tremendous crush of people in the courtyard, and overhead, hanging from balconies, cheering women and children tossed rose petals, gardenias, and rice. I backed to a vantage point behind a column. The band entered, encircling the priest. They tweeted, bonked, brayed, pounded, clanged, and danced till what I saw was welded into a pulsing screen of color-making noise.

I climbed back into the crowd, making my way toward the musicians. I got down on my back and shot up at the drum-thumper, who was dancing with several Small Boys. I silhouetted them against the sky, allowing, I hoped, just enough exposure to let the scarlet of the bandsmen's caps bleed through the milky blues and purples of the dusk. The faces were completely dark, just ecstatic shapes shaking and singing in the viewfinder. I shut out the sound and concentrated on the shapes and their rhythm, using the beat to guide my lens.

Meanwhile, Yvonne was submitting to a *mandi,* a magical hand tatoo which the women applied with a mixture of mud and hot vegetable oil.

As we were leaving, she stared at her tatooed palm and asked if I thought it was indelible. "Oh definitely," I said, "you'll have it forever." And we laughed.

Yvonne and I took a plane to Jaipur, the capital of Rajasthan. Sam, who was beginning to feel like a Milky Way left in the glove compartment, cooled his heels in Bombay.

We had already seen several of India's mistakes. Refreshingly, Jaipur was not another one. The city had been laid out in the eighteenth century by a maharajah who'd imported Jesuit architects to build an observatory, which was still standing. Except for the dung houses of remote villages, these stones for measuring the sky were the only strictly functional designs that I noticed in India. They were completely abstract, their functions replaced now by the gears and circuits of a more precise age. They sat in the courtyard of the old palace, casting shadows only scholars could decode, like toys left behind by the precocious children of giants.

We stayed at a modest state-run hotel with a pool at the end of a lawn, where peacocks called and strutted in the low-light hours. We bought some jewelry in a shop across from the observatory. We drove past hollyhocks and young mango trees. How nice, the luxury of domesticated plants. Here and there, hills turned to dunes.

We returned to the pool and spent most of the day lounging like seals. Yvonne stroked back and forth, holding her head up, grinning. In high school, she said, she had belonged to something called the Aqua Belles. An Aqua Belle always had to keep smiling, no matter how much water she swallowed.

Before dawn of the next day we set out for Bikaner, a desert outpost. Our driver was very young and his English consisted of "Okie-dokie."

The sky was a clean pastel-blue, the air sweet with flowers and sage, the bullocks on the road not yet snorting and twitching from the torture of midday flies. In the early morning, the mind and the desert made peace—a truce rather—and were allowed to savor each other, in the manner of civilized antagonists. Dawn and dusk were the human hours.

But the tropical sunrise does not linger as it does in northern latitudes. The sun pops up and bursts like a bubble, full of chatter.

An hour and a half out of Jaipur, the temperature passed one hundred degrees. The trees, as we plunged further into the desert, became twisted, stunted and sparse, like anchors at the bottom of a drained lake.

Yvonne switched on her cassette player and played Linda Ronstadt's version of "Love Has No Pride." Its Western harmonies, now exotic, restored in my heart all the things I loved in a leisurely way: my loft, New York, fishing. I missed New York so much: jukeboxes, strangers' cigarette smoke, crumple-fendered cabs, fashion-crazed Newyoricans, my plants, my records, my fountain-pen collection. All the things, all the *things* that were my life.

Despite the clinical detachment most cameramen attribute to themselves, movies are a massively flirtatious medium. Cinematography, the actual doing of it, generally feels like one of the construction trades, though there are times when it calls for tender attention. You fall in love with what you photograph and you're instantly divorced; that's what it's all about. When it's going well, camerawork is a perfect silence, a silence with love in it. Too corny? Nothing is too corny for a cameraman. I reached over and touched Yvonne on the cheek.

It was the first time I'd touched her. Her eyes went wide as clocks. I couldn't be sure if she was open to this or in shock. Strategically retreating, I pretended it was the song that moved me, and said that of the three versions I'd heard, Ronstadt's was my favorite.

Yvonne said she liked Bonnie Raitt's.

Good, I said, a close second. Rita Coolidge's I liked least of all. It's such a simple song, like "Help Me Make It Through the Night," but it's a singer's song. Without real feeling, it just falls apart. It sounds dumb. That's why I can't listen to Rita Coolidge doing it; she makes it sound sing-song.

"I'd like to hear Maria Muldaur do it," she said.

"What do you get out of her?" I asked crisply. "I just can't believe her. She sounds like a little girl performing at a party. Not enough experience in her voice."

"She has wit and intelligence," Yvonne said.

The cassette rolled to Jimmy Cliff's "Many Rivers to Cross." Yvonne had recorded it back in the States for Sam; she thought he'd would appreciate the sound of a fellow Jamaican.

Well, bless her little AM radio heart, I thought. And bless mine, too.

It's been many years now since Bikaner, and much of it is still a blur. What can be said about a town where, between eleven in the morning and four in the afternoon, the temperature sits at 130 degrees?

Nothing moved. No animals. No cars. No people. Nothing. Bikaner was far from a ghost town, but everything there kept perfectly still or moved so slowly, so tentatively, that all motion had the painful deliberation of a cripple's. Even the mosquitoes in Bikaner, unlike the robust malarial anopheles we had to dodge elsewhere, were frail and weary.

We were the only guests at the Bikaner state hotel. The hallways were dotted with English sporting prints and over the staircase stretched a moth-eaten tiger skin. In cooler months the hotel served as a lodge for big-game expeditions into Bengal. The houseboy was noticeably ancient, the oldest person I'd ever seen. I asked him for a Coke and waited for the fan to stir the air.

Up to 110 degrees or so, the heat is merely hot. You tend to be listless, short of breath, dry in the mouth and, if you don't get enough salt, your head hurts. Beyond 120, you've made a quantum leap into a new layer of experience. You drift continually between a state of semiconsciousness and complete unconsciousness. The idea of unleashing sprints of energy, as you must often do in film work, is unthinkable. We had come to a terrible place.

We had come, in fact, to take pictures of the Rajasthan Canal, the largest irrigation project on the planet. Two items of interest: the canal would make the desert green and it was being put together largely by hand labor, a bucket at a time. It was a big shot.

We lunched with two Canal Board functionaries, a couple of characters out of V. S. Naipaul. They made favorable comments on the soup and drank Cokes while evading questions about when we could film.

The Rajasthan desert includes India's border with Pakistan; Yvonne had been working for a month in New York and Delhi on security clearances, with assurances that all would go well. The officials knew nothing about the letters she showed them; their names did not appear on the documents. "But who are *you?*" Yvonne asked.

There was a magistrate, they said, in Bikaner whom we would have to consult. "But who is *he?*" Yvonne said.

At four-thirty in the afternoon, with the sun crisping my scalp and bleaching Bikaner a pale sepia, we found the magistrate. He was playing miniature golf on a course of his own contrivance in the middle of town. A Small Boy in a loincloth stood behind him holding a putter. When the magistrate tapped the ball, the little bearer ran after it, dropping the putter, then retrieved the ball and putter, all in a jerky run. The magistrate never moved from his spot, nor was there any hole to be seen.

No, the magistrate could not sign anything allowing us to take pictures of the canal. "I'm very sorry, Madame."

He putted, the boy scampered into the dust.

I was lying under my water tap when Yvonne entered, sat in the wicker chair, put her face in her hands and burst into tears.

I wrapped a towel around my waist and sat on the floor opposite her chair. She returned my look, hung her head, and sobbed.

"Would you like some water?" I asked.

"Oh, you're such a gracious host." Her chair squeaked.

I undid the top of the thermos and poured some water. It was hot. She didn't look up when I handed it to her.

"Do you know how much money I spent just to get us out here?" she moaned. "Five thousand rupees."

"Well, we'll make it up someplace else. Don't worry about it now."

"The bastards."

Had we met casually, I'd gladly have made a pass. The problem was that, having already achieved an advanced level of intimacy by sharing the brutal labor of this production, I was in no mood to treat her casually. By some strange inversion of the sex-work-ambition equation, I knew that *not* making a pass at Yvonne was the way to be true to her. Maybe I was warping cause and effect; maybe it was the heat. Maybe it was conjugal atrophy—I felt as if we'd been married for ten years—or maybe it was just plain priggishness. I was in any case frozen. The torturous part was that I suspected Yvonne was going through the same thing, afflicted with the same numb pride. No question about it, film was the stronger sex.

"Listen," I said, "when this over, we can start a new film company. We'll call it Quivering Blob Productions."

"A subsidiary of Slobbering Fool Films?" A mouse ran under my bed. We both saw it, said nothing. Then she sighed, the farewell signal. "Okay, see you in the morning."

"Okay. Goodnight."

"Thanks for the water."

Yvonne went for the door.

Below, in the courtyard, our driver was sleeping on a pal-

let next to the car. Both he and the car looked inexplicably
frail. It was wrong and dangerous and crazy, I thought, for
any of us, for anything, to be here. I walked to the bed and
passed out dreaming of the first salmon I'd caught.

Dr. Mathur was a courtly man who wore his white suit with
an ungainly, academic air. He'd lived all his life in Bikaner
and his presence was reassuring because it demonstrated,
contrary to the prevailing evidence, that a human being
could survive in this place.

With his help we filmed two classes in child care at the
Bikaner hospital. There was a class in breast feeding and a
class in how to sterilize a formula bottle over a buffalo-dung
fire. Dr. Mathur suggested that on our way back to Jaipur
we might like to film some scenes in Raisler, a Tribal village.

As is common in northwestern India, all of Raisler's
dwellings and sheds were sculpted completely of cow dung,
a cheap material with efficient insulating properties. When
we arrived at the first house, two women were repairing the
doorstep with a dung-and-water plaster. Children, their eyes
drooling and swarmed with flies, followed us. They smiled
when I photographed them, but they didn't brush the flies
from their eyes. Perhaps it was brain damage: malnourish-
ment over so many generations, hereditary syphillis . . . Perhaps it was a merciful adaptation.

On the portal of a newlywed couple's house, we filmed
magical paintings of Lord Krishna. Then we went to the
town well, where harnessed camels dragged buckets of
brackish water up from two hundred feet and where men
filled the jugs carried by women, who were forbidden to
touch the well itself.

By ten-thirty the sun was already too strong to move under. The bullocks sat down.

I tried to shoot a sequence of a woman carrying her jug

from the well, but Dr. Mathur's well-meaning white suit popped up in every shot. The woman returned to her hut and sat down to spin some yarn from camel hair and goat's wool. I tracked her left hand, which swooped around the bobbin in what seemed an unpredictable rhythm. Yvonne offered an orange to the woman, who at first refused, telling us through Dr. Mathur that she was letting us take her picture because of her affection for us.

"Affection?" I asked.

"Yes," Dr. Mathur said. "You know, I don't think these people have a word for love."

Our plan was to sleep until four in the afternoon, when it might be cool enough to start back to Jaipur. Dr. Mathur advised us to make our move when the wind was down, because sandstorms often swept the dunes across the road.

On the drive back the hotel, the wind from the jeep's motion washed us. Yvonne and I exchanged a few ideas on the logistics of living for several months with a family and documenting their life. The conversation trailed off. Film was not going to do anything for those villagers.

It came to me that we were touring the lives of millions of people, taking pictures of them, and that tomorrow they would be dead people. I'd seen them, the men and children hunkered by the roadsides, glazed and stupefied, without even the strength to beg. Benares was too much into death, an English hippie had said at the airport. I'd thought him ridiculous and in a way I'd been right. It was ridiculous to say that millions of people were predestined to starve.

India, if understood, is absolutely terrifying. Mercifully, India passeth all understanding, so we refer to it as mysterious, inscrutable, or we call it a phantom. It suits us to have a place like India. But my mind, secure in the schizophrenia of Western survival ethics, was not fused for the load. My camera stared because that's all it knew how to do.

* * *

By five o'clock, the sun was low and reddish through a dust storm in the east. Ten miles out of Bikaner, the engine boiled over. The driver, grinning boyishly, told us by signs that he'd forgotten to bring extra water. Our last swallow sloshed forlornly in his canteen.

There was nothing desert-island romantic about our predicament. In a couple of hours, toward dark, there might be a truck or two. By that time, though, we'd be delirious with dehydration.

This was not going to happen to us! Discomfort, exhaustion—all right. But to drop alone in the desert—that sort of thing happened only to Tribals or actors in corny movies. It was unthinkable. But there were no escapes on the horizon, no James Bond ingenuities. India was not a movie; India was the way the world was; she was not some other way.

With the appalling giddiness of final despair, we climbed a dune with our still cameras, playing out the script of this never-rehearsed thing by thinking to die on higher ground. I was laughing and taking a picture of Yvonne taking a picture of me when I caught sight of what the driver was up to. He was pouring the last of our water *over,* not into the radiator, and it was steaming uselessly away. I shouted and scrambled down the dune and yanked the jerry can out of his hands. I twisted off the radiator cap, searing my fingers, and managed to get a few drops into the radiator.

I slammed the hood. The jeep lurched and rolled downhill, frightening a camel. We packed our cameras and for six very slow kilometers we followed the camel until he came to a roadside well.

The camel sat peacefully by the spigot, his expression a weary smirk, while we doused ourselves. The day's assault had ended. The rest of the drive was pleasant. Wild peacocks darted vividly against the emptiness. Occasional

pockets of coolness. After dark, a desert truck stop. Drivers
with transistor radios. Bodies were still, in repose, or, when
someone moved under the blue moonlight, they coasted, like
meditating statues.

Later that night, by the pool in Jaipur, we sipped lime
and sodas. Every few minutes a blue flash, followed by a
distant thump, silhouetted sections of the town. Lights in
the hotel flickered, died, flickered and glowed again. A
bearer approached with another tray of drinks and told us
the striking railworkers were sabotaging the transformers. A
little boy in a loincloth paraded with a green-and-yellow
parrot on a leash. He would sell it to me for thirty dollars.
Flash, thud, flicker, bang, darkness. A backdrop of leisurely
chaos. Another sip of lime soda.

The shape of a man appeared, accompanied by introduc-
tory shuffling and coughing. "I am K. K. Jain," he said,
emerging against another flash. "I am Director of Public Relations for the entire state of Rajasthan."

Mr. Jain called for a chair. "Please be sure, Madame, that
I will be of any help you require. It is my job to see that
proper connections are made. Any help at all."

"K. K. Jain?" Yvonne said, recognizing that the gentleman's name was also the name of an Indian religion.
"That is certainly a Jain name. I have some good friends in
Bombay who are Jains. But they are very naughty Jains;
they smoke and drink."

"Oh. Then I too am a naughty Jain, Madame."

He made small talk for twenty minutes, interrupted only by
Yvonne's requests please not to address her as "Madame." He
talked about the heat, about his wife, about the price of silk,
about the peacocks, attaching himself to us with a skein of
non-sequiturs. Something about Mr. Jain suggested that in
another culture he would have been comfortable with a big
cigar. His eyes and mouth were under separate controls. He

stared with increasing dismay at our inappropriate *pajamini*. "Well, Madame," he said finally, "I am ready for dinner when *you* are."

In the dining room, it came out that one of Mr. Jain's concerns was the possibility that we were CIA agents. Merely mentioning the subject, of course, meant we had already been judged. He looked at us squarely for the first time.

"There was an incident . . . a very bad thing some years ago. CIA people running here and there telling people they were professors. It was very bad. Two friends—I knew them—lost their posts."

I assured Mr. Jain that while CIA agents were certainly inept, it did not necessarily follow that they were crazy. Consequently, when you came across two pajamaed Americans trying with all their might to get to the heart of the Rajasthan desert in the middle of May, you could with absolute certainty cross them off as just a couple of crazy filmmakers.

Yvonne, eyebrows curling, peered over a forkful of what the Indians call vegetable cutlet. K. K. Jain seemed relieved.

Without Mr. Jain, we wouldn't have been able to get to the places we needed to film. Even with him, it wasn't easy. Not always swift to see cinematic virtue in simplicity, he displayed a natural gift for crowd scenes. For one closeup of a baby being inoculated, he marshaled two streets full of people—a cast of thousands. Pans, zooms, follow-focus, elaborate crowd cues, move the tripod here and there. A closeup of a baby getting inoculated.

Typically, we would pull into a location with a van or two, meet the local officials, have some tea, meet their wives, have more tea. As much for personal sanity as for professionalism, I took to playing the heavy, and Yvonne the foil. Our routine went like this: when K. K. inquired of Yvonne, "What is wrong with Mr. Duke, why is Mr. Duke just sitting there, Madame, why isn't Mr. Duke drinking his tea?"—or alternatively (and a little petulantly), "Madame, now why is Mr. Duke outside playing football with the small boys, Madame? Doesn't he like his tea?" Yvonne would answer in a loud, peeved voice: "Oh, that Mr. Duke! He is so naughty. Mr. Duke can't stand talking and sitting around. Mr. Duke doesn't like officials, not magistrates, not even ministers. Mr. Duke, you know, is a cameraman. You know how they are."

The local officials, the tea, and the wives soon thinned out, and we were able to get a little work done.

I must report that this technique, relying as it did on the British abhorrence of a "scene," was not uniformly effective, perhaps because we lacked the proper colonialist flair. The next day, we trailed K. K. eighteen miles into the desert only to find about thirty officials, each with a frozen grin, lined up in front of a low building that comprised four empty rooms.

I sat in the van until K. K. came over. "What is this, Mr. Jain?" I asked.

"It is the local health center, Mr. Duke," he replied briskly. He ordered the bearer to fetch tea.

Four Small Boys helped set up the tripod. I placed the camera on it, called for smiles all around and panned the camera with a flourish, never once hitting the "on" switch.

"Say 'Cheese,'" I said.

"Seize!" they chorused.

Everyone applauded: the officials, the Small Boys, Yvonne, K. K. I applauded too. Tea and oranges were produced.

On the drive back to the hotel, I tried to nap in the front seat, next to the driver. Yvonne was lying across the seat behind me.

"Are you not married, Madame?" K. K. inquired.

"No," Yvonne replied, still horizontal.

"Why not, Madame? How do you manage?"

She sat up and continued in a polite, rehearsed tone. "I have been married so many times in previous lives, Mr. Jain, that I don't need it anymore. In this life, I am going to be by myself."

The van bounced sharply. "But how do you manage?" K. K. persisted.

"I have lovers. And I work."

K. K. smiled an incomplete smile, partly because of his astonishment at being privy to the exotic sexual practices of a strange culture, and partly because he seemed to find her views foolish. He linked himself to me with his smile.

"And what do you think, Mr. Duke?"

"I think it's okay. I think that's the way things are going in the world these days. No one owns anybody else. I think that's what people in the West are trying to work out."

"But who will raise the children?" asked K. K. "You know, here, the Tribals . . . we cannot teach these people family planning. The families live together in one house. When the man goes to the field in the morning, his wife brings him lunch and he enjoys her right there, under a tree. There is no time for a condom. How can you have family planning like this?"

"There are all kinds of possibilities," Yvonne said. "It's very hard, there is always a lot of pain when things change."

"Is it so complicated?" K. K. said. "We are a simple people."

"Oh no, you're not," Yvonne said. "Nobody is." Which led her, somehow, to a defense of arranged marriages. "The search for a perfect mate is foolish. If you know in advance that it's all arranged and that the person you're supposed to spend the rest of your life with is someone else's choice, it has nothing to do with personal satisfaction. Then you don't expect so much and you look to other things for satisfaction." She mentioned Leon Russell's manager and his girlfriend, how "they decided one day they were in love and had to go to Afghanistan." On the word "decided," she looked me dead in the eye as if to say: look, I know we can go as long as anyone else doing our jobs; you're tough and I'm tough, too. Anytime you want to lay down the guns and take me in, I'm willing, but I want the whole thing.

K. K. was silent for a long moment. "But isn't it nice, Mr. Duke, when you come home, to have someone there who says hello, sir, and brings you a glass of water?"

"Yes. That is nice."

We were eating breakfast bananas at the Wellington Club when Sam walked in with a newspaper. The headline announced the real reason for our banishment from the Rajasthan desert. Somewhere within a hundred-and-fifty-mile radius of the Bikaner magistrate's putting green, two days after K. K. Jain had ushered us out of Rajasthan, India had detonated its first atomic bomb.

We drove to a village hospital and filmed the birth of a baby, something that happens forty times a minute in India. On the way back to Bombay I sulked in the front seat, camera in my lap, eyes half shut, closing out the world, a technique I'd practiced during hundreds of takeoffs and landings, which have never ceased to terrify me. Only the smallest corner of my nervous system believes there is any reason for the plane to hang there in the sky. But I've disciplined myself to accept the consensus and the statistics.

Our driver passed on a hill, nothing unusual for an Indian driver. Main roads in India, such as they are, are arenas for anything that chooses to move: cars, trucks, carts, people, cows, chickens. There is occasional observance of the English convention of driving on the left, but Euclidean traffic is simply not an article of faith in the Third World. So our driver passed on the hill doing forty, but he kept the car in the lane of oncoming traffic, maybe because he was too flushed with triumph to follow through.

Half asleep in my daze of disgruntlement, I noticed an oil tank truck climbing the hill toward us. Just as in all those landings and takeoffs, I corrected my instinct and thought, No, I'm safe, it's not going to happen. Then the truck was very big and I knew it was going to happen. You're going to get hurt now, I said. *Whunk.* My sense went their separate ways.

What I perceived was a profound shudder, the wet dog of my existence slowly shaking itself dry. Then came the skid—a low, hysterical scraping—and Yvonne's gasps and screams, and the clangs and growls of strong pieces of metal suddenly changing shape.

Coming to, I noticed clinically that I was unable to account for all the parts of my body. And then I noticed that the pain which seemed to be happening everywhere was happening in my right leg. I remembered that the leg in which all this pain was happening belonged to me and I screamed.

I saw something in closeup, blurry at first. I was looking at the windshield, shattered in a spiderweb pattern, bright blood smeared at the center, my blood. I was curled up in a fetal position, pinned by the detached dashboard. The camera was still in my lap. The lens was in the driver's seat. The interior of the car had been rearranged beyond recognition.

What had happened was that I'd broken my ankle and suffered a concussion which deprived me of vital signs—no pulse, no breathing—for about three minutes. They'd left me in the car for dead. I smelled smoke.

The driver had caught the steering wheel in his throat, broken a collar bone, and wandered off, crying, furious at the truck driver. Through the windshield, I could see Sam pacing up and down, trying to support his left arm. It was broken in eight places between the shoulder and elbow. Yvonne was out of the car as well, her blouse soaked with blood, talking to the driver of a car who said he wanted a hundred rupees to help us. I scratched glass splinters from my scalp and cheek. I rolled out of the car.

A Volkswagen pulled up, driven by a young Indian who spoke colloquial American. He recovered my sandals from the smoldering wreck and said he'd gone to school in Minnesota, where they'd called him Poncho. Bob Dylan was from Minnesota, Poncho said, did I know Bob Dylan? Not really, I said, but I'd like some morphine. Poncho knew of a dentist nearby who might have some.

We lurched through the bazaar of a small town. Faces pressed at the windows. I was beginning to fade. A smiling man approached with a hypodermic, swabbed my arm, jabbed it . . .

Sam and I spent two weeks in a ward with seven merchant seamen, all of them English-speaking except for Sinbad the Fly Swatter, an Ethiopian Muslim who had some Italian. Sinbad, whose real name was Ali, had crushed his hand under a hatch. When asked how he was coming along, he'd refer to his pain, in a Ronald Colman accent, as "excruciating." To his cast he'd taped a flyswatter, which came to be regarded as a symbol of authority around the ward. Since we were all in some degree of pain and had to help each other out, we all became good friends.

"I used to be in love," Sinbad said one night. "But it didn't work out. Her parents didn't like me because I was a sailor. Now sometimes I stay home on leave for six months at a time, but always, after a while, I have the urge to get another ship and go someplace else. Or to see Singapore again, to see if it's changed. It doesn't change, but I can't help myself."

A couple of the sailors had families, and one of them talked about buying a ranch in Australia and settling down. No one spoke of the sea as something they looked forward to anymore.

I was unable to urinate for three days. "Neurasthenic shock," Dr. Singh advised with a smile that was perhaps too reassuring. Finally, despite the risk of infection—the hospital floors were foul—they catheterized me without anesthesia on the assumption that Americans, something like fish, did not experience pain. Miss Shrivastara, the Goanese nurse, tickled my ear with the feather of a crow who'd been shelling a cockroach enormous enough to be mourned as a pet and made me a present of extra morphine.

Father Fernandes, an aged Portuguese priest from the Stella Maris Society, asked in liquid English if there was anything he could do for me. Did I still practice the faith? I said no. Oh, you're in trouble, my boy. I said, aren't we all, Father? Aren't we all? I asked if he would get me a Sikh bracelet. Why? I admired the Sikhs, I replied, and the simple steel bracelet they wore as a reminder to speak the truth always. Yes, he said. It shakes when you raise your hand, it is a kind of reminder, isn't it? He pulled up the long white sleeve of his cassock, exposing a bony forearm and a Sikh bracelet of his own.

Yvonne, who'd come through okay except for cuts and bruises, made arrangements to go on to Sri Lanka. She turned up with a couple of friends from Bombay society, an assistant cameraman and a gorgeous woman in a scarlet sari who magnetized every man in the ward. I tried to be cool, though I realized I was staring all the time at the woman's dusky navel.

"When we crashed," Yvonne said, "I knew I had to get it

together one more time. I sat under a tree. Oh Guru, I prayed, what are we going to do now? And suddenly this shaft of light, like an arc lamp, came down over the car. I jumped right up. The car was next to a twenty-foot cotton-wood tree. I needed shade, I had this tremendous need to get out of the sun for one minute. I was thinking of Sri Chin-moy, not so much as a person, but as a wind through the ages. He's not much of a person, really—he's, like, lumines-cent, a real spiritual master. Before I left, he said, 'I'm going to give you a *tilik*. We usually make them with red dye. I'm giving you one of light. You have my protection and bless-ing through the journey. It will be a silver journey. Silver means purity, but also freedom from jealousy and attach-ment to ego.' The light energized you, Duke."

I told her my big toe was numb. She said her thumb was numb. She was on her way to the radio station to record a show. But the manager called to say sorry, Madame, strik-ing technicians had set the station on fire and would she please send him some commemorative stamps from the States.

She left me a book, beautifully illustrated, about Akbar, the Moghul lord who never smiled.

A few days later, three ladies from the Stella Maris Soci-ety arrived with a Sikh bracelet. Oh yes, Father Fernandes is not well, you know. He is so good. He spends all day walk-ing along the docks, talking to the boys.

No matter how I squeezed and pushed, the bracelet was just too small. I tried it on my left hand. It stuck on the lump of my thumb joint. I sucked in my breath, squashed my fist and pushed the bracelet down, tearing skin from the thumb knuckle, exposing a white flap of flesh, then blood. The bracelet slipped over my hand and hung on my wrist.

The hospital faced the Bombay shoreline, and I took to

sunning myself on the balcony, often in the company of Sinbad, who'd sit on his prayer rug and try to converse in Italian. We exchanged the odd "que bella figura" regarding
Miss Shrivastara. Sam and I staged frisbee tournaments with
stale toast. The last three days of my stay, I took my turn as
custodian of the flyswatter.

On my last morning in the hospital, I sat on the balcony
at daybreak watching our crow dissect another cockroach.
He and his mate lived in a coconut tree in the courtyard. He
was so efficient, so determined, taking only what he needed
with four or five vigorous pecks and leaving just the wing
husks. He flapped back to his nest, I stared at the Arabian
Sea. Towering monsoon clouds were moving in; there would
be showers any day now. Miss Shrivastara tickled my ear.
"What are you looking at?" she asked. "Home," I said.

Not yet, something echoed.

Sri Lanka is so lush that when you move, you get wet. You
get wet on top because a monsoon shower is pouring great
lashes of water on you. You get wet on the bottom because
the mud and the grass squooshes underfoot. You get wet on
the sides because water from fronds and ferns dribbles on
you. You get wet on the outside and you get wet on the
inside because at the slightest exertion you break into a
sweat that soaks your clothes. I packaged my cast in a plastic garbage bag.

We drove to the highlands to film a tea plantation. A mile
below, the sun dialed haloes in the river. Above the water
ran a duplicate river of dripping steam, every meander
matching. Moisture ticked under enormous high-altitude orchids. The hot eyes of individual blossoms stared back at
me. There was sweat on my forehead, as if I'd wept upward,
and my shirt was soggy from the climb. And there, lower, in
a strand of pale lavender mist, on the porch of a grass-

walled cabin, stood a tall woman dressed in black. She waved and shouted hello in what sounded like an Irish brogue.

Her name was Sister Mary Rosary. She stood over six feet tall and her freckled hands belonged to a plowman. Other nuns peeked from the cabin window. "Would you like to hear some music?" Sister Mary Rosary asked the instant she heard my last name.

She gestured regally; a young nun lugged a hand-cranked Victrola and a stack of 78s to the veranda and set it on a table next to the rock garden. The first selection was "The Rose of Picardy," recorded by John McCormack in 1917, a few years before Sister Mary Rosary had left Galway for the Eastern missions. Hers was a common sort of Irish exile, now obscure, but not irrelevant. The nuns jigged. I waved my crutches. We toasted each other with strong tea.

In a silence between records, Sister Augusta, very old and very bent in her wheelchair, was wheeled onto the porch.

Sister Mary Rosary said, "Sister Augusta is very close to God." Clearly, Sister Augusta was dying. "Would you like her blessing?"

Because of my bad leg, I was unable to kneel. I approached the wheelchair and bowed my head. Sister Augusta made the sign of the cross in my hair and uttered a soft squawk, incomprehensible but somehow precise. Her smile was a trembling pastel crease.

This was a mulberry farm, Sister Mary Rosary explained, pacing in a circle, her habit twirling; the nuns made their living raising silkworms. She pointed to a wall map captioned *Foreign Missions, Less Polar Regions*. The map, its lacquer cracked like old clay, was sprinkled with pins. "Raising silkworms . . . the cocoons are very beautiful . . . the spinning of their silk . . . there's a lot of mothering to it, as you might imagine."

Smiling blindly, Sister Augusta rose from her wheelchair. After forty years in the Sacred Heart Leprosarium, Sister Mary Rosary whispered, the old sister had contracted a rare form of tuberculosis and had retired to spend her last days in the misty hills, which reminded her, especially at dawn, of the Connemarra she'd never see again. Her prosthetic knee joint made a popping noise with each step. It was as if, in moments of locomotion, her starchy black habit deliquesced into a sarong, to the accompaniment of a tiny drum. The other nuns, harmonizing expertly, sang along with McCormack's rendition of "Danny Boy."

We worked, days passed, and then the plane took us away. We stopped over at Zurich, that perfect plastic flower of a town, whose every citizen looked forty-eight years old. We ate yogurt, watched TV, and savored the privileged coolness. The lights, the phones, the hot water, the cars— they all worked. Amazing. At the airport, I chatted with an American missionary in baggy pants who, after twenty-three years in the Asian missions, was returning to bury his mother in Alabama. When he saw me fumbling with my francs to pay the airport tax, he offered to pay it for me. Obscurely embarrassed, I refused. Civilized again.

"I never been in a car crash," the New York cabbie said. "What's it like?"

"It was an out-of-body experience, all right," I said.

We were still wearing our *khadi pajamini*; somewhere between Sri Lanka and Switzerland, Yvonne had also acquired an old-fashioned bonnet.

"Yeah," the cabbie said. "It gives you a chance to remember all the things you did wrong—right? A friend of mine, his horse won a big race, then he drops dead of a heart attack, my friend. So if you're a human being, anything can happen to you. So you gotta take your time, don't hurt yourself."

A road gang was repairing the potholes in front of my loft. A curly Sicilian leaned on his smoldering tar broom. I tipped him twenty dollars to carry my equipment upstairs.

When Yvonne got out of the cab at her place, she left behind an expensive microphone and the parasol she'd carried all the way from Sri Lanka. Two days later, while hobbling across Canal Street, I heard someone call, "Hey, dja get your microphone yet?" It was the driver of the cab Yvonne had left the equipment in. He pulled over and gave me the police department receipt. The microphone was recovered, but not the parasol.

Three months later, our film on India's population problems opened the UN conference in Bucharest. The *New York Times* noted that the conference, owing to summer swelter and warring factions, was "underpopulated."

Yvonne and I never did become lovers. We've worked often together in the years since Inida, mostly on industrial films. There's talk of a two-week job in Jakarta soon. A coupla weeks of living cautiously, I guess.

Murder in
the Carwash

"I'm trying to remember who we killed yesterday."

"Name began with an *S,*" Tyrone said.

"With a whip and a barbecue fork, wasn't it?" Teddy Churchill sat in the back of the van, latching and unlatching his seven equipment cases, average weight forty-five pounds, groping their entrails for his watch. The sky was rainy and cool with interesting clouds. The wind whipped the Hudson into whitecaps.

"I lost my watch." Teddy took a bite out of his bialy. "I took a shower and I lost it. I can't believe this. I got too many things, Tyrone, I'm losing my mind."

"Try to remember the last time you had it on."

"Listen, you don't understand—the thing I take pride in is being organized. This is twenty seconds to meltdown. This is where I start throwing things. We're talking nanoseconds here."

Teddy had looked all over his loft for the watch, picking

things up and slapping them down in a series of pounces. He'd stood his answering machine on end, scattering a roach family. Every cup, every paperclip might have been a lid on lost secrets.

"Today's the murder in the carwash," Tyrone reminded him.

"I just hope I don't have to get wet. Water on this equipment is the kiss of death. They didn't tell me anything about water."

Tyrone, the gentleman Teamster, was cast against type. He was soft-spoken to the point of being honey-tongued, his eyes were mild, his mustache precise. He had driven Paul Newman's camper on *Fort Apache, The Bronx*. Today he was trucking Teddy upstate to shoot Steadicam sequences for *Blessing in Disguise,* a British horror film.

Yesterday was the tracking shot through two hundred rented chickens to reveal a dead white dog and bare bloody feet attached to a dead man with an eight-inch stilleto sticking in and out of his neck, hysterical poultry rocketing all the while through a blizzard of their own feathers. The crew had debated whether to replace the actor's eyebrows with chicken feathers. It was decided, after a discussion of the fine points of horror, danger, sadism, irony, and the overall mechanics of film emotion, that feathered eyebrows might tip the director's hand and defeat the horror.

"Yeah, that was some shoot, that *Fort Apache* thing," Tyrone was saying. "Never stopped for a light, alla way through the Bronx. Bricks and bottles flying. A real gentleman, Mr. Newman was."

And the day before yesterday was the corpse facedown in a lobster tank, the lobsters nipping the deceased's drowned face.

"The thing about Mr. Newman . . ." Tyrone continued. "You ever notice he's got no ass? His pants hang straight down."

"Yeah. Like Sigourney Weaver. A major disappointment."

"Yeah. Remember what's-his-name, the production manager on *Fort Apache*? At the end of the day, he looks around and he goes, 'Okay, where's Mr. Newman's ass? Nobody leaves the room till we find Mr. Newman's ass.'"

"Here it is!" Teddy uncovered his watch in one of his accessory cases, and a lovely piece of work it was, a Tourneau: thin black anodized body, a perfect circle dial, sturdy black hands and numbers, chaste white face. He'd customized it, of course, by adding Velcro tabs to the wrist band for swift attachment to his Steadicam. It was a picture of the time as well as an elegant mask for the machinery that made it tick.

Tyrone pulled the van into the carwash on 9W, next to Pal's Chevrolet, in the middle of a sixties mall which had begun to dilapidate.

Nigger Rig Roy uncapped a bottle of Yoo-Hoo with his molars and extended his belly ahead of his handshake. Nigger Rig Roy was the first assistant cameraman on a mixed crew of English and New York technicians. The crew were the usual universal fisherman: complaining, bantering, horny, and cynical. The Brits were lean, suave, and fair. Nigger Rig Roy had a blue terry cloth cap and bushy inverted-V eyebrows. He'd salvaged several dozen eggs from yesterday's chicken sack location, which he'd brought along, hard-boiled, today. "The assistant director kept shooting off his shotgun to get the chickens to fly. It must've been the deaf ones that laid the eggs." He handed Teddy one of his new business cards.

Kandid Kids Studio * Capturing Today for Tomorrow & Always * Quality Photography & Postcards * Brochures * Calendars * Display Posters * Banners * Greeting Cards * Programs * Sports Cards * Publicity Photos

* Weddings * Portraits * Framing Pictures * Note Paper
* Publications * Church Printing * Bulletins * Specialty
Cards * Letterheads * Menus * Table Tents * Golf Score
Cards * Advertising Cards

"I do printing, but it's basically a silver recovery business. This is my black-and-white card. I got color ones too. You got to keep busy. Eggs, silver—whatever. I save them. You got some short ends, send them to me, I'll give you a cut."

An assistant cameraman is in a position to keep the "short ends," the odd bits of film not long enough to run efficiently through the camera. Photographic film contains silver salts, which caused the price of film stock to shoot up 75 percent during the precious metals inflation of 1978–79. Film laboratories generally have machines for recovering silver as a byproduct of photo-finishing. Nigger Rig Roy had a secret cottage alchemy of his own.

"I suck the silver out of the film," he said without irony. He reminded Teddy to smoke his pipe downwind, please.

"Suck this," Teddy said.

He unpacked the Steadicam counterbalance, a black box the size of a construction boot. On the side, hand-lettered in silver paint, it said *CHURCHILL*. The letters leaned, as if rocket-propelled.

"Okay, Roy. Now I need a stand, a sidearm, two sand-bags, and a blowjob."

"You'll just have to wait. There are no grips here yet, just Teamsters."

"Hamsters?"

"Teamsters."

Teddy tapped his pipe on the tailgate. They exchanged silences.

The wreck of a Cadillac totaled in one of last week's stunts was being towed to the back of the carwash. It had been partially pancaked, and there were long scrape marks gouged along its side and hood; it had evidently skidded some distance after the initial impact. Nigger Rig Roy narrated the story of the nearly tragic car stunt with swoops of his flattened hands, like a fighter pilot.

"The car was supposed to just miss the tree. It was supposed to come off the ramp at an angle, like this, on two wheels. That way it would've cleared the tree by this much. But something went wrong and it came off pretty much straight, like this, you know, so it hit the side of the tree and took out the Arri I had mounted there. It was pretty close for a couple of people. You could've got a lot of parts for your Arri, though, Teddy."

Teddy squinted in an effort to see inside the compressed passenger compartment clanking by.

"I better go find out if you're gonna be inside or outside the carwash," Roy said. "I don't want your equipment getting wet."

"This is definitively the big time, Roy. We got a cellular phone in the van, I'm smoking a Sherlock Holmes pipe and these people are paying me cash. But I want to settle down. Not even my plants want me to come home. My fern hates me." He crumpled a couple of cigarettes into his pipe. He wasn't carrying pipe tobacco because he was trying to give up smoking again. He cast an eye on Ramona, the svelte ballerina he'd spotted among the extras.

"I've fallen in love with a movie star, Roy. Kristy McNichol. She is the *one*. Not since Ava Gardner. Remember Celeste, the Turkish ventriloquist's daughter? She turned out to be incredibly sincere, especially in bed. These ladies that keep popping up on the set, though, they all tend to be in turbo-bimbo land. Seduction is out of the question; they're too far gone."

Ramona waved and smiled, porcelain-shiny, and glided toward the wardrobe wagon. She was carrying a crash helmet.

"Plus she's got an ass like a New England boiled dinner," was Roy's evaluation. He hollered: "Carwash is closed today, sweetheart. Stop by tomorrow for hot wax."

Teddy changed into hightop sneakers with ankle supports. Bedford Argyle, the director, walked by while he was standing in his socks.

"Not wearing shoes today, Teddy?"

Bedford complimented Teddy on the rushes for yesterday's slaughter-in-the-chicken-shack scene. Bedford was a young Englishman with brick-colored cheeks, opaque sunglasses, and long feral hair. This was the next-to-last day of an eight-week shoot and he was in a state of giddy surrender. Actually, Bedford Argyle was a Polish émigré with a British accent. His charm derived from having seen the worst (Russians with automatic weapons peeing in his garden), gracefully accepting his sentence of exile and whorish success, and sailing on. Teddy had seen him on his day off, unshaven, in dark glasses, pedaling an old bicycle, pointing out comical birds and chatting about baseball with his young son in the handlebar basket. After invasion, exile, change of name and tongue, this film life was fair enough. Which may be why émigrés get so many Oscars.

"You're gonna be *in* the carwash," Nigger Rig Roy announced. "Walking alongside the car, but on the dry end."

The carwash stood empty, puddles shining, a ragged line of coffee cups on the lone windowsill.

"Spitoon architecture," Bedford said. "It stinks."

"You ever work with tigers?" asked Nigger Rig Roy. "They stink. They stink like goats."

Somewhere a phone rang insistently, the sharp echoes grating off the cinderblock walls stained with slime and moss that flourished in the constant moisture.

Bedford hunkered down at the dry end of the conveyor chain used to tow cars through the wash. He sighted toward the wet end, contemplating the design of the shot. Teddy hunkered next to him. Spacey Tracy, the assistant director (her trademark was always wearing a bow), pushed a wall-mounted button; the conveyor chain jerked into motion. The puddles trembled. Halfway to the other end of the garage-cave, long rubber scrubbing strips wiggled, hulalike. The squashed Caddy lurched through, snout gleaming. The roar of the drier fans swamped conversation. There was nothing to do in the industrially induced deafness but stare and think about it. Tow, scrub, wiggle, spray, blow. Bedford studied the contraption till it dawned on him that steam should be added, so that the squashed Caddy would be seen emerging from a scary mist.

"You know what we call something like this in East Canarsie?" Nigger Rig Roy asked.

"No." Bedford wrung his scarf. His concentration was blown, and he was politely infuriated about it. "What *does* one call something like this in East Whatever-it-is?"

"We call this a nigger rig."

"I see. Thank you. Now in this movie *some* of us will continue to work on, a child—that is, a little kid, a little girl, I mean—has been killed by a bloke named Costello. No, wait. *Costello's* kid has been killed by this gang of blokes whilst they're robbing the armored car. So Costello has to kill all the robbers who killed her. One bloke, he's very sorry he did it, you see, it was an accident, but he has to die anyway, I think."

"Great," said Teddy. "Got it."

"It's got to be dreamlike."

"No problem."

"Luvly."

The corpse in the car had been spray-painted to death,

fluorescent pink. To save wear and tear on the live talent and since the corpse had no lines in this scene and only had to sit there with mouth agape, teeth snapped and blood drooling down his day-glo chin, the corpse would be played by a torso dummy who perched for the moment on an oil drum in a corner, quite still. The idea was for Teddy to dolly in toward the car as it moved down the line, revealing at the last second, through a mephitic veil of steam, a glimpse by the floating Steadicam of—*aieee!*—the spray-painted corpse behind the wheel.

He strapped on his Steadicam vest: plastic shoulders joined with webbing like football shoulder pads *cum* corset. He tightened the straps till he gasped. He inserted the Steadicam arm into a notch in the front of the vest. It was roughly the shape of a human arm and it had muscular-looking springs and an elbow. Instead of a hand, though, there was a ring. The camera itself stood a few feet away on its docking stand.

Teddy still had to remember, after years of experience, to tell his own hands to do nothing. Just relax, face the machine like an amputee. He was still in awe of its intricate black assurance.

Sticking from his chest was an arm with a ring at its end instead of a hand and it wanted to be connected to a black rod about the thickness of two fingers. The rod, in turn, was linked by a gimbal—a planetary ring—to another rod, a vertical one, on top of which sat the camera. At the bottom was the battery sled, which functioned as a counterweight. He made the connection and stepped away from the docking stand. The device totaled fifty-five pounds and it took him a second to relocate his center of gravity.

Yes, there it was, the stress of the weight, between his shoulder blades, as if someone were determined to press them together till they touched. The sensation was restricting, but not painful, unnatural, or even unpleasant. The camera, in the low mode, floated in front of his left knee, virtually weightless, responding to a feather touch. The gravity-defeat effect was stunning. He could not force it; he coaxed it to move, Christian ethic sort-of-thing.

Gino, the Teamster captain, rode his Mercedes through the carwash for a free scrub. Teddy lit his pipe to incense the arena. A hellish shine kicked off the black puddles.

Outside, in the parking lot, a swarm scene was building. Forty-three crew members tossed ropes, rigged tarpaulins, coiled cables, chomped donuts. A small electrical fire had developed in the front of the squashed Caddy. Gino the Teamster and Nigger Rig Roy stood around in a stench like that of burning hair and debated, like experimental barbers, whether to use water on it, or foam.

Legendary Rooney, the soundman, requested the removal of the Caddy's trunk lid so he could run some microphone cables through it. Gino did not fucking want to remove the fucking trunk lid unless it was absolutely fucking necessary. Gino was short and slope-shouldered, a serious projectile. He lunged across the trunk, tackling Legendary Rooney, flattening him.

"I'm a little grumpy today," Gino said when he simmered down. He pried off the trunk lid and added to the artistry of the scene by shredding strips of door paneling with his teeth.

"Lunch!" Spacey Tracy called. "One hour!"

"Are youse from the movie?" the McDonald's waitress asked as she wiped the table.

"Sort of," Teddy said.

"When're you gonna ask me to be in the movie?"

"It's just a lot of people playing dead."

"I can do that."

"This cake is almost as good as sex," Nigger Rig Roy said.

"I don't think sex is all that great," said Teddy. "You haven't shot Steadicam. Is that chicken salad from yesterday's location?"

"Waste not, want not."

They wandered into the showroom of Pal's Chevrolet, where a dozen other crew members were already browsing. Teddy paced around a white Corvette, stroking its rump. The sticker price was $24,000.

"Day's pay, Roy. Real fancy. I like the square back, it's sexy. It's like an animal. I remember the first time I saw a car. *Saw* it. '55 Roadmaster. I was coming out of the Rexall with one of those brown bubble gum cigars; I sent in the most wrappers so I got a big one." He popped his eyes to *sooo*-big size. "I got so sick of that stuff. So anyway I'm coming out of the Rexall and then I see it, with the circle dashboard and the holes in the sides of the hood for dragon flames to come out. And the New Look fins." Pacing around, stalking the Corvette. "I used to go on trips with my parents and sit looking out the back window, having a contest to see who'd spot a New Look with fins first. 'I got it! I got it!' All trip long, 'I got it!'"

They trudged uphill to a larger mall. Nigger Rig Roy handed Teddy his bag of potato chips and said, yeah, it was true, he was having an identity crisis too, working full time as an assistant cameraman and trying to develop his own business on the side, which reminded him of techniques for buying off Teamsters on low-budget films, how far out of town you have to shoot to give them the slip, how to avoid slashed tires next time they spot you, and it was getting to be a show business war-story conversation, sprinting past hilarious atrocities, so Nigger Rig Roy, who seemed all of a sudden to have reconciled nostalgia and glamor and bucks, recalled the farmhouse he'd lived in with eleven other radicals while organizing GIs at Fort Dix.

"I don't know why we weren't all killed. We had a plan but the plan was stupid. We were armed. We posted sentries on the roof; we had telecommunications and alarms. We had screens on the windows so they couldn't throw bombs in. We had blacks, Vietnam vets. We'd come home and do acid every night. One day we went out and made a test—fired rifles at the house. The bullets went right through and out the other side. We took a can of food—beans—and threw it at the window; it went through the screen. I don't know why we weren't all killed.

"They came one night, these rednecks that were after us, they were in the woods. I put my daughters in the bathtub. In the bathtub because lead wouldn't go through the bathtub. The vets went out in the woods and shot them up. *Powpowpow.*"

Water roared in the drainage ditch separating the mall from Pal's Chevrolet.

"You look at that and you could be someplace beautiful," Teddy said. "You ever go tubing, Roy? They drop you off ten miles upstream and you float with your ass in an inner tube. When I take a bath, I try to deal with the water taps with my feet. Any disco skater should be able to do that."

"We're back in!" Spacey Tracy barked over her bullhorn. "Positions for Murder in the Carwash, everybody."

Teddy flipped up his goggles and massaged his eyelids. "Yuh sure do look purty today, Miz Spacey."

"The time is now thu-ree-thirty, Teddy. Pee-fucking-em."

"It's only noon in Hollywood, ma'am."

"Yeah? This ain't Califuckingfornia. Let's get it right this time, shall we? Honk when you're ready, asshole."

Under pressure, Spacey swore like someone who'd majored in it. Teddy didn't take it personally; it was part of the crew's shared defiance. Twenty years ago, when she was ten, Spacey had been worth a lot of money; she'd been the cutest thing on the silver screen. The cry to kids across the land was, "Why can't you behave yourself like Spacey Tracy? Spacey Tracy doesn't wipe her mouth with her fingers." When Spacey ate ice cream in her first movie, she ate it more stylishly than any child in history. Her secret was to eat the cone with her teeth, not her lips; so her dimples remained spotless and polished as apples, to which the flacks invariably compared her cheeks. But she claimed to have lost everything in a quiz show scandal.

Teddy spit in his goggles to keep them from fogging and squeezed the bulb of the bicycle horn taped to his crash helmet. Again. Honk. The set quieted down to a bullfight hush.

By five in the afternoon, two takes had been accomplished. Teddy wasn't happy with either of them. He huddled with Bedford Argyle, who'd taken to wearing a parka, not because of the chill, it was clear, but wearily, for amniotic reasons. The grips hustled in, shoulders rolling, whistling, hooting 'Lez go, lez go, lez go Mo,' pushing the squashed Caddy back to position number one. This was professional moviemaking. You want it moved, we move it. We know how to do this. The same thing was happening over and over, but this was not just a parade that couldn't decide which way to turn. This was respectable plunder. Teddy nibbled his nails, adjusted his gloves and his goggles. The steam machine wheezed.

After five takes he Zenned out enough to anticipate the pace of the car. Spacey Tracy whistled him back to the first position. "Roll 'em," she said with an illustrative grind.

Take seven did it.

"Luvly," Bedford said. "Toodle-oo."

"Toodle-oo? That's it? You won't need me tonight? Well, goodbye. Too bad. I wanted to spend more time with you guys."

"You're history," Spacey said. "Pack it up."

The steam machine made a noise like Daffy Duck enunciating *Schenectady*, then fluttered and died.

Thstrange, Teddy thought, how many cartoon charactersth have sthpeech defexths. Or, to put it another way, the idea of the Duck has exerted a powerful influence on the cartoon imagination. His eyes felt peeled.

Nigger Rig Roy hadn't gotten a chance to unload the exposed film in Teddy's magazines. So they'd had to move with the first unit to the next location and unload there. They stood in the dusk waiting to find out where this was and how they were going to get there. There were no vans available. They waited next to the squashed Caddy. The only other thing on wheels was the honey wagon, a trailer of portable toilets.

"It's all on the clock anyway." There was a marooned edge to Teddy's laugh. "Wait'll they get my bill."

Gino started the Caddy with a roar and a rumble. Teddy jumped.

"Race car movies. That's what I wanted to do. Caress the Porsches with a super wide-angle lens, right? You know what you get? You get noise that deafens you, fumes that asphyxiate you, warm six packs, and a herd of crazy scumbags running around trying to kill themselves."

"Let's see. We could load this shit, so to speak, in the honey wagon."

"We don't have to ride in the honey wagon, do we, Roy? I'm a class act." Teddy brushed his hair with a brush that came out of its own zip-lock back in his kit. He looked around, scanning the sea of things for whatever had triggered his panoramic instinct.

"My entire sense of reality has just come unglued, Roy. This is the kind of place I have dry dreams about. Stores and cars, that's all it is. Look at them all. Everywhere you look, the old, the elegant, the crafty—it's fading. And people live with this other shit. Everything in this place is dead, you notice that? The plants in the car showroom were dead."

"Yeah. You ever take acid? I don't feel thirty-nine. I'm going to start saying I'm twenty-nine. That's how old I feel. A lot of people out there are still swimming around. I been on dry ground for years, my friend. Think how much money we could make hypnotizing people into thinking they were ten years younger. I'm not kidding, Teddy."

"Yeah. What's next? Holographic modems, networked. Goodbye reality."

Tyrone the immaculately groomed Teamster circled back to ferry them to the next location, a curve on 9W overlooking the Hudson. There was a cement factory in the foreground, bisected by New York Central tracks—shiny ribbons of reflected skylight. The dark trees, like Italians, kept touching one another. The Hudson was the same matte-blue as the sky, and in the south, toward the city, a full moon was rising, a pale flat disk.

In movies, this was the Magic Hour, the ten to twenty minutes at the close of a clear day when just enough falling light remained for the emulsion to record colors with some fidelity. It was called Magic Hour because it was brief and because its illusory light made heroes of everything—the landscape, the sky, passing strangers. It was the light of most religious paintings, the light of pretty force; it was lullaby light, the light of legendary rearing stallions and Shane's farewell wave. And since Magic Hour was the only kind of light that could not be mechanically controlled or prolonged or duplicated, it was, for a film crew with exteriors on its schedule, a time of frenzy. A battery of three cameras bristled, filming Teddy knew not what.

His magazines had once again leapfrogged ahead of him to yet another location, this one twenty minutes further on, an alleyway next to a rail depot.

It was pitch dark when they arrived. Cop cars, Mars lights flashing, warned civilian traffic away. Teddy stood in the glare of a worklight. The romance of night encampments, here it definitively was.

A woman holding the hand of a small boy walked up and asked what was going on. Teddy told her he didn't really know, he was just a second-unit Steadicam operator hanging around waiting to collect some equipment.

"Hey, well I'm just a housewife with wet hair, and my son said they're shooting a movie over here and he dragged me out of the house and I had to drive over about a ton of broken glass to get here."

Two gigantic jackknife cranes trundled down the alley. The grips argued about how high they'd stretch, two hundred or a hundred-and-fifty feet, and how to rig the lights on them.

"See, you got to get the lights high at night," Teddy explained. "You got to have moonlight for everybody." The cranes clanked. He looked up. The real moon was streaking through high mist. He felt he was being peeped on from above. "See, lady, it's the delicacy and the indelicacy of the whole thing."

DuffyVision

I woke up brooding about money and the perfect woman again, namely Zazi.

I'd slept in the Technicolor shirt Zazi had given me as a divorce present three years ago. It was an early synthetic, probably rayon, and it was printed with photographs of sporting scenes, hand-tinted, faded now, like a movie of equivalent age. Preservation is a problem.

I draped the shirt across the ironing board. There was a run in the left shoulder and a moth hole just above the belly. The predominant color was pale blue (skies with clouds; blurry fast-running streams). A football player, number 14, followed through on his punt. His arms were stretched wide, his eyes up, helmet tilted over his brow, right foot straight ahead, his left foot off the ground, laces blown back. This was his airborne instant. This was also Zazi's message about men, a selected short subject coming at me across the ironing board, and something of a relic by this time.

Fodo, my crow, flapped to the top of the skylight. I set out a bowl of sunflower seeds. Fodo settled on the sprinkler pipe, strutting back and forth, making plans and giving me the eye.

I put the shirt on, slightly threadbare but still warm from the iron, sucked in my stomach, renewed my cameraman's vow of invisibility and dashed through a thundershower to Sammy's, a Bowery seafood eatery that featured a singing banjo player and stupid food.

The restaurant was done in a dim grotto motif. There was only one window and it was curtained. The thunderstorm lightninged; the window lit a cigarette. Good decor, I thought: it's guilty here. For the silhouetted assignation look, you light the walls, not the people. Sex was darker and usually adulterous in the olden days, so say the movies.

Lately, truth be told, I'd been living mostly off surveillance jobs which I got by way of Rocco Barnello, the fireman who inhabited the loft two floors below mine. Barnello was a shutterbug who documented arson jobs for the fire department. "I know as much about movies as the little lady knows about the ol' in-out," he said, but hey, he knew what he liked and he happened to know some guys who needed some work done. Last Saturday he told me about this guy Brigante, who was this big-time lawyer, defending this heavy-boogie dealer coming up for trial. So that's where I was headed now, to meet the client, take a lunch, scout the location, etc. Which was fine by me, because it was bucks and besides, what are movies if not the all-time gangster art form?

Nevertheless, from what Barnello had told me about Brigante and the nature of his clientele, I thought it would be wiser not to use my real name. I decided on Duffy. What kind of cameraman was this guy Duffy? I wondered, giddy with precautions. For the past four months, Duffy's sub-

scription to *The American Cinematographer* had arrived
soggy. The rest of his mail came in windowed envelopes.
Old Blind Duffy, Legendary Blues Cameraman. Got dem ol'
Dear Occupant Blues. Duffy was a journeyman. He fitted
me fine.

I made my way through a bow-shaped party with a knot
of dancers in the middle. An unlaundered Third World
aroma wafted from the kitchen.

The wine cork plopped in Brigante's glass. He picked it
out, licked it, then his fingers. He straightened his canary-
yellow Joe Garagiola Golf Classic cardigan. He was in his
fifties, glossy and tan. He had high cheekbones, a flattened
nose and small military ears. He scratched his neck.

"Great shirt, Mr. D. Colossal shirt. Say hi to L. S.
Nussbaum. Say hi to his twin sister Rochelle S. Nussbaum."

"Hiya," Rochelle said in a flutey voice. She smiled, shivering nicely. She slid a Kool out of the pack on the table,
struck a match, and floated the flame contemplatively toward the tip. She looked north of my eyes, at my hairline.
"You been a cameraman all your life?"

"Not yet."

"I'm totally impressed." Her legs were long, her shorts
were short.

L. S., her twin, had a face like an autographed cast—
beat-up, funny. He wore a tietack high on his shiny tie, and
a blue cashmere topcoat. "L. S.," he amplified, "that stands
for Louisville Slugger." He folded his gloved fingers in front
of his balls. "You know anything about Costa Rica? I'm
thinking about going to Costa Rica. They got waves." He
rippled his eyebrows and fingers.

A chunk of blue ash toppled from Brigante's cigar. "So
howya doin', Mr. D? You a good cameraman or what?
Whassis?"

Instead of a résumé, I had handed him by mistake one of

the religious handouts I'd gotten from a sockless fanatic on Grand Street, two pages about the birth of Marxism in Ethiopia, with a border of hand-drawn stars. I have a collection of such things.

Brigante's mustache went limp as he fingered the Ethiopian history. "Now lemme just ask you this, if I may. Is this normal horseshit or what?"

"Excuse me, who gets the rare?" the waitress inquired, nibbling a strand of her hair.

"Rare's over here, sweetheart," Brigante said. "If I gain another five pounds, I swear to God, I'm going to have to flush $8,000 worth of clothes down the toilet. Cause between this and the flu and everything else that's going on, I'm just a dead fuckin' duck. Excuse me, sweetheart."

"Gimme French taste and bocan," L. S. said. "Ooops, I mean . . ."

"L. S., do me a favor, tell that banjo player to go home and practice, he's giving me a colossal headache."

Rochelle, in a gathering gesture that included my knees, fondled the plastic roses. "Phooey, with flowers, if you want permanence, you get plastic."

No, the roses were real. I spotted pollen on the doily. Also, reflections of the white ceiling fan, erratically revolving, in the table wax. Cameramen are the only true private eyes: you're literally the first to see the world become a movie; you get in the habit of regarding life as an exclusive screening. Your eye becomes a convex lens, like a glass ball in a reflecting birdbath, taking everything in but making it all seem far away. DuffyVision. Meaning that I still had my photographic clarity, but lately it had been costing me a lot in the way of emotional miniaturization.

The waitress unscrewed a jar of macadamia nuts. The nuts hopped when the vacuum burst. I stopped feeling invisible and sectioned my pancakes into a crude map of the

USA, gobbling the Baja Peninsula first. "So," I said, "you
want to describe the job?"

"Sure, sure. The other night, it's four-thirty in the ayem
and I'm in this joint here having two microwave steer-
burgers. I drive up in the limo, my shirttail's hanging out, I
feel like a bum. The Korean guy that runs the place is petri-
fied I'm gonna rob it. So to put his mind at ease, I play Ms.
Pacman while I'm eating. But he's still nervous; he's having
fits he's so nervous. So I bought the place."

With the banjo player silent, the restaurant seemed more
spacious. L. S. mimed a gun with his finger and blew on the
barrel. "*Bla-doom*! That's the end of him and his big
mouth, right chief?"

"Yeah, thanks, L. S., you do nice work."

L. S. laughed shyly, took his seat and seemed to think
about food.

Brigante rotated his cigar band abstractedly. "Barnello
says you're the best, Mr. D. He says you got the Oscar for
Best Boy, right?"

"Wro—"

"I saw the Oscar show," L. S. said. "It was so fuckin star-
studded. But it was a little too fuckin' esoteric for me."

Rochelle whispered confidentially to him, as if his head
were a big furry microphone into which she was delivering
eye-witness commentary of some complicated but boring
event, like a coronation.

Then I saw it, I understood their design, their blunt twin
symmetry, their mirrored mannerisms. Because twinning is
the simplest way to solve problems of composition—with
the force and rigidity of folk art. A lamb on the left, a lamb
on the right, as in nineteenth-century quilts. Plus I was getting into the initialed symmetry of this situation: L. S., R. S.
. . . left side, right side . . . L. S. and R. S. went on trading
saucy information about me.

As a matter of fact, the book on me is that I'm too gangly to be smooth, but I'm fast, I'm cheerful, I travel well, and I'm absolutely fearless.

Take for instance how I met Zazi. She was in line with her great-aunt for the Easter show at Radio City Music Hall. I was a doorman, seventeen years old. It was practically my first job in show business, so to speak, and all the doormen had to know how to say, *Hay un mejor selección de sillas arriba a la izquierda*—"There's a better selection of seats upstairs to your left"—and when I said that Zazi smiled and wrote down her address in Mazatlán and stuck it in my uniform cap, which her great-aunt slapped her for. Three months I worked overtime to save the planefare. Zazi met me at the airport, there were frogs all over the runway, and she drove me to a hotel where the elevator operators were on strike. Her great-aunt said I had to stay in the hotel but Zazi said I could visit her at their house on the hill. The next morning I rented a convertible with no brakes and drove through town trying to read her directions. I get lost right away and it starts to rain in sheets but I figure if she lives up on a hill, the hill has got to be *up,* so I take the first road that goes up and pretty soon it turns into no road at all, more like a raging torrent with rapids and boulders, and I'm roaring through people's backyards, with laundry and chickens flapping against the windshield, and I can't get the top down, and these bald dogs are nipping at my bald tires, and the convertible stalls and rolls back through somebody's kitchen, it must have been, and these two giant Aztec-looking guys come out with machetes and I figure this is it. These guys aren't interested in a *mejor selección de los sillas arriba a la izquierda,* this is human sacrifice—right here, live, in the twentieth century. So when very politely the Aztecs ask me where I'm headed, I point up with my eyes and say "Zazi" (she'll appreciate my dying with her name

on my lips), which is like "Shazam" because the two Aztecs
break into big grins and pick up the rear end of the car, just
the two of them, aim it uphill and wave bye-bye with their
machetes.

The rest of the road runs through red flowers. When I get
to Zazi's there's a breeze and a lawn guarded by iguanas,
who hiss, and a cottage overlooking the phosphorescent bay
like a coloring book, and the sun is out again, it's sparkling
on the wet banana leaves.

The great-aunt says we have to get married. I am stunned
by how much this appeals to me. For six months we live on
the hill. Our bedroom has a view of three volcanoes. We
make love every day at two o'clock. I learn to merengue.
Zazi says I dance like a missionary. We eat candied yams
and swim in the bay with the pelicans till she wins two
thousand bucks in the lottery and we move back to New
York, where I get a job carrying cans for Candid Camera.
This is a snap, I say to myself; the rest is going to be film
history.

"By the way," said Brigante, "while we're on the subject
of Oscars, what do you say—*win* it or *get* it?"

I was developing, in Brigante's presence, the tendency to
shrug a lot. "I say get it. So you want to describe the job,
Mr. B?"

"Right. Get *it* before it gets you—that's what I say. Barnello says you deserved it, the Oscar. But what does Barnello
know, that dago fireman?"

"I cannot eat this wop slop," Rochelle remarked about
her bowl of minestrone.

"Incredible," said Brigante, breadcrumbs dotting his lips.

"What are you laughing at? The way I eat?"

"Incredible. You make a noise like a sponge when you
chew."

"So do you. Did you ever listen to yourself? And you
blow on your soup."

L. S. uttered his laugh again, a strange undeveloped titter. When he sliced his French toast, the plate took a tiddly-wink hop, spattering syrup on his topcoat.

"Oh no!" Rochelle said. "Now look at you. You're gonna be greasy for the rest of your life!"

Brigante asked her if she wanted something else to eat. "Something that won't get in the way of your gum?"

"I don't wanna eat, you know what I mean? I just don't wanna, is the point."

"What? You say something, Mr. D? You know, I hate talking to a shrugger. They're the only people that can make me shut up. And lemme tell you something else. There's two other things I can't stand. People without taste—ninety percent of people got no taste—and cynics. So don't be a cynic. Barnello tells me you're a genius, a solid citizen, a hot prospect and a nice guy. By the way, what kind of a name is that—Duffy?"

"It's my name," I lied.

"That's the whole story? Makes you sound like a generic Mick. Listen, why don't you change it to something classier? Like Kennedy. Get yourself elected to office. Then shot. Hey, sorry. Forget it, that's a terrible idea; there's too many of them Kennedys around already, creeping all over the place, getting themselves killed and killing themselves, running the conscience of some fairy tale country they think the rest of us oughta live in." He clinked his cigar against the glass ashtray and the ashtray clinked against the table, *clink-clink*. "You know, my father used to go to the drugstore to buy me Christmas presents. Close the barbershop at seven o'clock and go to the drugstore. My analyst says that's how come I like the rackets. He's wrong. I don't go for those stereotype kind of things. I *love* the rackets."

"You want to describe the job, Mr. B?"

"Take the latest one, Joe, Bobby's oldest son. So he's not a junkie. Very good. But why should this rich kid be presi-

dent, or even councilman? If this were 1960, okay. After
Eisenhower, anyone with an active sex life could get elected
anything. Lotsa teeth, lotsa hair, lotsa money . . . But Joe—
this rich kid who inherited high-class hobbies like sailing
and politics? What has he got to say to us now? That he
likes poor people? *Likes* them? Is this *noblesse oblige,* or
what? Can this guy really remember that he comes from
conniving saloonkeepers? Lemme tell you something, Mr.
D. The rich—the truly rich, the zombie rich, the Rockefel-
lers—they only want bloodless things: power, control,
thumbs-up or thumbs-down, the power of life and death,
the ultimate pleasure, stuff like that. The Kennedys got their
dynasty and all that stuff but they still dream the slobby
dreams of peasants—women and money." He jammed his
fists against the table as if attempting to levitate. "Which is
why I want them to try again, *because they're me!*"

Absolutely fearless, sure.

R. S. carried her Coke outside to a pimpmobile with "Ari-
zona, Land of Enchantment" plates. And the plates, in a frame
that named a dealership in Santa Monica, said SHIRL E. These
characters were definitely scoffing the law.

L. S. opened the door with great respect. R. S. looked
down in her purse, then, all eyelashes, up at me. Most people, my theory was, felt less interesting than their cars, so I
asked her, "What kind of car is this anyway?"

She checked her face in the fender. "Uh, Catholic, I
think."

"Yeah, world's largest living car," Brigante said. "Get
inna back."

"I mean Continental," said Rochelle. She made a cozy
show of squeezing in beside me, thighs rustling. She un-
peeled a deluxe taffy. "We're twins but he's only four minutes older than me, you know."

"You look a lot younger."

"Yeah? Rilly? Thanks. I'm a twin, but people regard me as one of a kind. At least I get the feeling they do. I'm a blend."

We drove to the Bronx. It was a harmless evening with lots of Saturday cars and thickening fog. The windshield wipers ticked domestically. I had a hard time following the conversation, which went on in a vaporous and slightly hysterical vein (the topic: Brigante's upcoming gum surgery and his gallstones, painlessly passed last Tuesday after months of torment; plus Rochelle was just recovering nicely from minor surgery for polyps, so she was planning to start smoking Gauloises again as of tomorrow noon). But I enjoyed the cadence of it, which was relaxed and generous, despite the noise, the careening lights, and the traffic. The lights of cars coming toward us were stationary till just before they flared past. I'm a true fan of fog. Tricky to shoot but dreamy to watch.

"I got them night driving blues . . ." L. S. sang—croaked rather ". . . black as I can be. Got them night driving blues till you come back to me. Night driving: *woo-ee!*"

Brigante palmed a vial to his nose. "Nice snow. It's fun. It's Florida." He passed it back to Rochelle. She sniffed and blinked. I snorted a capful. Zing. Fearless again.

Brigante stroked the wine-velvet upholstery. "Nice, hah? Made with material left over from the Pope's jockstrap, you know what I mean? Scuse me, sweetheart. By the way, any calls this afternoon?"

"No," Rochelle replied over the dull jingle of pills in her purse. She touched her hair with her fingernails. Her nail polish matched the upholstery. "Oh. Sherman from Washington called."

"Sherman from Washington?"

"Sherman. From Washington." She assumed a legal demeanor.

"That's what I like—a neighborhood mind in a world-class body."

"You want to describe the job?"

"Ask not what you can do for your country . . . *Ask not*? Remember that? These days it's *Don't ask*. My uncle Nunzio, he used to play bocce on the court down by Houston Street. A hop and a skip and the jingle of change in his pockets—I'll never forget it."

L. S. drove artistically, but he had the handicap of being in various ways at war with his nose: blowing it, plowing it, thinking about it, turning it left and right in the mirror, squeezing it. A garbage truck (Allegro Sanitation) stopped short. L. S. frowned and went bug-eyed as Beethoven.

"Scumbag trucks! Lack of consideration like that tears my guts out!" His fat face turned purple, bulging with wrath, eyes on the verge of popping out of his skull. I wondered briefly if this had ever happened. It must have. Everything has happened.

Brigante leaned forward and said very slowly, "Number one, L. S., you're stupid, right? Am I right or am I wrong, L. S.? Number two, you're a fuckin' dimwit." He itemized these arguments on his fingers, bending them back as he called off each one. "You are too dumb to talk, and you are too fat to fight and therefore if you don't just shut the fuck up and do your fuckin' job, I'm going to take you out of this car and beat your head till it's soft."

I slouched and considered the situation a little more horizontally. Was it time to pray? No, I couldn't be fervent under these conditions. Prayer's not for pressure situations, that's just a bullshit theory. Unless prayer is a last good look at things, like during takeoffs and landings or on the subway at night.

L. S. parked precisely. Around the streetlights, moths swirled like unseasonable snow. Fog fizzed in at a chink in the door. I could feel the night on my head. Brigante inflated his nostrils.

"Okay, lemme just describe the job, if I may. Is that what you call it in the motion picture industry—a job? I thought it was more like a, like a location, or a whadayacallit . . ."

"A *mise-en-scène*," said Rochelle.

"Medicine?" L. S. said. "In your purse."

"Shaddup, shaddup! I'd be very grateful if all you guys would just please shut the fuck *up!*" The volume of the man blew my eyebrows out of order. "Okay. So the cops were sitting in a car exactly where we're sitting. Two hundred and twelve feet from that stoop over there with alla spics on it. It was a rainy night. They're watching my client, the cops testified—get this—the cops see him walk up the stoop carrying a briefcase, and when the alleged perpetrator emerges a few minutes later carrying the same briefcase, only lugging it lower, they surmise, the little crime stoppers, that the briefcase is about four million dollars heavier. So they radio in for a warrant and bust him and sure enough they're right, the briefcase is heavy and there's a lot of money in it. The only surprise is it's five million dollars heavy instead of four." He massaged another line into his gums, which made me hungry. "The indictment weighs thirty-five pounds."

"But gee, how could they see how heavy the briefcase was?" Rochelle began.

"On account of the cops are lying, that's how come they can see so good, sweetheart. They can see so good on account of they got tipped what they were going to see and where they were going to see it."

"And it was raining and everything."

"And it was raining, right, and everything."

"Boy, what next?"

Brigante gave Rochelle a pat on the cheek to settle the contents of her head. His eyes clicked, left-right. "So what I want to know, Mr. D, is how much is it gonna cost to shoot a movie of a man with a briefcase walking up that stoop, from two hundred and twelve feet away, through the windshield of a car on a rainy night."

"Well, Mr. B," I coughed once and muffled a second one. "You got to bring in lots of lights and a couple of firehoses, three maybe, to make rain, which means you need Teamsters."

L. S. flicked an irritant off his tie. "We'll take care of the Teamsters."

"Yeah," said Brigante. "Because if I show a picture of that to the grand jury, they'll know the cops had to be lying when they said they had sufficient cause to bust my client on the basis of what they could see, cause they couldn't see shit. 'Scuse me, sweetheart. So how much? Just gimme a rough idea."

"Ten-twelve thousand."

Brigante moved his eyebrows. Rochelle spilled her Coke. She raised her hips to clear the spreading stain.

"Oh, instant bummer!"

"Shaddup, will you please, sweetheart."

"Oh. It was shaddup from you yesterday and it's shaddup today."

Brigante squeezed his eyes shut, contemplating something more profound than the upholstery. "You got to talk up, Mr. D. I'm a little deaf in this ear. Thickened eardrums I got on account of the ringing and roaring of the engine in an open cockpit. I keep a little stunter—it's a biplane—out in Teterboro. Remind me to take you up for a ride sometime. So look: no headaches, no horseshit, no aggravation. Just regular business. How much?"

Fearless, absolutely. I had no idea why I'd changed, but I knew I had. Well, sometimes I knew. Since the Oscar, which left me with the infected feeling of nothing to be but a winner—since the Oscar, I haven't always been sure if I was a guy or a gadget. Since Zazi, really.

"Yo! Mr. D! How much!"

"Eight th-thou—"

"Eight thou? You got it, Mr. D."

L. S. started the Lincoln a little too fast for me to believe anybody. The directional signal made the sound *linquent, linquent.* Brigante angled the rearview mirror and checked on Rochelle, who was still wiggling away from her Coke spill. "Hey, don't worry about it, sweetheart. As long as I got a face, you got a place to sit."

L. S. glared jurisdictionally. He swerved the Continental to the curb. "Okay, that's it. That's my kid sister you're talking to."

"Okay, okay, okay, L. S.," R. S. said. "Take it easy."

L. S. bolted out and popped the trunk. He ran around to Brigante's window with one of his Louisville Sluggers, cradling it like a precision instrument. The rattling of his gold watchstrap was louder than anything else.

"Whaddaya got there, moron?" asked Brigante.

"A thirty-two Mickey Mantle. Geddada the car."

"You gotta be more subtle in your thinking, L. S. What happened to the Rocky Colavito? It's a lighter stick, the Colavito, but it's really wicked around the upper temple area." Brigante reached out and knuckled the side of L. S.'s head. "Whaddaya, under the influence of stupidity again?"

"Geddada the car."

"Whaddaya talking, geddada the car? You ain't the king of me, L. S."

"Oh yeah? You ain't no king of me neither."

"Oh yeah?"

"Yeah!"

Yeah, well, in the name of the Father and of the Son, I prayed. . . .

"*Yeah!*"

Zazi and I spent a week in Hawaii once, where macadamias grow ankle-deep, on the way back from a UN assignment in Japan. Teenage beauty queens carpeting the beach at Waikiki, Kansas-blond every blessed one of them, oh Lord . . .

"*Yeah!*"

. . . braces glinting in the sun. Yeah, so in the name of the Holy Ghost, too, who so seldom gets a chance to show what He can do.

Yeah. *Since Zazi.* Here's the picture: before going out in the boat during our second Mexican honeymoon, waiting for the darkness to settle and expose the phosphorescent reefs, Zazi and I park on the pier and watch the pelicans soar and plunge and soar again. The phosphorescent bay, it seems to me, is not nearly so mysterious as the pelicans. Zazi and I disagree on this with a stubbornness new to our young marriage. To me the pelicans are wizards; to her merely animals, ungainly in their hunger. The glowing bay, in my opinion, is nothing more than a tank full of tropical fish or a movie screen accidentally arranged, although as we shove off from shore in the glass-bottomed boat, I begin to get higher expectations, catching sight of the huge, slowly flapping wings of a manta ray, six feet or more from tip to tip, slithering away to deeper water, its shadow on the shallow sand like the shadow of a cloud. Everyone is impressed, including the vacationing Irish Monsignor who asks, shouting over the splutter of the motor, what my name is, and hearing "Duffy" (my disguise is ancient), did I still practice the faith, as if it might be an occasion of sin to skim across the waters of a diabolically glowing bay with a lapsed believer. But it's Zazi who's beginning to have her doubts. She wants me to believe in the bay. But I won't, it's too much like a movie. The bay glows. So what? So she left.

At first I thought it would be only a year, the grief. Then

a year went by in time-extending romantic schemes and I said, well maybe only two years. Then it was three years and I said in midnight candor, this is hell. That's when it began to fall apart, I guess, the benign marriage of eye and money, and in its place I saw a mirror-window and, dully reflected there, like the shadow of the manta ray, a naive likeness of myself, gracefully fleeing.
myself, gracefully fleeing.

But it wasn't always bad grief, I learned things. I learned to like being miscellaneous. Last December, for example, when Fodo escaped through the roof vent of my van, I walked a mile down the road calling his name—*Fodo! Lunch, Fodo!*—till he heard me and flapped down on my shoulder. The crew applauded and went back to work. I mainly kept busy with my next few futures. Which is okay, but sometimes a very vicious circle. How many haircuts had I had since she'd left?

"Oh yeah?"

Rochelle must have been used to timing the volleys; she found an opening. "Okay, okay, okay, L. S. Come on, now, Okay? Your nerves are shot. Whyncha just stop being so puritanical?"

L. S. shined his shoes, one after the other, on the backs of his pants legs, scratched doubtfully at his stubble and poked the knob of the bat in his chin, creating a horizontal dimple. His thought processes were slow enough to watch. "Hey, whaddaya talking about the Puritanic? The Puritanic went down years ago."

I kept my next appointment with Mr. B on the scorching roof of a warehouse on 110th Street. He was wearing a clerical collar under his green plastic trenchcoat and he was feasting from a casserole dish of steaming pasta.

"Hey boss. Lookit."

"Lookit what, L. S.?"

Louisville Slugger Nussbaum lobbed a wine bottle into the shaftway, bombarding Christmas tree skeletons at the bottom.

"Be that as it may," Brigante said, "here's where the cops were watching my client from." His client in this case was a not-so-rich Newyorican dealer.

I aimed my camera at the doorway of a bodega ten stories below and a block and a half downtown. At this distance, according to the testimony of the arresting officers, an alert human eye could detect a six-pack of beer being carried out of the bodega in the arms of the perpetrator.

Brigante snorted wine straight from a wickered Chianti bottle. "Now the interesting thing about this six-pack is that one of the bottles was riding a little higher than it should've been—half an inch, maybe an inch." He illustrated by tweezering L. S.'s left earlobe and hoisting him to his tiptoes. "You know why it was higher? Because at the bottom of the carton, pushing up the bottle, was supposed to be a bag of smack. Which there was. Well, whaddaya know?"

L. S. rocked back on his heels and loitered in the body language of befuddlement—the ball scratch, the ear tug.

"Now that may be a very turbulent grocery store, but how the fuck are they supposed to see the inch difference in one beer bottle ten stories up?"

"No way, Mr. B."

"I don't mind the cops lie. They all fuckin' lie. The judges lie. But they are so *stupid*. Some of these guys are *embarrassing*."

I started unscrewing the camera from the tripod. "Pictures lie too."

Brigante raised his hand. I braced myself for a blessing.

"Take the picture anyway. What can I tell you? Juries are romantic. Everybody who's bored is a romantic. I'm a romantic."

A romantic. Fifteen hundred bucks, not including film and processing. You charge for the mystique of it.

"Listen, here's what I got, Mr. D. I got Rochelle. I got forty thousand feet of archival film on the Vietnam War. What can I do with it, this is my question. I gotta fire my fund raiser, this I already know. He looks at the film and he says, mighty footage! But I can't get him on the phone. I want forty half-inch cassettes at forty places around town, I can't waste time. You want to take a look at it? I get Alan Alda to narrate it, right? He's a Fordham grad. I used to hang out with his old man. Lemme buy you a drink."

"Hey boss, lookit! Lookit!"

"Lookit what, L. S.? Lookit what?"

L. S., cranking underhand, lofted a bottle to an altitude that caused me to squint. The back of Brigante's neck, pivoting with the bottle, splurged like a sausage around his Roman collar. The bottle soared, arched, flashed, plummeted, and crashed soundlessly on a heap of mattresses and Christmas tree skeletons.

"Everything's beeyoodeeful in slow motion, right boss?"

Brigante bought me a kidney pie and a piña colada in the Glocca Morra on 23rd Street, a limbo for cops that featured napkins with shamrock appliques, a jukebox with bagpipe waltzes, a Crazy Jane–type improvising phone calls without quarters ("Hi Ethel, is Bob there at all?"), a woman in a red dress shooting miniature pool with a guy in a three-piece suit, and a cranky Chesterfield smoker at the end of the bar, Wally Walker the professional veteran he must have been, because he was telling those Jap torture stories of his non-stop to O'Malley, the bartender, who was swabbing steins beneath acrobatic pinups that seemed to somersault from everybody's imagination. L. S. stayed in the car, steamed because they didn't have Space Invaders. Rochelle was said to be on "a working vacation" in Florida.

A bare seven-and-a-half watt bulb hung between me and Brigante, slightly higher than hat level, casting dark-side-of-the-moon shadows on cheeks and eye sockets. In the Industry this is called *Godfather* lighting because Gordon Willis, who shot the *Godfather* films, was the first cameraman to notice that certain kinds of guys conduct certain kinds of business under low-wattage lamps slightly higher than hat level. Brigante played to the light with a shrewd, jaunty air. His white Roman collar had become soiled from touching it between stories. He unsnapped it.

"Every five years or so," he was saying, "I throw myself into free fall, you know what I mean? But I got friends."

"A priest should argue from the example of his own life," the veteran shouted.

"Like Saint Augustine," the bartender added.

Brigante cleaned his nails with a corner of his collar. "Just stick to putting real liquor in your drinks, O'Malley."

"I pour an honest shot."

"Nobody pours honest shots anymore. You could put anything in a piña colada, nobody'd know the difference."

"I had a real piña colada once," said the veteran. "At Newark airport. I never found another one. I tried Kennedy, LaGuardia . . ."

"But seriously," Brigante said, "in the life of any saint, of course, the most important scene is always the death scene. Now Jesus—there was a great director. 'Pick up your bed and walk,' he said to the cripple. 'Follow me.' *Those* are directions. Still . . . I don't know . . . the question is, how to say it in a film? I keep thinking, you got to use the beauty, use the beauty."

"I was under the impression you were a lawyer, Mr. B."

"I am. I was. Till yesterday, I think. Before that I was a

priest for twenty-two years, but I quit. *Then* I was a lawyer. Now. . . . Remember my client with the briefcase fulla money and the stoop in the rain and the thirty-five pound indictment? When the case got to court, it came down to whether or not the briefcase belonged to my client. My client denied it was his. The prosecutor put the owner of a certain midtown luggage store on the stand. He asked him, 'Do you recognize this briefcase?' The luggage guy said, 'Well, not that particular one, but I know the type. I'm the only one in the country that imports them. I sell about six a year.' 'And is there anything special about these briefcases?' 'They have a three-number combination lock on them which you set for yourself. I always tell the customer, set it for your birthday; that way you'll never forget it. December 12, 1942 is 12-12-42, something like that.' The prosecutor took the briefcase, showed the jury that it was locked. Then he put my client on the stand and asked him his birthday. Forty years. I'm looking for a new line of work. Something a little more . . . I don't know . . . more creative, maybe."

He discarded the collar and ordered another round of piña coladas. He began to whistle softly and tap the dial of the Hopalong Cassidy watch on his wrist. "I'm not a collector, I'm not compulsive about it. I'm what you'd call a passive collector. There must be a word for it in Japanese or something. Friends just understand I appreciate certain things, and they give me a lot of gifts. You know those Crime stopper handcuffs I got? They were a present from a guy I was in the seminary with. So now what?—this is my problem. The thrill is gone."

He confessed that he watched Merv Griffin. Sometimes he sat through entire telethons, and he kept up a correspondence with Jane Fonda, Jon Voight, and Donald Sutherland (who painted his toenails purple).

The woman in the red dress chalked her cue.

And lately, he'd been running into a lot of stars who were coming back from L.A., on their way to L.A., or thinking about going to L.A. Last week, for example, who should he run into on West Broadway but Meryl and Bobby. Then uptown, in the Dakota, he met Lauren Bacall. "Well, I didn't actually meet her. She was in the elevator. It was dim, I didn't recognize her. But when I heard that voice . . ."

"Hey, Ava," the three-piece pool shooter shouted, "enough with the chalk already. Just let's shoot, okay?"

"Yeah, just let's shoot, Okay. I need something new. We *all* need something new, am I right? Hah? Something really new. You know what the trouble is, Mr. D? It's a creatively bankrupt time, the eighties. Lawyers, shrinks, politicians, poets, crooks, cops—nobody's got any new ideas. They're all doing the same thing they did fifteen years ago and it don't work no more. It's falling apart. I always ask myself the following question: waddle we do? Waddle work?"

"Blessed are they that hunger and thirst after justice," the veteran at the bar shouted, gnawing the handle of his umbrella. "Especially thirst."

Brigante heaved his piña colada at him. Over by the bar, after the mirror shattered, not a thing moved except O'Malley, idiotically wiggling a finger at his own reflection in the splintered glass, below which, somewhere behind the bar, the bombed-out veteran made weak scratching sounds. I hopped into a half crouch.

"Settle down, Mr. D. Settle down." He left a fat tip on the bar, snapping the bills.

The veteran climbed back on his stool. "I don't know what day it is. I am an alcoholic and I do not know. I got fifty-five cents."

Brigante clucked some coins in his plastic cup. "Now you have a dollar." That was the most convincing priestly thing about him, that he would give money to a lost soul, count the change, and make it sound amusing.

"Thanks, Father," the veteran said.

"Forget it, O'Malley. I'm nobody's father."

I rode up front with L. S. Brigante sermonized from the back seat.

"We may be flying blind, but this is our daily lives, that's all. I'll be calling you in a couple of weeks. I got to take a trip, see some people. I got something cooking. Meanwhile take some pictures you really believe in, Mr. D. Use the beauty; you know how to use it." He dropped me at my loft.

Fodo had gotten loose again. That moron crow was getting senile; all he wanted to do was peck at the air conditioner. I lassoed him with a towel on the second try and carried him to the fire escape and let him peek around. Then he flapped to the neighboring fire escape, where he sat, shivering and regrooming his sinister dignity.

I ironed my divorce shirt again. It had become a ritual way of polishing my memory. Next to the football player, a bird hunter walked in an open field, black boots barely topping the grass. His shirt was red, and so was the collar worn by his bird dog. A shotgun was resting, cracked for safety, in the crotch of his right arm. In his left hand, he held a dead bird, a pheasant, mistakenly tinted white. The hunter squinted under the peak of his corduroy cap and smiled the experienced stalker's half smile, satisfied, sensing more kills.

I never heard from Brigante again. Both of his clients, I read in the *Post*, went to jail and were murdered in their cells. Take a picture you really believe in—that's something I've been trying to do for a long time. There's a certain Zaziness to it.

The Gentlest
Object Imaginable

"Uplink, downlink, hard disk, modem, whammo bubble memory—this guy's hot, Duke. Super tech."

Teddy Churchill was calling from Philadelphia. He was talking about Garrett Brown, inventor of the Steadicam, a camera stabilizer that has revolutionized the look of films and the way they're produced. He was spending the weekend with Garrett working on the prototype of a new invention: the flying robot camera.

If you wanted to set a film or video camera in motion before the appearance of the Steadicam in 1978, you had to put it on your shoulder, where it would invariably wobble, or on a dolly, a heavy sled that runs on tracks and requires tending by two to four men with Popeye forearms. With Steadicam, you put the camera on the cameraman; it goes where he goes, smoothly.

The 7:30 A.M. Amtrak to Philadelphia whizzed southward. The February sun rose reluctantly over assorted septic rubble: vacant foundries, tilted telephone poles, smashed panes in sawtoothed skylights, squashed cars, graffitied walls and the Tacony-Palmyra bridge, its box-girders labeled TRENTON MAKES, THE WORLD TAKES in letters twice the height of a man.

I blinked at an idea—of Steadicam as a symbol, as an extension of the nervous system, and this new flying camera of Garrett's as an extension of the imagination, like the boyhood dream of flying come true. The Amtrak train, on the other hand, symbolized the writer's snooze, the ground-level present and the crumbling of the northeast industrial corridor.

The pay phone at the 30th Street station was warm and perfumy from the previous customer. Teddy said hello in a mock British accent. "It's unbelievable, Duke. It flies, it shoots, it's wild! Hurry up, we're testing it at ten."

The cabdriver explained that the gentrified neighborhood we were driving through—its brick facades fresh as baby skin from sandblasting, wrought iron fences curlicued, stoops swept—was called Society Hill. Garrett's house stood in a mews row. There was a designer-gray Mercedes 300 SL turbo diesel in the courtyard and a scarlet Japanese sports car too exotic to identify. In the overcast these machines glowed with more life than drab mortals like myself, huddling colorlessly against the cold.

Teddy opened the door just as my finger touched the bell. He was wearing a camouflage T-shirt with the logo of Cine-Tech, a Florida camera repair shop, over his heart. "It's run by a German named Egon," he said. "See the Panaflex on the back? It's great, huh? He doesn't sell them, only gives them away to the right people."

The first two floors of the three-story house were connected, in duplex fashion, by an open staircase. The design of the house, with its dramatic stairs and strong verticals, seemed configured to lead the eye up and down and down and up in a homey maze. There was a tall blond bookcase— a recreational display, really—full of magazines and photo books. The decorations—towels, books, toys, snapshots taped to the refrigerator door, all of them apparently as stray and disorganized as straw, actually the stuff of the nest—these were feminine. Gentrification meant girlfriend interiors in a grandfatherly neighborhood.

Garrett was on the second level making breakfast. His Oscar statuette for the Steadicam stood at the end of an eye-level shelf.

"I think we've met," he said, graciously mistaken. He resembled, at forty-one, a mellow Max Von Sydow.

He said he was late with his article for *The American Cinematographer* about a shot he made last summer for *Return of the Jedi:* Steadicam in the redwood forest of northern California.

"It was fun. They built me an eleven-pound Vistavision camera. We shot at three-fourths frames per second. Undercranked that way, it would look like I was traveling more than a hundred miles an hour when they screened the shot."

He spoke like an enthusiast, his precision habitual rather than rehearsed. Garrett was fluent in several technologies, spoke enough pidgin electronics to tinker with computers, TV monitors, walkie-talkies, radios, or automobiles. He made it his business to master these things because they are dialects of the visual lingua franca of the time. If you're making a complicated movie, Garrett is the guy you want on your side. Mr. Fixit, Mr. Gee-whiz homespun genius technocrat. Impresario and pitchman, very much the man with the plan.

We reminisced about *Popular Mechanics* fantasies of the forties and fifties: rocket cars, housewives with helicopters in their kitchens. . . . I wondered if there were other inventors whose work inspired him. "No, I don't have a role model. What I am is an old-fashioned entrepreneur. I think of Edison sometimes, but of course he worked with a lot more people. He did have a great sense of knowing what kind of invention was needed. That's important. A lot of inventors have great ideas for things nobody needs. There's just not a big market, for example, for a car that washes itself.

"I consider myself a good mechanic. I mean in the old Newtonian sense. The Steadicam is a very Victorian gadget; it's mechanical. Today people tend to want black-box solutions, like that thing." He tapped the Canon copier perched on the kitchen table. "There's nothing new about it, at least not about what it does. It *is* a wonderful ergonometric design, it's modular; everything's in a slip-in, slip-out cartridge. The Germans and the Japanese are wonderful at this sort of thing. It's packaging. But the ideas, the big new ideas, they're still in this country."

Garrett attended Tufts for three years, "majoring in sleep," then departed the classroom for the life of an itinerant folksinger. In the early sixties, he and Al Dana, now a jingle writer in New York, played three hundred college concerts and recorded an album for MGM. "Then I sold Volkswagens for a while. A friend at an ad agency suggested that advertising was a good bolt-hole for ne'er-do-wells. I got interested in the production side of things and pretty soon I had my own company, small offices in New York and Philadelphia. We did a lot of Subaru commercials. I got into hanging the camera thirty feet below a helicopter, flying the lens six inches off the ground, looking up at the Subaru, stuff that hasn't been done before or since. I began learning about the problems of isolating the camera from sources of vibration. The whole idea is to isolate one object, the camera, from another—the cameraman, with his random momentary input: from his stumbling, tugs and falls. The Steadicam is a clever gadget, but it requires skill to operate. It's a little like a skateboard that way. You can't just hand it to somebody and say, here, go do a flip turn.

"There were several prototypes of the Steadicam. They all worked, but they tended to be murder on the operators. Some were eighty pounds, torture contraptions, made the operator look like he was having eye surgery in an abortion clinic.

"Finally, to be alone and think things through, I checked into a motel for a couple of weeks. Isolated the inventor. I got my best ideas walking up and down the corridor with borrowed mops and brooms and pails in my hands. There came a moment when I knew it was going to work and be a famous gadget, win an Academy Award. I knew it. I was flying. I haven't been up there since."

John Russell strolled into the kitchen, carrying a pipe. John is a North Hollywood craftsman who specializes in customizing and refining film equipment. He sat down at the table, spilled some ashes and lit a cigarette. He was close to sixty with the pot belly and energetic wrinkles of an individualist who cultivated bad habits because his work, however craftsmanlike and lucrative, was still anonymous servitude; he smoked with bravado in order to signify, for a start, that he could, despite his backstage status, keep up with the vices of the young.

"Even old people look good in California," Teddy whispered. "Like great fifties cars." John had made the many modifications on his Steadicam. John's work—a special mounting plate here, a video plug there—had a clean, polished look, a good cut above the usual garage machining, with its rinds of untrimmed lathe work, that you find on many customized cameras.

Garrett had flown John in to tune up the hardware for his

new invention. He wanted to keep his promise to Vittorio Storaro, the Italian cinematographer renowned for his sinuous moves in films like *Last Tango in Paris, 1900,* and *Reds.* Garrett was supposed to take his new flying robot camera to Rome this summer to make a shot of a falcon swooping down on the falconer's wrist—from the falcon's point of view.

Ellen, Garrett's girlfriend, descended from the bedroom level. "Oh," she said, spotting me halfway down. "Did somebody else sleep over?"

"Go ahead," Garrett said. "Go ahead, eat." His twelve-year-old son Jon forked a sunny-sided egg on his plate. He had hesitant eyes and a downy mustache; he was on the verge of having to affect manful behavior. I gave Garrett's eight-year-old daughter "a tiny one," as she requested, and offered the platter to John Russell.

"Lord, no," he said, snuffing his cigarette and maneuvering a match to his pipe. "Talk about snow—would you believe sixteen inches last night in Barstow?"

"I know Barstow," Ellen said. "That's desert all around there."

John's pipe would not ignite. He set it on the table next to his pack of cigarettes. "Course that's high desert. Now Santa Fe's a great town, oh yeah. I love Santa Fe. They shot *The Lone Ranger* there."

"Who shot *The Lone Ranger*?" Ellen asked.

"Uh . . . Laszlo," Garrett said. "Was it Laszlo?"

"No," John said. "Vic shot it."

"Oh." Teddy rolled his eyes. He was standing behind me with another plate of eggs in his hand. *The Lone Ranger* crew was legendary, even by the merry measure of a Hollywood crew on location, for its rowdiness.

Garrett excused himself to take a call from Steven Spielberg, who booked him for two weeks in Sri Lanka at

the end of April. He'd be shooting Steadicam sequences for
Indiana Jones. "Scampering across rope bridges"—he
smiled—"diving into caves. Life is sweet. I get to spend a
week or two on lots of movies, then move on. I don't get
stuck for six months in Shreveport."

Not many movies get shot in Shreveport, but it does happen. Garrett's expertise made him something of a hired gun,
a quick hit man, and spared him from stupefying stays in
the Moot Point Holiday Inns of this world. He pondered his
coffee cup as if waking from a dream and coming to a more
complete sense of himself.

"There are great gaps between the things we take for
granted. I have blind spots about my personal life, but I'm
good at mechanics. I doodled a lot when I was a kid. I was
always good at taking things apart and fixing things and
figuring out what was needed. In high school I heard about
sleep-learning so when we got an assignment to memorize a
poem I recorded it on tape. This was before the days of
cassette machines; the tape was very long, too long. I had to
record the poem very fast to keep the length down. Even so
the tape was all over the room. When I woke up, all I could
remember was the first line." He finished his coffee standing
up. "Let's go," he said before we'd quite completed our
breakfast.

Teddy wiggled into his thermal underwear. John put on
his cowboy hat and adjusted the angle of an iridescent
feather in its snakeskin band. As the ranking technician, he
rode up front with Garrett in the Mercedes. Ellen would
drive Garrett's daughter to her mother's house in the scarlet
Japanese sports car, then pick up an urn to brew coffee for
the crew. Teddy and I squeezed in the back of the Mercedes,
young Jon shoehorned in between.

Driving through Society Hill, Garrett wiggled his long fingers into pigskin driving gloves. John Russell lit a cigarette.

Garrett guided his hand to the ashtray and activated the electronically operated sunroof to evacuate the smoke. Teddy grabbed Jonathan in a headlock and screamed, "You are a spy from Panavision! You vil del uz evryding you know. You vil *talk*!"

I mentioned a story I'd shot recently: on the track at Abilene Christian University in Texas, Billy Olson, the world's champion indoor pole vaulter, had braced his wing-broad shoulders and squinted his small eyes and sniffed the breeze like a bunny and sprinted for the bar and hoisted himself till he stood for a photographable instant on his hands at the tip of the pole, which whipped him over the bar against the clean southwestern sky—a thrilling sight, especially in slow motion.

"That's something we could do with the new Device," Garrett said. "I mean, have the Device vault the pole."

"Does the Device have a name yet?"

"No. There's a crane which calls itself SkyCam, which is too bad. SuperCam? The root means 'above.' I don't know what we're going to call it."*

Jonathan turned to me. "Are *you* a spy from Panavision?"

"There's a need for a new camera," Garrett continued. "Helicopters own the space above a hundred feet—above five hundred feet, if noise is a consideration. Lower than that, they blow things around, and they can be dangerous. And a helicopter shot is something, even with the weather on your side, that you settle for.

"Cranes can lumber along, get you to about thirty feet. But these tools are major distractions. What is the ideal camera? It would be silent, infinitely maneuverable. Remote control we'll take for granted. It'd be fast: twenty–thirty

---

* The legal problems have since been cleared up; the Device is named SkyCam, and Garrett and Ellen are married.

miles an hour. Inconspicuous. It's not going to do you any good if it's as big as a Zeppelin. The ideal, of course, is invisibility. But invisibility is tricky. What you want to wind up with is the gentlest object imaginable.

"Safety. Safety is something you don't think about up front, but we've had to think about it. The National Football League, for example, is very conservative. For years they wouldn't allow a sideline camera. Now they're standard. Imagine this camera pursuing a ball carrier. What an appalling, wonderful shot. It'd get out of the way with about the same speed and maneuverability as a human being. We've decided to have two operators—one to actually move the Device, the other to make sure he doesn't hit anybody with it.

"Uses. Most of our sports and entertainment takes place in stadiums or halls. Today a director is able to use only about one percent of the volume of these spaces. He's restricted to shooting at the telephoto end of a zoom lens, which gives you that remote, compressed, creepy-peepy look. Take a political convention. We know the coordinates of Senator Claghorn; we can fly to him in seconds. Boxing, anywhere in the ring, slightly above eye level. Skiing: the lens could start ahead of the slalom skier at thirty miles an hour and watch him go through the gates at sixty."

He slipped into his dreamer-pitchman mode. "For the past seven years I've been working on a human transportation device. I think it'll sell a billion." He swerved his Mercedes surefootedly onto the athletic field of Haverford High School, his alma mater. Film technology may be taking the corners on two wheels, but not this technician.

Larry McConkey, Garrett's operating engineer and the son of novelist James McConkey, was unloading a red van. Everyone lugged blue canvas equipment bags into a home ec classroom on the ground floor.

Larry began attaching the Device to its docking stand, a thin, even scrawny, aluminum pole with tripod legs. You didn't have to be an engineer to appreciate its *Star Wars* panache: it was essentially a black rod about one inch in diameter and four and a half feet long. Toward the middle of the rod was a gimbal, a balancing joint in the form of planetary rings, to which angular sensors, voltage regulators, and small servo motors were attached by screws, Velcro tabs, color-coded wires, and, in a few cases, by rubber bands. At the bottom was another gimbal, with more rings and motors. Below this gimbal dangled the camera, which, for purposes of recording today's test, was a small black-and-white home video camera.

Larry nibbled his mustache and hovered around the Device, bobbing and probing, now with a soldering iron, now with a jeweler's screwdriver, now with Allen wrenches. He kept up a conversation, the kind a playful father might have with a speechless child, or a compassionate ventriloquist with an strange dummy; cooing to it, shouting at it, pretending he was deaf—anything to get the kid to sit up and show some life.

"How come this motor just went *eeek*? How'd you sleep last night? Boy, did I sleep. The sleep of the working man." He yanked a small shiny pulley that was still wearing a fluorescent yellow $7.50 price tag. "Oh my God," he said, "what happens next?"

Teddy and I hauled one of the winch motors out to the field. Each winch drum was wound with a couple of hundred feet of stainless steel aviation wire and weighed more than a hundred pounds. Three winch motors would be used today; a fourth would be added next month, when the computer came on-line. The winches functioned like giant fishing reels and the light towers like fixed rods to "play" the Device. A computer's quicker than human response would eventually add more control. Teddy and I trudged past the fifty-yard line.

"Whoops," Teddy said. "Too far."

We set the motor down with a thump on the first row of benches in the bleachers.

A compact young man named Carl walked up and said hi. He was wearing a telephone lineman's belt and climbing boots. Teddy, in what he called "a test of knotsmanship" helped him secure a pulley to one of the poles.

"I got a deli restaurant," Carl said, goldrush fervor in his voice. "I got a truck. I do electric. Construction's pretty steady. I got two kids. I leave at five-thirty in the morning, get home ten, eleven at night. I don't hardly see them at all. I don't have any emotions. This thing's gonna go."

"What's the name of this winch motor?" Teddy asked.

"We call it the, uh, spool-motor combo," said Carl. "But we should call it something sexy, like . . ."

"Like 'that scumbag motor'?"

Carl clipped a rope to the end of the aviation wire on our winch, hitched it over his shoulder and climbed the eighty-foot light tower in back of the bleachers, towing the rope and wire after him. When he got to the top, he safetied his belt and rigged the wire through a pulley which he secured to the pole. Carl moved on to two other light poles far across the field, where, like an amiable Disney spider, he repeated this procedure. Teddy and I gawked at the spokes of his mammoth web or three-sided clothesline, at the center of which the camera would hang.

"There are two kinds of people here," he said. "Friends and those interested in a second career. I'm interested in a retirement." He opened his Swiss Army knife and trimmed the clothesline. "Money sure is slippery stuff."

"I just saw a flake of the white stuff," Jonathan said. The wind was raw. Every few seconds we felt the tick of a snowflake.

"Let's call it SnoCam," Teddy suggested.

The Device was still on its docking stand in the home ec room, and Larry McConkey was still chatting it up. The four servos on the topmost gimbal were twitching and whirring, causing the main rod to swing erratically. The Device was trying to find a way to keep its balance. "Mystifies the shit out of me," Larry said. "Upside down and a hundred and eighty degrees out of trim, huh? That's slick, kid." By turning set-screws the size of pinheads, Larry could adjust the speed with which the servos reacted to variations in trim. The servos would take their final instructions via radio-control, from a model plane joystick Larry had modified.

The Device, despite its jittery excrescences, retained the aura of a wand. Garrett kept backing away from it, adjusting the antenna on his walkie-talkie, until he was out the door.

"The Device makes use of winch technology," he explained, "the kind of thing you see in logging operations. Steeplejack technology, too. And good old Euclidean geometry. Newton and Euclid, it's their kind of machine. The hardware . . . well, with prototypes, it's best to work from crude to fine. Otherwise you can overlook the weak points."

Garrett presented himself as an old-fashioned, self-taught inventor in the Tom Swift tradition. His materials were simple and, for the most part, off the shelf. His machines were dauntingly hardware-intensive: watching the Device go together piece by puzzling piece, one was struck by the Rube Goldbergness of it all.

But in response to Garrett's enthusiasm, or perhaps because of a tic of hope in the topography of chaos, one suddenly remembers the *idea;* that this new camera is supposed to fly, that it is about to dance in the volume of space described by the tops of the light towers and the ground of the playing field. By the simplest extension of that idea, it could do this anywhere that you might attach winches to trees or girders. And because the camera will do this unattached to a cameraman, it will feel like it's doing this on its own, despite its wires, winches, and endless wheels within wheels. In the presence of the naked idea and its quotidian complications, one feels awed, detached, and confused, like the drowsy emperor waiting for the missionaries to wind the clock; one senses a strange surrogate freedom, giddiness almost. Because something in you is going to fly with the Device.

The trick, the plain geometry of the metaphor, is this: we are at the end of an old brute force technology, technology based on blowing things up, whether it's gas in an internal combustion engine or atoms in a bomb. All we really know how to do right is make things go *bang*! But if we manage not to erase ourselves with the old machines, something new is going to happen. Garrett Brown's work is a bright homespun banner of our interim technology, nervously trying to outlive the century.

John Russell had inserted red earmuffs under his cowboy hat and was standing over a winch motor with two miniature electrical connectors in his hands, bringing them together and drawing them apart with exquisite determination, testing something, the old grizzly threading a needle. His paws seemed too big for the task, but he was getting it done.

"Larry," Garrett said, suddenly inside again, "why don't you open a couple of windows in here? It's brutal going in and out of the heat. Young Jon, why don't you take a walkie-talkie with you to the bakery and get some donuts?"

Garrett wired me with one of his sleek new Japanese walkie-talkies, threading the antenna through the loose wool of my cap. Wordlessly, he plucked a cigarette from the pack in John Russell's vest. John transferred his connectors to one hand, removed the pack, dumped it on the workbench and flipped a switch on the winch motor, which sounded a violent *pung*!, as if echoing his annoyance at the removal of the cigarette. Garrett studied the cigarette in his hand; he seemed to be wondering if he should count it as one of his fingers. His fingers were long, his nose was long, his face was long, his body was long. His eyes were brown, opaque, and perfectly round, blinkless with concentration.

"Scumbag motor!" John said. "Who's got the hammer? Who's got a cube-tap? Who's got the vice-grips?"

"Should I be hacksawing this thing?" Garrett pointed with his unlit cigarette to the motor mount.

John leaned across the table with a flaring Zippo.

"There is one word for this machine," Larry announced, "and that is rinky-fucking-dink. All great things are rinky-dink in the beginning. Is this thing in trim? Let's dock it." He taped four penlight batteries on the top gimbal.

Ellen and Jon served coffee, crumb cake, and donuts. I neglected to angle my walkie-talkie mike out of the way before munching, so it got candied with confectioner's sugar.

I went outside with Garrett and Carl the climber to complete the rigging of the winch motors. Garrett handed me the end of a rope, pointed to a utility shed and said, "Tie it there." I tightened the rope by pulling hand over hand. "Pull," Garrett said. "Pull manfully." He squelched his walkie-talkie. "We're ready to fly out here, guys, whenever you're ready in there."

At the north end of the field, a touch football team was warming up. The snow was becoming a storm. Larry Mc-Conkey carried the Device toward the center of the field, cradling it until he reached the fifty-yard line, where the wires from the light towers converged. They were temporarily anchored to a tool chest weighted with ninety pounds of pipe wrenches. Carl detached the wires from the chest and clipped them to the upper gimbal of the Device.

Garrett folded his arms diagnostically. "Prototypes are some fun, huh?" He wrung his driving gloves. "If I was in Rome, with a bunch of Italian guys standing around, they'd think this was normal." He took a step toward the Device, arms still folded. "Fortunately, gravity is on our side. Its own weight makes it want to right itself."

"First time you ever said anything nice about gravity," Teddy said.

"Anybody got a small piece of wood?" Garrett asked. I handed him a couple of toothpicks. He taped them to the camera and wrapped the antenna around them to keep it from dangling in front of the lens.

"Fabulous tech," Teddy said. *"Fabulous."*

Garrett strode to one of winch motors on the sideline. "I'm going to take the tension up, Larry," he said over the walkie-talkie. "Till it floats, okay?" Electrified, his voice was at once public and confidential, like Larry's when he'd been nursing the Device inside.

"Nnnh . . . okay." Larry gripped one of the suspension wires. Snowflakes sparkled on his mustache and the black aluminum gimbal. "There's some kind of intermittent problem with the power here. Vibration coming through the catenaries. Could be the wind." Larry addressed the Device: "C'mon, stop that! You listening? C'mon. Tell me what's wrong. Tell me; show me a sign, servo." *Pung!* "There it goes."

The Device, now supported by wires, hopped gently from Larry's hands and drifted at eye level toward the forty-yard line. Garrett reeled in the slack. The servos quieted and the Device hung plumb, twitching feebly now and then to counter the force of the wind, which had hushed. It was on its own for the first time. It wiggled and spun and peeped around, a puppy with new admirers.

"Like one gigantic video game," Carl said, leaning against the bleachers. "Cosmocam."

Larry walked to the red van parked on the sidelines. He upended a plastic milk crate and set his joystick console on top of it alongside an eight-inch video monitor. The console was decorated with the skull-and-crossbones insignia of the First Air Cavalry and its motto: "Death from Above."

Garrett hunched over the main winch motor at the south end of the field. To accomplish anything more than a monotonous swoop, he would have to use his walkie-talkie to coordinate synchronous movements with the other two winch operators. Teddy manned one, Carl the other. If any of the winches braked too soon, the Device, rudely tugged, would backlash. If braked too late, it would lose support and plummet to the field, where frozen ruts and cleat marks were acquiring snowy white fringes.

The Device was hanging ten feet off the ground. Garrett stared at midfield like a bombardier. "Stand by." His voice had dropped a notch. He flipped the power switch on the winch. It grunted, hummed, growled, the motor's power wanting release. "Ready? I'm taking it up." He dialed the throttle. The winch began slowly to roll, reeling in cable. The pulleys screeched. The Device ascended. When it came almost level with the top of the light towers, Garrett brought it to a halt by dialing down a rheostat. "You getting a picture there?"

"Yes." Larry was ogling the hover shot of the field on the monitor. "Great picture."

"Stand by. Here we go."

Garrett released the brake and whipped the throttle of his winch motor ahead, hoping the other motors would operate synchronously. The wires whinnied.

Eighty feet in the air, the Device catapulted toward him. Then—though we all saw the plunge as a floating because human beings, unlike cameras, do not record catastrophes unblinkingly, and because we could not, as accident victims cannot, believe that life is so simply and swiftly disposed of—it crashed. Once, twice—before Garrett could engage the brake—it bounced on the twenty-yard line.

"Sonofabitch." He snapped off his driving gloves, heaved them at the winch and stalked out on the field.

A couple of servos had been jarred loose but nothing was seriously smashed. The camera, nose down in shame, continued to transmit a picture of Garrett's black sneaker tapping furiously on the frozen turf.

I slumped with Teddy by his winch motor. We leaned back, elbows against the bleachers, oblivious to the snow. Our cheeks, chins, and lips were frozen. Conversation sounded drunken. "Id's a dezperad siduazhun, Doog. But id's going to worg. We're nod going do be dinuhzorz."

For the next six weekends, heavy rains drenched the northeast corridor, threatening terminal rust. For what seemed forever, the meteorological motif was a chronic Kurosawa downpour, a soggy movie symbol of the human condition.

On the morning of Sunday, April 17, Manhattan puddles were glazed with ice. But the sky was china blue and the temperature was climbing. It was going to be a great flying day.

I took the train with Teddy and his identical twin brother Jack, himself a successful commercial cameraman. Garrett greeted us at the station, waving hello through the sunroof slot of his Mercedes. He sighted the Churchills' duffel bags and commended them for bringing enough gear for Prudhoe Bay.

He was wearing a black sweater with *The Shining* in red letters across the chest, just under the silhouette of a pouncing eagle in sparkly silver thread. It was Garrett's balletic camera work in the maze sequences of Kubrick's film that made the Steadicam famous.

Teddy and Jack, having just purchased updated models of

the Steadicam, discussed modifications. There might be a problem, Jack thought, with the leaf capacitors, or the video tap, or . . . Garrett's son Jonathan, in the back seat, slipped a golf ball down Teddy's shirt.

Teddy, unfazed, announced that he and Jack had been having the same dream about forced landings of jumbo jets on interstate highways.

"Without having talked about it before?" Garrett said.

"Right," Jack said. "But the problem is not the highway . . ."

"It's the tollbooth," Teddy said.

"Yeah, I know," Garrett said. "You don't want to get stuck in the exact change lane with a 747."

We stopped at a McDonald's for Egg McMuffins and danishes. Garrett railed against the electrocuted hotdogs he'd been noticing on the Jersey Turnpike. "You look in the window and there's this frozen wienie. I mean like a rock. Hit it with a hammer and it'd shatter. You put in your money and these two electrodes grab each end of the hot dog and zap it and out it comes, still solid at the ends and mushy in the middle. You look around and the only human being is a guy outside pumping gas, not even close enough to give you a sympathetic shrug."

At 10:00 A.M., the sky was still cloudless, wind puffing from the northwest at ten to twenty miles an hour. "On a day like this," Garrett said, "we ought to be able to score a demo."

"We're talking Sputnik here today," Larry McConkey said as he unloaded the Device, sporting a new science-fictiony antenna, from his van.

A bearded young man named Larry Cone was setting up his portable Osborne computer in the scorekeeper's booth at the top of the bleachers. It was not clear why he had been exiled so far from the sidelines, where Garrett and Larry

McConkey would be operating the joystick controllers. There was no better reason, perhaps, than that the booth perch was aloofly there and looked like it needed occupying.

"Hi," Larry said. "I'm software." He'd driven down from Cape May with his wife Marie, who had just started a skin care business, so she and her husband would both be able to work at home.

Larry Cone had written the software—the computer's strategy—for handling the winch motors, four of them this time, one at each corner of the field. There were two major sectors of control; one the equilibrium of the camera itself —the way it hung in the air. This was Larry McConkey's concern. The second sector, its flight—its walking on wires— was now in Larry Cone's hands, or rather in the hands of the computer he had programmed. Ideally, his software, interfaced with the joystick, would allow the camera to move anywhere, any way. And because the computer digitalized each move, analyzed it and memorized it infallibly, the camera could rehearse swift, intricate maneuvers at a leisurely pace, then repeat them at two times or five times or ten times the rehearsal rate.

"But you have to locate the geographic center of the field with fantastic accuracy," said Marie, pacing off measurements on the field. "With the wrong coordinates, the computer might think the ground was lower than it actually was, and what you'd see is the Device burrowing into the field, still thinking it was airborne."

Teddy was threading a power cable through the bleacher seats. He stared perplexedly down at the coils of cable, then straight ahead at the stands, then up at the scorekeeper's booth.

"What we should do," his brother Jack suggested earnestly, "is get a pole vaulter out here." He went off to play hardball catch, without a glove, with Jon.

Armand Francart, a machinist from Landenberg, Pennsylvania, handed me his card. *Quality Is Not Our Goal—It's Our Standard.* Armand, in his navy blue blazer, starched white shirt, rep tie, twill pants, blond cowboy boots, and shiny hair, looked more like an agent than a machinist. He was standing in for John Russell, who was in Hollywood catching up on backlogged work. From his blazer pocket Armand produced a set of snub-nosed pliers for Larry McConkey, who was busy repositioning the penlight batteries that powered the servos. Teddy stood by with scissors and tabs of Velcro.

Garrett assumed his arms-folded, fist-to-chin diagnostic stance. "Arrives in a station wagon," he intoned in a commercial spokesman's voice, "sets up in minutes." He retrieved his hand from the gears of the upper gimbal, which were grinding exceedingly fine. "I've just found another place you don't want to put your finger."

He asked his son Jon to put the baseball away and bring coffee. The grownups were not playing now, they were measuring.

Garrett conferred with Larry Cone about the computer's data rate—its capacity to get enough information to the winch motors so that their spooling and unspooling would be smooth. The idea was that if the flight was considered as a line, and the line considered as a series of points, the more points the computer could tell the motors about, the smoother the flight. Garrett wanted pinpoint control, meaning twelve, even thirty-two pulses, or messages, per second. The best Larry could promise was three. Each pulse, each updating of direction, called for nine separate mathematical functions for each motor. Camera movement, therefore, might be fidgety. The alternative was to settle for a "soft" joystick, a trade-off that would make for smooth continuous movement, but slow starts and slushy stops.

Larry proposed installing a "hard math chip" in each motor to assist the Osborne with some of the heavy number crunching. Garrett nodded like an auctioneer nodding at money. He grasped at once that the hard math chips, at a cost of $250 apiece, would bring him close to the ideal: a one-to-one ratio between instruction and response, rather like the rack-and-pinion steering on his Mercedes. But today's flight, whatever refinements the crew might dream about, would have to be guided by a Model T data rate of three pulses per second.

Larry McConkey was soliloquizing again, sleeplessly. "Coffee. He's getting coffee. I guess it's that Brown instinct. I should get my Ph.D. in Velcro-ology. Dirty Doc, that's me. A Velcrometer would be useful. Heh-heh. See, we can still laugh. I ask you, is this show business?"

"This is show research," said Garrett.

"In many ways," Larry said, "I'd rather be whittling those little balls within balls in ivory than balancing this machine." The servos hummed. "Lookit it go. Sounds semi-slick. Starting to *look* like something, momma!"

"This thing's going to be so stable," someone said, "you could leave your cocaine on it."

"Arrives in a tractor-trailer," Garrett amended, "sets up in one geological epoch." He switched on the video camera, color for this flight, and went to the monitor on the other side of the van. "Can you point the camera at something besides the sun, Teddy? I'm getting a blow-out on the video." He put on his walkie-talkie headset and called Larry Cone. "Are you on the air, Larry? Put your ears on."

"I'd like to reinitialize," Larry said, meaning he wanted the device and the winch motors and the computer to agree on ground zero. "It'll take about five minutes."

A softball game was getting under way on the adjoining field: cheers, smacks of ball-in-mitt.

"Say when, Larry."

"Two minutes."

"Stand by. We're flying in two, assuming this extension cord here works."

The van was a sink full of wires, wool caps, coffee cups, dead batteries, papers, bungie cords, foam strips, blankets, candybars, screwdrivers, and Larry McConkey's stepped-on lunch. Larry, a model of unflappable alertness and good nature, took his seat at the console, shoveled tacos and potato salad into his mouth and combed his hair with his fingers, all the while watching the monitor, the Device, and Garrett's hands for a clue to the next move.

"I'm going to fly it level across the field," Garrett said. He eyeballed a little boy pursuing a fly ball at the south end. "I'm going to chase that kid."

Slowly—elegantly, almost—the device began to sail downfield. It was behaving quietly today; the pulleys chirped distantly, the servos hummed softly. Perhaps the grace of it—it was gliding now with a swan's assurance—stunned us into deafness.

"I'm going to a slightly faster stick." Garrett pinned the joystick, the camera lurched forward. The winch at the northwest corner unspooled too fast; its line went slack, bellying nearly to the ground. The Device hovered less than a foot above the field. The other three wires remained taut; miraculously, the Device leveled itself at once.

"Number four motor is way overslack, cable's dragging on the ground. Is the pulley slipping? Let's spin the drum. Reverse it to get back in position. Is everybody's brake on? Please respond in order."

"Number four has always been a nasty motor," Larry Cone reported.

John Seitz, the electrician, found another problem; the new "sputnik" antenna was broadcasting a signal powerful enough to interfere with the "Watsons," the angular sensors that controlled the leveling servos. They chattered irritably from battery drain.

"The trouble is," John said, "there's so much metal around here, everything's an antenna. It's a little like when you get close to a radio station, people start receiving Michael Jackson in their fillings. So we have to perform a little dentistry here. If we take care of this, we're golden. We never grounded this Watson case. Let's have the ohmmeter."

Armand the gentleman machinist produced a roll of aluminum foil to shield the Watsons from the antenna. A patch here, a patch there: the Device began to glitter. Armand stuffed his hands in his blazer, muttered, "Let's go, let's go, let's go," to no one in particular and retreated to the bleachers, twiddling his thumbs fretfully.

It was 2:45, still clear, but the wind was picking up. A sort of Sunday doubleheader boredom was setting in. The camera remained live while swinging in the breeze; the picture on the monitor might have been taken from a day-tripper's rowboat idly drifting in midair.

"All right now gentlemen on the motors . . . is everything set for automatic?" There was a rushed, anxious note in Garrett's voice. "Stand by. Everybody hit their reset buttons. Larry, can you do a reset to zero? Brakes on?"

The wind stiffened. The Device moved, but stutteringly, bridling at the resistance. Number two motor was freewheeling now; the Device, still wondrously stable, was flying on only two wires.

"Duke," Garrett said, "take a walk out on the field . . . anywhere on the field."

We know your coordinates, Senator Claghorn, and we can fly to you, just above eye level, in a matter of seconds. . . . Out of respect for the role I was suddenly playing, I tucked in my shirt and removed the toothpick from my mouth.

Then, alone on the field, separated from the crew and the joystick console, no longer a bystander, I caught sight of it, the Device, above me, way over there, off to the left, thirty yards away now but closing slowly, serenely in pursuit, a floating, freshly hatched eye. In the middle of a chilly football field in the sinking light of a spring afternoon, I was caught, watched, trapped, a Hitchcock hero, glamorously paranoid.

My tendency till now had been to anthropomorphize the Device, to notice its resemblance to a fledgling bird, or to outer-space it, call it R2D2, pat its shiny little noggin. After all, it was only a machine, a creature of human ingenuity, and for all its gears, gimbals and foil shielding, there was something Bambi-pathetic about its mimicry of animal movement. When I'd been watching *it,* that is. Now it was watching me and it didn't feel like a bird of anything especially cute. It felt quite smart, determined. I fought a reflex to avert my eyes. It was in the superior position, as the future generally seems to be, no matter how tentatively or clumsily it contrives to happen. Didn't the Wright brothers build their airplane out of bicycle parts? And that nice guy over there with his computerized joystick—fifteen years ago it'd been a guitar—was he turning cinematography, one of the last romantic cowboy trades, into a desk job?

The sun went down, the mercury-vapor field lights flickered on, the sherberty blues and pinks drained from the western horizon, the crew dismantled the motors, coiled the wires.

Garrett, happily exhausted, read the label on a bottle of champagne and said, "Now theoretically the camera could follow this cork. . . ." It popped in the direction of midfield. The crew flinched merrily. Garrett still had a debriefing to preside over, and there was a lot of gear to pack for tomorrow's flight to Sri Lanka.

The Test

I took the 'A' train to the union office to sit on a panel judging applicants for cameramen's cards.

Curly, the business agent, greeted me at the door. Curly did not chomp a cigar, nor did he have a pot belly. He was young and skinny and held a graduate degree in labor relations. He did seem to swagger, though, even when standing still.

I took the quiz sheet to the mensroom and tried to bring myself up to speed. Let's see: one-half double fog filter on lenses shorter than 45mm . . . for longer lenses, a one-quarter double fog'll do. Crystal control with angle adapter knob, zoom support bracket in a block of amber, sheet metal over silica gel, floppy diskettes for motion control, corals, graduated neutral densities, polarizers, Harrison diffusions, Tiffen fogs, nets, scrims, babies, juniors, seniors, Fays, reflectors, Lightflex, foam core . . .

I couldn't get the mensroom key to work. I went back to the office and said, "Hey look, Curly, I can't pass this test and I can't get this key to work."

"There's a trick to it." He escorted me back to the mensroom and kicked the door open. I asked how things were going with him.

He tilted his shoulders and straightened his tie. "Okay, okay. I don't know if you're sensitive to these political things . . ."

"The political thing I'm sensitive to is that I'm three months behind on my dues and I just received my suspension notice, which was followed by your call to be on this screening panel."

Back in the office, Mo and Shep, my fellow panelists, were reminiscing about a cameraman of their acquaintance who'd torched his own studio for the insurance, got some new equipment, got a divorce, got into therapy, got a new girlfriend who kept him sane, and now was getting a little work from the agencies again.

Larry, the first applicant, showed a sequence from a student film in which a young couple was interrupted in the middle of necking by a wristy actor wearing a Donald Duck mask. Larry's final sample was a commercial featuring a coin rolling toward a bottle of cough medicine.

The lights went up and the oral part of the exam started. Shep put his questions aggressively. Mo was firm in his avuncular way, very much the custodian of correct answers. Larry got stumped on the difference between a one-half and a one-quarter double fog filter. "But I'll tell you this much," he said. "You need a carefully structured filter system to be creatively free."

"Right." Mo folded his arms like a Persian executioner. "Send the next guy in."

Sal, the second candidate, was burly and blond, wore a gold earring and had an affable "Hi, guy" manner. His reel opened with scenes from a documentary about killer whales.

"What's the biggest problem shooting underwater?" Shep asked.

"Turbidity."

Turbidity, right. This was like watching guys going to the gynecologist.

Val, the final candidate, showed us several rock videos. "Now this next thing is about Men and Women and Drugs and the Future," he explained punkly.

We flunked Larry, passed Sal and Val. I emptied ashtrays and dumped coffee cups, lifting one gently from the hands of Curly, the business agent, who'd been dozing at his desk.

"Don't wake him up," Shep said. "He's taking his test."

Steady Teddy in the Fourth Dimension

The whale must see one distinct picture on this side, and another distinct picture on that side; while all between must be profound darkness and nothingness to him. Man may, in effect, be said to look out on the world from a sentry-box with two joined sashes for his window. But with the whale, these two sashes are separately inserted, making two distinct windows, but sadly impairing the view. This peculiarity of the whale's eyes is a thing always to be borne in mind in the fishery.

—Moby-Dick

"Wake up, Duke. It's me, Deep Teddy. I'm in a phone booth outside the White House. It's all happening right now: 3-D Panaglide West Coast comedy chase film right in front of the White House. I've been down here since Monday and it's still going on. *Under Pressure,* that's the working title, and we're shooting the sequel at the same time. It's called *Under More Pressure.* Don't worry about planefare, I got money up the *wazoo.*"

I packed my still camera and caught the nine o'clock shuttle. Lulled by the authoritative rustle of politicians' newspapers, I scanned, in my own copy of the *Times,* the obituary of Joseph Ruttenberg, winner of four cinematography Oscars, dead yesterday in Los Angeles at ninety-three. One of the last of the pioneer cinematographers, "Mr. Ruttenberg was noted for his knack of making black-and-white photography seem almost three-dimensional." His credits included *A Day at the Races, Gaslight,* and *Julius Caesar*—titles that summoned up a luscious style of cinematography.

The three-dimensionality spoken of by the *Times* was an effect easier to achieve in the black-and-white of Ruttenberg's day than in today's color. In black-and-white photography, you're dealing with tones of gray: looking back on it, it was a relatively simple trick to orchestrate lighting, camera movement, set design, costumes, and art direction to "stack" or layer planes of light and shadow to suggest depth. Color, with its additional variables, is more of a chore to control. And the *Times* was talking about the *suggestion* of depth rather than 3-D's palpable feeling of space between foreground and background.

With the possible exception of Smellovision, 3-D has a history more eccentric than other special effects, mostly because it insists on installing part of its hardware—those goofy cellophane glasses—on the viewer. Behind the scenes, 3-D cameras have the reputation of being as nimble as a '47 Packard. 3-D technology has always been dinosauric, poking its snout into the movies' Flash Gordon idea of the future. But there is, after all, something essentially dinosauric about movie production: so big, its brain so far from its tail.

A simple twitch, for a beast so awesome, can take a lumberingly long time between idea and execution. Still, to take all that hardware—cameras the size of refrigerators, not to mention studios and egos the size of airplane hangers—and produce the illusion of refinement. . . . This is the movie way of billboarding our dreams.

Washington's pale monuments poked through the tawny smog. I funneled to the front of a crowd at the White House gate and told the guard I was looking for the film crew.

"There's about fifty of them here every day," he said.

"They're shooting a comedy. . . ."

"There's a lot of that around here, too, lately. Might it have something to do with those trucks across the street?"

There it was, right over my shoulder, the woolly mammoth: six tractor trailers disgorging equipment and Teamsters with coffee cups.

Teddy, wearing his Panaglide harness, a sort of breastplate to which the camera would be attached for certain shots, was chatting up a *zaftig* lady Teamster named Audrey.

"This afternoon they want me to run up and down a rotten pier. Wait'll you see what happens when I say no. I don't work near water—quick-release harness or not. What are they going to do—get six grips to dive in the Potomac after me?"

Audrey consulted her watch.

Freddy Moore, the director of photography, was reclining on the grass, sipping coffee, eyes flashing to whatever music his Walkman was delivering.

Everyone on the crew looked more or less like Freddy, who was the very model of a professional film refugee: stained leather flight jacket over Hawaiian shirt. He smiled without removing his earphones. Teddy mimed a lengthy introduction, mouth silently working, hands emphatic. Finally, Freddy noosed the earphones around his neck.

"What do you do and how much do you make?" he asked.

"Not much," I said. "And not much."

Teddy and Freddy shared an interest in personal computers. They began lamenting the hobby-compulsiveness of it all. Last month, for instance, Freddy had innocently entered a Los Angeles mall and emerged moments later with a $2,800-printer for which, he discovered when he tried to plug it in, no local store stocked the correct interface.

"Interface," Teddy murmured with a fellow mechanic's compassion.

"Yeah," Freddy sighed. "Innerface."

I was curious about the name—*OK FREDDY*—stenciled on his high-legged folding chair, which stood empty on the lawn.

"It seems that years ago there was this extra in Hollywood called Okay Freddy. He had an enormous schlong. Used to work as a waiter at fancy parties, walk around with it on the hors d'oeuvres tray, garnished. Whenever they needed a reaction shot for one of those cast-of-thousands crowd scenes, the assistant director would stand him on top of the scaffolding and say, 'Okay, *Freddy*!' which was the cue for Okay Freddy to whip it out. And that's how C. B. DeMille got all that gaping religious awe." Okay Freddy Moore ignited a Lucky.

"All those fruitcakes with the protest posters are ours," he continued, waving at the extras: the warpainted Indian, nearly seven feet tall, in overalls, the old lady in pink dress and sneakers, the bucked-toothed blind man with a blank picket sign, the punk in studded black leather, pirate earrings, and spaces between his teeth, which he kept baring, overplaying the fang effect.

"All kinds of freelance crazies on the set today, too," said Okay Freddy. "This morning, guy walks up to me, very straight-looking guy in a suit, he says he's going to chopper down a Marine fire team right on the White House lawn, arrest Reagan. 'I'm a Jewish attorney,' he says, 'and I'm going to prosecute him.' Prolly a cop. I says, 'Okay, I'm delegating you to be the first assistant director in charge of the second unit. Stand over there.' I don't know where he is now. Prolly joined the Marines."

I looked around for familiar life forms. To my left, the production manager was flipping audibly through a wad of twenty-dollar bills. He handed a few to his assistant. "Better make that *two* hundred Big Macs," he said.

"See, you got focus and convergence," Teddy said, starting my first hands-on lesson in 3-D. "Vertical and horizontal convergence." The words, like the camera itself, were familiar, but they were defined here in a special dialect.

Teddy swung the matte box—the frame that holds filters and blocks stray light—away from the lens. Lenses, rather. There were two of them, side by side, one slightly higher than the other, like a cockeyed set of binoculars wielded by the awkward kid at camp.

Optimax III, the version of 3-D marketed by the Panavision company, comes in a nine-pound box about the size of a Rolodex. The box fits directly into the lens turret of a standard 35mm-Panavision camera. On the front of the box are matched lenses which split the 35mm-image in two, horizontally, in a format known as Techniscope. This crams two wide frames, one on top of the other, into one conventional 35mm-frame. All true 3-D systems, of course, rely on two two-dimensional pictures which are eventually blended, via those glasses, to create the stereo effect of primate binocular vision—a single three-dimensional picture.

"Okay, let me tell you about convergence: look at Okay Freddy over there. Now hold one finger up in front of your face. Keep looking at Okay Freddy."

I saw two fingers, one Okay Freddy.

"Now focus on your finger."

I saw one finger, several Okay Freddys.

"When fish start buying tickets to movies," Okay Freddy said, making eyes at the side of his head with circling fingers, "the problem will be different. Or bees."

"Oh, wow, yeah, bees," Teddy buzzed.

Except for the occasional tuning of the convergence knob, there was virtually no evidence that this was anything but an ordinary 2-D picture. Older 3-D systems have used two cameras, closely yoked, or one camera rigged to expose two rolls of film. The advantage of Panavision's Optimax III is that it greatly reduces the number of moving parts, as well as the bulkiness of the equipment.

"But 3-D's got about as much future as Channel J," Teddy said. "It's a hum job."

"But this *is* an odd movie," Okay Freddy said. "Half the characters are invisible half the time. Blue fluid makes them invisible. That's the stuff the lobster dropped. Or maybe it's the flying knives."

Teddy's Panaglide was rigged, something like an outboard motor, on the tailgate of a pickup truck. He was to drive past the White House in pursuit of four actors who would chase each other, knock each other down, shriek and fight, limbs cranking at Keystone Cop angles.

Teddy would not have to wear the Panaglide for this shot. Clamped to the tailgate, the camera would smooth out jounces in the pickup's suspension and produce an astoundingly long and complex dolly shot. Teddy, himself strapped to the tailgate by means of a safety harness he'd adapted from auto racing, would try to keep the action in frame. We drove across Pennsylvania Avenue in heavy traffic, back to the Gate of the Jaded Guard.

Okay Freddy cruised the sidewalk with his walkie-talkie, occasionally communicating with Teddy, who was backing up the camera truck against traffic, but more often reporting to his personal CIA on the status of nubile tourists: "Ap-

proaching the south gate . . . short-shorts . . . braces . . .
stand by. What is this—a School for the Blonde?"

One of the blondes asked him what movie this was.

"This is *The Robe Part VI*—the day everybody gets cru-
cified."

"It's a TV deal or something," a civilian protestor explained. His placard, emblazoned with a mushroom cloud,
called on Mr. Premier Gorbachev to do something about
disarmament before it was too late.

The extras sprawled against the fence. Some dozed, others
thumbed plump paperbacks.

"Who is this man?" the scowling assistant director asked
Okay Freddy about me.

"This man is a totally harmless tourist," said Okay
Freddy. "See his dinky camera? Put him in the movie."

It wasn't easy keeping an eye on things while maintaining
the discreet boredom expected of an extra. The cameras
rolled. Two actors screeched to the curb in a station wagon,
jumped out, ran up to another actor, knocked him down
and started beating him up. But he got away and they all
chased him down the street, to the astonishment of the pick-
eting extras, me among them, and the genuine alarm of
bona fide tourists in their path.

"Brilliant, Duke, brilliant," Teddy said, sailing by fourth-
dimensionally on the tailgate. "Just don't look in the camera, okay?"

The next setup was on the south corner: actor vaults a
police barricade, knocks down an elderly blind news dealer,
jumps into a car, and drives off.

"*Fuckface! Bill!*" the director shouted, clapping his hands
to summon the peg-toothed Punk. Then, without lowering his
voice, the director explained the shot to Teddy. "*Okay, it's a
tableau, see? Guy runs in, knocks the guy on the head, runs
away! You have very little to do except photograph it, see?*"

Teddy peered into the viewfinder. "I've seen Helen Keller compose a better frame than this."

Lunch. The crew mingled with pedestrians, nothing magical in their demeanor anymore, athletes merely mortal off the field. I helped myself to the glistening buffet laid out alongside the trucks: noodles, lamb. On the sidewalk, a battalion of brown ants was disassembling a Big Mac. The Punk was juggling his lunch.

The temperature was sixty-five, balminess imported from California along with most of the crew. We selected a comfortably sloped section of the lawn and lolled in first-class idleness. Lately, Teddy, a New Yorker, had been scurrying from movie to movie, exercising his specialty for a few days at a time.

"See the tires on that truck?" he asked. "How clean they are? The Teamsters clean them with Coca Cola." He emptied his wallet on the lawn. "Look at the green on that fifty." It was fresh as a new leaf.

"It's unreal," I said.

"It's real." He leaned back on his elbows, mellowing. "Well, it's party-party-party, I guess, and cowboy-cowboy-cowboy. This is my thirty-second picture in two years. It's wonderful. You never really get tired of it. I went to Rhode Island School of Design for a year, did well in art, could draw the shit out of anything, flunked liberal arts, went to Parsons in New York City, studied industrial design, shot stills for a school assignment, bought a Nikon, quit school, got a job with a picture framer back home in Princeton, joined the Army Reserve for six months, saw *David and Lisa, Yojimbo, The Seventh Seal*—like that, moved to New York City and got into film. My father was a ham radio operator, had his own call letters since 1933. But we weren't really mechanical, my brother and I. More into fantasies. Putting wasps into matchboxes, squashing them in vices for the sound effects. We were boys. I used to love to hang out in the Village. The energy level of the city, it's like an animal. I lived on St. Mark's Place before the Electric Circus. The first person I met was Richie Havens. He was an artist then. He never had teeth. We used to hang out in Washington Square Park and draw. When you have that innocence and enthusiasm . . . Remember how we used to think we'd find some great bunch of people? I never found one in New York.

"The film business . . . it's a lifeboat. Once you're in it, you look after each other."

We walked to the camera truck. Teddy fiddled with the Panahead, a camera mount that allows the camera operator to steer the lens smoothly and with precision.

"I can sign my name upside down and backwards with this thing. Of course it helps to be slightly dyslexic, which I used to be."

In the sixties, when recreational machines became small and portable, Panavision, under the leadership of an ex-actor named Robert Gottschalk, decided to make a quiet, lightweight camera that would match the performance of the bulky studio Mitchells. It was the kind of thing you might have expected the Japanese to do. But it was Panavision, an American company, that left Mitchell in the dust. In June 1981 Gottschalk was hacked to death by his boyfriend in Los Angeles. Panavision, now a subsidiary of Warner Communications, continues to supply cameras for most of the features shot in the United States, and it is a measure of the fresh hopes for 3-D that Panavision has thrown its weight behind Optimax III.

The light was getting low and blunt. An overtime discussion flowed through the crew like water sloshing in a barrel. Lots of beard-scratching. Teddy got trapped in a conversation—became the target, rather, of a monologue delivered by a bag-lady with a fanatically peaceful face and cardboard-fringed black boots. She stood rigidly still and told a story that vined around H. L. Hunt, JFK, and two reporters, German and French, at whose side she happened to be standing the day JFK was shot. Her picture was taken, along with theirs, and transmitted around the world, skewering her with the fate of being a paranoid encylopedist of one the century's famous catastrophes. She wished us victory and peace and shuffled away singing "The Battle Hymn of the Republic."

"It just goes to show you," said Teddy. "You can be absolutely crazy and absolutely happy."

We caravanned to a new location on the bank of the Potomac under the Key Bridge. There was a view, two miles upstream, of Watergate and the Kennedy Center. We parked in a sheltered yard, railroad tracks embedded in cobblestones, the Potomac shining through fresh-budded elms. It was quiet, it was perfect—an idyllic nest under the hum of traffic: racing shells, splintered oars, water lapping, tilting masts, reflections rippling, bugs spiraling, fish nets hung up to dry, dandelion seeds drifting, high school girls hoisting their rowing sculls onto a dock and into a shed through whose unhinged wooden door they were silhouetted and haloed by the shine off the water.

On the dock, Okay Freddy blocked out the action of the upcoming scene by wiggling his fingers.

"Here's the lobster, here's the ball," the propman said. He was carrying a plastic lobster who was in turn clasping a blue plastic sphere in his claws.

Teddy paced the pier to check for rotten boards. He ordered the carpenter to build an eight-foot plywood ramp to cover some shaky spots. He started setting up the Panaglide, adjusting his vest with an Allen wrench, pipe fuming, deep in his urgent battlefield-surgeon mode.

"No Panaglide, Teddy," the assistant director interrupted. "We're going to Plan B. Take it off, you're out."

Teddy sizzled, a commando with his mission thwarted. "Good drill. Now I've got to kill something."

The freight train announced itself with a clang. A locomotive was very slowly nudging four coal cars our way. Okay Freddy and half a dozen crew members wandered out to marvel at it. Teddy led the ceremony, sacred to little boys of our generation. Reverently, he placed a penny on the track.

"Anybody got a nickel or a dime or a quarter?"

The coins spread flatter and flatter as each set of wheels rolled over them, until they could barely be distinguished from the tracks. The locomotive bellowed its farewell *moo* from the phantom American herd.

"That nickel's looking like half a dollar," Okay Freddy said.

"But you can still see the face on the dime." I peeled a penny, now waferishly two-dimensional, off the tracks. The brass shone through grease still warm from the weight of the wheels. The edges were sharp enough to slice a finger.

The stunt coordinator turned up in a black rubber suit. He tested the depth of the water at the edge of the dock. One of the actors was evidently about to get wet.

"Hey, here's the writer!" a woman said in back of me. "See his pen!" It was the bag lady, magically arrived, still smiling. Behind the hanging fishnets, she and her boyfriend—an elderly gent in a three-piece houndstooth suit—held hands and watched the bad guys chase the good guys across the dock. The bad guy in the black outfit—the Punk—fell in the water and bobbed right up, flashing his fangs and combing his hair.

"I just got stepped on by two different people," a voice blared over the walkie-talkie on Okay Freddy's belt.

"Stay off the radio, please," the assistant director's voice squawked. "I am talking with a police officer."

Okay Freddy crooned into his walkie-talkie. "Could I have two cheeseburgers and a thirteen-year-old to go, please?"

"Okay, *Freddy!*" Teddy said.

Eyes for Miss Piggy

"We're waiting for the Pig to get dressed," Ezra Swerdlow said. "Then the thief."

Ezra was a smiling, sharp-eyed man in his thirties, young for a production manager on a major film like *The Muppets Take Manhattan*. There was something very *heimische* Brooklyn about him, and something, too, that made me want to salute. "You got five minutes," he advised Teddy Churchill, the second unit cameraman, "then we move."

Teddy, pipe sparking, was rigging his Steadicam near Bethesda Fountain in Central Park. The day was lush: sunlight dappled the Winnebagos, and around the fountain itself a solo rollerskater boogied, flashing a sixties peace *V*.

"Well," said Teddy, ritually flashing back, "the good news is that last night I got my double-sided, double-density disk drives for my PC. They're quiet. The bad news is I need more tobacco or I'm going to have an oral crisis."

Frank Oz, the director, arrived to discuss the morning's

work. Listening to his throaty Midwestern resonance, I closed my eyes and saw Fozzy Bear, so endearingly insecure, so frantic to please. Frank was a tall, thin man in his forties, emphatically unbearlike; he wore a faded soccer shirt whose horizontal stripes saved him from looking skinny. His collar curled rakishly. His hair was a neatly trimmed hedge on the sides of his head. His salt-and-pepper mustache was trim, too—drawn almost—so that it perfectly described the line of his upper lip while reinforcing it. His eyebrows were joined by a deep vertical furrow developed by flexing his principle muscle, a powerful talent for concentration and invention. Below this muscle were his eyes, direct and chronically merry.

Miss Piggy's purse, Frank explained, has been snatched by the thief. Miss Piggy pursues the thief on rollerskates. Teddy's assignment—while the first unit was shooting by the fountain—was to film part of this chase sequence.

Part of this chase sequence. Chase sequences are tricky to shoot because they're quilted from so many little pieces: cut to the pursuer, cut to the pursued, cut to the feet, cut to the skates—back and forth, back and forth. Since every camera setup takes time, the trick is to make a few setups look like many by slight alterations of angle. "The whole idea," Teddy told me, "is to disorient."

An additional complication: when Miss Piggy is seen in full figure, she is played by a young woman in a Miss Piggy costume. Closeups, in which the lower part of her body is not seen, would be shot later, with Oz himself manipulating her face. In the meantime, Frank was very concerned that Teddy stay far enough from Piggy so that her facial movement—or lack of it—would go undetected.

"The most important thing is that she's always hunched over, body tense, murder on her mind."

A pair of Miss Piggy's styrofoam thighs wafted by on a

wire coat hanger. Teddy scored some tobacco off the rollerskater. "How about the thief? How close can we be on the thief?"

"We can be *nostril*." Frank tweezered his thumb and forefinger and leaned into Teddy.

We piled into a van and drove against traffic to the Ramble, a heavily wooded section of the park notorious as a hotspot for muggers. Ezra Swerdlow turned to Billy the Grip. "You got a broom, Billy?"

"Yeah."

"You got the thief?"

"Yeah."

The thief was played by an athletic young man named Gary. Still in his twenties, he had the beginnings of a natural scowl. In a few years his face would have character, probably villainous. He confessed this was only the second day of his first movie job. He'd done off-Broadway, showcases, stuff like that. He liked the film life so far. "People seem very privileged." Below us, in a saucer-shaped meadow, extras with professional-looking pectorals were lounging.

At the Ramble, Teddy hopped out first. He strode up and down the paths, pausing at each turn to evaluate camera angles.

Ezra kept up with Teddy. Lynn, the script clerk, kept up with Ezra.

"I'll be sort of directing this sequence," Ezra said, unfolding his camp chair—*Ezra Swerdlow* emblazoned on one side of the webbing, *Production Manager* on the other.

"Just remember there are four levels of sweat," Lynn reminded him. The makeup department was standing by to spray more or less water on the thief according to his stage of exertion.

"I got some ideas." Teddy was hunching, bobbing. "I got some hot ideas. The hardest thing is to get these shots clean." He took half a step to his right to see if he'd be able to hide a couple of strands of phone wire behind a tree. Raw industrial modernity would be perceived, in a Muppet movie, as an intrusion. A Sidney Lumet movie would take a grittier view of Manhattan. "I don't want to see that fence, either," Teddy added. "Frank's into prettiness."

"Let's get these leaves outta here," Ezra said.

Billy, the grip, swept the path. His broom sent up golden dust in stalks of sunlight.

"This is all skatable, right?" Ezra asked Vic, the stunt coordinator. Vic was a tree trunk of a man, swarthy, with eyes so large and eyelashes so dark they seem mascaraed.

"He holds the record for falling farthest out of a building backward onto an air bag," Ezra confided proudly. "Two hundred feet or something."

One of the city policemen assigned to the production spotted an unleashed dog. "To me," he said with suburban equanimity, "it's unfair to have a dog in an apartment."

"I had two dogs when my husband died," the script clerk said. "Six months later, one of them died of cancer. I was left with a Yorkie. I couldn't deal with him. I had to deal with myself." She consulted her clipboard and cast a clinical eye on the thief. "We're going to make you, uh let's see, the most sweaty, Gary. See, you've already seen her gloved hands. So you're just hysterically fleeing."

The makeup man sprayed an appropriate amount of water between the thief's shoulder blades, on his neck, on his sideburns.

Miss Piggy was not in costume yet, so Teddy filmed Gary the thief alone. Gary scampered past the camera and bounded up a flight of stone stairs.

"Well, shit!" Ezra barked. "The purse! What about the purse?"

"Right," the script clerk agreed. "If he's a purse snatcher, so where's the purse, right?"

"Do we want to make him stagger a bit going up the stairs?" Teddy inquired.

"The running changes not so much in speed as in *intensity*," the script clerk advised.

It was finally decided that the pace of the thief's running ought to be *erratic*. Rather than stagger, he would simply break stride as he passed the camera.

The policeman had brought his young son along. He held the boy's hand as the thief ran up the steps four times.

"Okay" Ezra said. "Print one and four. Next case."

A hundred yards to the south, Teddy was planning another shot, but there was a broken lamp post in the way, and no tree to hide it behind.

"What we could do," he suggested, "is to have Miss Piggy bounce off the lamp post and make it so she bent it."

"You want to explain that to Frank at the screening?" the script clerk cautioned. No one wanted to be responsible for surprising the boss.

"I met a producer once," Teddy recalled. "The biggest thing in his life was he moved an aircraft carrier three feet. Of course, that was the last thing he did."

Miss Piggy skated downhill in a red skirt and lavender three-fingered mittens, arms windmilling. Vic caught her like a couch.

"Does she have eyes that she puts on?" asked Teddy.

Miss Piggy's eyes—plastic hemispheres with thin slits through which it was difficult for the actress to see—would be installed just before the camera rolled.

Teddy zapped his zoom control to find the right focal length for the next setup. "You know what Zane Grey says? 'She had eyes like burn holes in the jailhouse blanket. . . .'"

"Let's put the eyes on and shoot it," Ezra said.

"All set, Denise?" Vic asked. "Denise, are you all ready, sweetheart?" Vic's voice needed no amplification. He addressed his troops in the tone of one who was asking them to do something they could break a bone doing. He wanted them to understand that as long as they followed his clear and simple instructions, everyone would look good and no one would get hurt. Vic was the champion at taking chances. Vic had taken the record fall. Vic was there to catch them when they fell. Vic was their net.

From a plastic case marked *Normal Eyes,* the makeup man plucked Miss Piggy's eyes. Ezra called *"Action!"* Miss Piggy skated downhill full tilt. Vic planted himself off-camera to catch her at the end of her run. Almost at once, however, she tripped and slammed into the pavement paws first, scuffing her padded knees.

Leo, the first assistant director, took over while Ezra retired to his camp chair and approved $20,000 worth of bills which had just been delivered in an overflowing folder. Leo was an émigré seven years out of the Soviet Union. He spoke Russian, Polish, Hebrew, and English. He wore sunglasses and a bush jacket and moved deliberately. He had acquired in his travels the Israeli mannerism of never smiling while he worked, real work being mostly war. But when he took his sunglasses off, his eyes were young.

At the crest of another hill, Teddy was designing another shot. He wanted the thief to run downhill, then make a sharp left turn. The Steadicam would dolly toward him, pan with him as he whizzed by, snapping leaves from a branch in front of the lens. Miss Piggy would rocket from behind the camera and crash through the branch.

Denise, after her tumble, was tired. For the new shot, Miss Piggy would be played by Cheryl. "In the big time," said Teddy, "even stand-ins have actressy names."

Cheryl sat down next to a clear plastic bag containing Miss Piggy's head.

"What stage of sweat is this for the thief?" Leo asked.

"Early stage," replied the script clerk.

"Gary," Vic said, "this is easy. Keep it fluid. Lots of form." Last week Vic had instructed Gary to run five miles a day in preparation for his role.

Ezra finished his bookkeeping. "Let me know when the head is on. We want to shoot it—eyes, everything."

Miss Piggy's eyes were on her lap. Cheryl had just put the head on over her thin bicycle crash helmet. The makeup man poked his fingers in the eye holes to arrange Cheryl's hair, which had gotten snagged.

Teddy thought that when Miss Piggy crashed through the branch, leaves ought to fall. Billy the Grip was consulted. He didn't have a ladder that would enable him to get high enough to drop the leaves from a realistic height.

"Is that eighty-six on the leaves, then?" Teddy wanted to know.

"Could be too hambone, anyway," Ezra said. "Seriously." He turned to the makeup and stunt people. "This shot is from the back. No eyes on her. Unless they'd protect her."

"Put the eyes on," Vic said flatly.

Leo had developed a broad twitch in his left cheek. His eyes were blinking like signals.

We joined the first unit in the neighborhood of Bethesda Fountain. Teddy walked through a shot with Frank Oz. This would be a close two-shot with Kermit the Frog and an actress jogging along the path. It had to be close because just below the camera frame, Frank would be lying on his back on a sort of low-rider tricycle, his arm in a Kermit hand puppet and his eyes glued on a TV monitor at the foot of the dolly.

"Kermit's got to go like this." Frank guided Kermit in a shoulder-rolling bob which, from the waist up, looked precisely like a frog jogging. Teddy walked a few feet ahead tracking the action with his Steadicam.

The policeman's little boy peered through the viewfinder. "It's pretty dark in there," he noted with an accuracy alarming in one so apparently innocent. It was all one to him, the artifice and the honest magic. Later, during lunch, he would have his picture taken in Miss Piggy's lap, her styrofoam arms embracing him. Happily disillusioned, he would join the elite illusionists.

The set was beginning to draw a lunchtime crowd. The production assistants got busy corraling curious stragglers. "Step back, please folks. Work with us," said a young woman with a walkie-talkie on her hip and a hitperson's *sang froid* in her voice.

The boy and I were pushed back along with the civilians. At a distance of fifty feet, out of earshot, the crew gesticulated, all of them suddenly Muppets. A ten-foot-by ten-foot butterfly—a framed sheet of silk for diffusing the sun—was hoisted in. Teddy stood tall in the middle of it all, pointing, pantomiming his plan for the next shot, pipe fuming. He looked up, caught the little boy's eye, smiled, and mouthed—I thought—the words, "Th-th-that's all, folks." He flashed the peace *V.* The boy flashed back.

A Coupla Months of Living Cautiously

The peculiar and slow-moving "Emulsion J" somehow was able to render the human skin transparent to a depth of half a millimeter, revealing the face just beneath the surface . . . He has been zooming around in a controlled ecstacy of megalomania. He is convinced that his film has somehow brought the actors into being. "It is my mission," he announces with the profound humility that only a German movie director can summon, "to sow in the Zone the seeds of reality."

—Thomas Pynchon,
Gravity's Rainbow

> What I saw on the ground glass invoked in
> me a commingling of tenderness, pity and
> sorrow, to the exclusion of more searing
> emotions. Was there another American
> emotion to match it?
>
> —Wright Morris,
> *Photography and Words*

The elevator operator waited for me to make a remark
about the aroma of marijuana in his car. It was originating
from another passenger, a chained-and-leathered messenger
boy who proclaimed, between floors, to be the illegitimate
son of Orville and Wilbur Wright.

The men's room was swampy and flyblown as Bombay in
monsoon. This was 49th and Broadway, where a janitor
was hauling away garbage bags lumpy with God knew what
debris while the parthenogenic messenger boy, now in the
next stall, kept shrieking, "Sheba! Sheba!" This was not
Bombay, nor was it the Radio City Music Hall of yesteryear
where, in the course of my high school summer job, I'd
dreamed snazzily-uniformed dreams of all thirty-six Rock-
ettes, the mommy-est fantasy I'd ever wrought; nor was this
newsreels and twenty-cartoon shows at Loewe's Bay Ridge
in 1957—sly monster scenes for sly monstrous times, kids
stacked two and three in a seat, chins sticky with cherry
Cokes, Dirty Dot McDermott and Mattress Back Mahoney
playing stinkfinger with the Donnelly triplets, who were
sporting superhero capes for the occasion. No, Preview Theater at 1600 Broadway was not this, but it was going to the
movies, the most public of our private experiences.

More than that. It was the ultimate suspension of disbelief,
going into a darkened auditorium and believing, for ninety
minutes or so, that something was really happening up there
on the screen. A whole world ensorcelled by movies, by the

mechanics of rehearsed emotions—only French intellectuals and Indian villagers take this sort of thing seriously.

And cameramen. In the end we have to say our hearts are in them, the movies. As much as we know they lie to us, and we should know, we—like the French so easily awed by the latest savage trend, or like those hope-and-bread-starved Indian villagers—we believe in the movies, believe in them in a way so deeply that no amount of cynicism or rational argument or mature thought or irrefutable evidence or triple-time calculation can persuade us that what we see on the screen is not actually happening, or ought to be. We are in the habit of wanting miracles.

The entrance to the screening room was clogged with cameramen. Right in front of me stood someone who looked like he must be Michael Ballhaus, and was: expensive suede trenchcoat, gray temples, lively eyes, and the solid, courtly manner of a celebrity guest.

Ballhaus is one of the handful of gifted cinematographers fortunate enough to link up with *auteur* directors. The others: Storaro with Bertolucci; Almendros with Rohmer, Truffaut and Benton; Coutard with Godard; Willis with Woody Allen and Coppola, Bruce Surtees with Eastwood; Giuseppe Rotunno with Fellini. There are dozens of cameramen as mechanically masterful as Ballhaus, but until you make a collaborative connection with a great director, you're just another journeyman.

When the lights went down, draining color from the audience, the cameraman sitting next to me suddenly seemed a picture of Lou Costello, only with a suntan. It occurred to me, the way such things occur to cameramen, that I'd never seen a color photo of Lou Costello. Suntans don't show up so well in black-and-white.

The movie, in color, opened with Maria Braun's marriage in the midst of World War II sniper fire.

I'd never seen a color picture of Adolf Hitler, either, until a few years ago, during a public television seminar. The Library of Congress had furnished a clip of Hitler doing a jig on the terrace of his villa in Berchtesgaden. It's a piece of film that's been used many times in documentaries, but always in black-and-white, which seems appropriate for "history."

In fact, the original film was shot in color by Hitler's girlfriend, Eva Braun, who was a photo hobbyist. After the war, American Intelligence experts hired lip readers to find out what Hitler had been saying to his companions while doing his little dance. It turned out he was gossiping about Gary Cooper, whom he'd just watched in a western. The Intelligence people printed the scene in color and dubbed the soundtrack. So there was Hitler, in living color, talking movie trivia in an everyday voice. Agfacolor and modern methods of restoration made the monster appallingly human.

The print of *The Marriage of Maria Braun* was "hot"—too bright—and did not show Ballhaus's lighting to advantage. But Fassbinder's feverishness was a wonder.

The houselights went up and there came that moment of dazed shyness that distinguishes the end of a private screening. Ballhaus, a squarish man, removed his trenchcoat. Everything hung a bit too long on him. The effect was to cast him on the sagging side of relaxed. He smiled.

"Perhaps you might like to know a few things about the production." He seemed to speak around as well as through his mustache. His English was precise, very lightly accented. "*Maria Braun* was the last film I shot with Fassbinder, who at the time was doing a lot of cocaine—about three grams a day, I think."

There was probably no one in the screening room unfamiliar with the ammonia zing of cocaine, the radiator dribbling in the nose. Cocaine operates at twenty-four frames a second, twenty-four hours a day, synchronous with the frenzy of filmmaking. So much of moviemaking is, like the army, fatiguing and boring; sometimes you need more than coffee to instill the warrior confidence it takes to shoot around the clock. Take enough cocaine and you're always on, manically, like TV.

"After *Maria Braun* I couldn't stand it anymore. It was fifteen films with him in nine years."

There were the usual questions about filters and film stock. Ballhaus smiled and gave little away, as if all those years of steady shooting had earned him the right, at times, to a veteran's tranquil blindness. He wore his insouciance proudly, and it was charming. But his memory, when it occurred to him to be specific, was astonishing: the number of hours it took to scout a particular location, the serendipitous drifting of certain clouds. He sensed, finally, that the only thing anybody, even brother cameramen, wanted to hear about was Fassbinder.

"He was very . . . he had to be . . . what is the word?" Ballhaus struggled to convey, diplomatically, that the Christopher Marlowe of movie directors had been something of a monster. Fassbinder was a lens transparent to his time. He was also a scrofulous, tyrannical, drug-afflicted gay, the very model of the filmmaker *maudit*. Most Americans are a little bashful about being *maudit*.

"Competitive?" someone suggested heartily. "Egotistical?"

Ballhaus shook his head. "I will think of the word later."

This was a room full of professionals. We knew that the tools of our trade could outsee the human eye. But we viewed change with the caution of those who, culturally, were waiting to be replaced. A while ago, when Richard Patterson, editor of *The American Cinematographer,* suggested that the success of European cameramen might be attributed to their superior sensitivity and cultural background, his name vanished from the masthead and a full-page apology was printed.

I asked about the inspiration for a complicated dolly move in *The Stationmaster's Wife*. Dolly moves—being in precisely the right spot at the right time in the midst of heavy emotional weather—are the cameraman's essential thrill.

Ballhaus's eyes rolled after the memory. "Yes. There is an expression in German, I don't know if you have it in English: 'An angel flew through the room.' We were talking about the sequence and Fassbinder said"—Ballhaus fluttered his hands . . . "'It's like an angel flew through the room.' And so we tried to move the camera that way."

Exactly: Ballhaus moves the camera like an angel. Sinuousness—a spontaneous, sensuous control of motion more evocative of dance than machinery—is a hallmark of his work. Now that lighting is no longer such a big deal (lights are smaller and fewer), the issue becomes camera movement.

And lighting becomes playful. I inquired about his use of eye lights. One of the tricks Ballhaus likes to play, particularly with male actors, is to spot their eyes with a banner of light, like a bright raccoon mask.

"I like to use eye lights because I think it is important to see the eyes. And with some people you have to give them eye light because their eyes are—" he hesitated, looked in the eyes of his audience "—dead." It sounded like the word he'd been searching for to describe Fassbinder. The issue is feeling rather than just looking.

I lit a cigarette. *The Marriage of Maria Braun* is, among many other things, a great antismoking film. Maria worked so hard, she was so heroically addicted to employment. She would've enjoyed a happy Hollywood ending if only she hadn't also been casually addicted to black-market Camels. Poor Fassbinder. Cocaine is a Nazi drug, heartlessly speeding the love pump and turning the brain to remorseless *übermenschen* black-and-white. It's unfair, perhaps, or ghoulish to wonder why he needed so much of it.

I knocked on the half-shut door of Roni's hospital room. Her purple cowboy hat hung on the bedpost.

The first face I saw, directly across the bed, was familiar. A doctor, I assumed; he looked like Victor Jory. Roni lay in bed, awake and smiling. Her husband Barry, calm and serious, stood at the foot. He was a production manager. When Roni's X rays showed lung cancer, he flew home from Dallas, where he'd been working on a Mike Nichols movie.

"You've met Barry?" Barry said.

The man who looked like Victor Jory stood up. I reached across the bed and shook his hand and turned to Roni. Both Barrys departed.

"He stops by a lot," Roni said. "You make him nervous."

"That's him—the scumbag? I didn't recognize him." The second Barry *was* a doctor—the doctor my wife had run off with.

"Look . . ." Roni said. She extended her hand; the thumb wouldn't move. Last Sunday, when she was trying out her new typewriter, her fingers had stopped working, a symptom that the cancer had intruded into her brain. She'd lost weight; the serious pain was starting. Suddenly I saw my troubles in a weeded-out way.

What do people talk about at times like this? Dying is unmentionably blunt. So we talked, mercifully, about dumb shit. How was the latest Eastwood, the new Elmore Leonard? We held hands firmly. She looked like an old, old woman sliding out of life.

Roni had been the dubbing editor for Bergman, Bertolucci, and Wertmüller. Like many film workers, she dreamed of a freer career as a solo artist. For years she'd been working on a screenplay of her own, trying to graft the grace of Colette, her favorite writer, onto the life of a free spirit from Jersey City. Roni with an *i*; she'd learned to dot her *i*'s at Barnard.

Three years ago, the day I drove my daughter to college, Roni gave birth to a son, Jonah. Because of repairs on their loft, Roni and Barry lived at my place for the first few days of Jonah's life. I shot home movies of Roni breastfeeding under the skylight. Her baby replaced mine. Now everything was falling away from her but her heart.

On the way to the door, she staggered like a marionette. "I envy you going away," she said, thinking I must be going off on location again. The drugs were thinning her hair and her awareness. "You can change your identity, Duke. Maybe I'll be stronger when you get back."

I bought a new pair of running shoes for the New Directors' party. New Balance, purple, pretty expensive. I'd always owned the gray ones, but they tend to get dirty too fast. Nestor Almendros was supposed to be coming.

Moby Dick, the albino porn star, bribed the security guys with a bottle of 'ludes, strolled into Zazi's loft, and rubbed his eyes as if blinded by the effort of being clothed. He flexed by the punch bowl, notched his high-heeled boots on a bar stool and nibbled the ends of his sunglass frames. His hairpiece was a unique achievement in taxidermy. I've shot my share of low-budget nudies, though never with Moby. Used to shoot them with a shower cap on.

The loft, a survivor of the South Street Seaport restoration, had an eye-level view of the Brooklyn Bridge, so close you could hear it humming. Very immediately Manhattan. The kitchen was fussy-Victorian: bric-a-brac, ferns, puckered velvet lampshades, sepia Steichens on faded lilac wallpaper. There were two Art Nouveau clocks that kept improvisational time. In the bedroom, kaleidoscopically reflected at the end of a mirrored corridor, was a bedroom set, reportedly Jean Cocteau's, full of twisty columns, and a sullen Rothko. Zazi's ex-husband, a set designer co-famous with his wife (who was heavy enough in lower Manhattan real estate to interest Hizzoner), had art-directed this habitat himself.

Zazi's unusual name, also the name of my first wife, struck me more like a thud than an echo. This Zazi had short hair, dance muscles, a high-voltage Hawaiian shirt, and gold jazz shoes. She was just getting over the flu, so she had no appetite for the chocolate-dipped strawberries, which were sweating.

"Excuse me for asking—is Zazi your real name?"

"Yes. My father named me after a girl he met in Brazil."

"Your mother must've been a good sport."

"She divorced him later but *not* about that."

Francisco, the Magnum photojournalist, phoned to say he'd be late. Just back from Beirut, he'd been mugged in the subway; slugged as he slid through the turnstile, wallet lifted.

Zazi did everything—smoked, answered the phone—with a pinkie pointed at some sexual destination in the near future. Each puff had delicacy.

I joined a pale young English director sitting by himself in a striped sling chair.

"I live in London, in the very shadows of St. Paul's cathedral." He smiled, savoring this location very privately, meshed his fingers like a homosexual, then mopped his brow with a paper towel. "I can't seem to get my balance." He flopped cadaverously on the couch and pulled a blanket over his head. He rose, staggered, stalled, said "ooooh," and whoofed his cookies on my new sneakers. I got him outside and sat him on a fish crate while I woke his chauffeur, who resembled Henry Kissinger asleep over a crossword puzzle.

Francisco the photojournalist showed up wearing silver
suspenders and hotdog photojournalist sneakers, white-and-
blue foot rockets. The first thing he did was call Magnum to
have them cancel his American Express card, which had un-
limited credit. "You could buy a helicopter with it," he told
the room when they put him on hold. He jittered in his
fancy floating shirt.

Zazi stood by the sink digging into her supply of sponges.
The pale director, she said, had just made the most depress-
ing movie anyone had ever seen; he'd been throwing up all
week. "But these photo*journa*lists, they're the *worst*. Such
baby *heroes*. They all like going out to some *war* somewhere
and coming back and quibbling about who *appreciates*
them. Francisco's okay alone, but my parties are *too*
postmodern for him. All that's left for *him*, I suppose, is to
surprise us with his *suicide*." She bowed her head to my
chest, crushing my crush-proof Dunhills. "So Duke . . . are
you good for anything tonight?"

I wasn't sure yet, so I said hi to Mort, an analyst with
pink cheeks and prophet hair. Mort hinted at having treated
famous film people and announced robustly that he was trying to get drunk. I said hi to Annette, who introduced me to
Ben, who asked if I had any scripts, preferably "Disney material." I said hi to Jay, who said that Almendros's film on
the persecution of gays in Cuba was bourgeois and evasive. I
said hi to Marjorie, who was writing a piece on the New
Numbness for *Esquire,* plus a screenplay called *Confessions
of a Kept Man.* She'd come with Eliot, a serious film critic
wearing a Cub Scout shirt he'd bought in Bombay. He'd just
seen a shitload of stuff from Eastern Europe; everything else
was overwritten, especially comedy. Or underwritten. I said
hi to a short dark actress with a fascinatingly imperfect profile and a black dress which, being French, could be seen
through despite its darkness. She seemed to act mostly with

her upper lip, like Jeanne Moreau. Eliot the critic paid her
solemn attention and kept perforating the conversation with
expert opinions.

"Lots of short people at this party," Mort the analyst
said, his jacket off by now. "Lots of people who don't know
they're alive. My stepfather was a great collector of violins."

I introduced Mort to Marjorie. "*Greystoke*'s the all-time
film about separation anxiety," Marjorie said. "Tarzan's father dies three times: his natural father dies, his gorilla father
dies, and his grandfather, who calls him his son, dies."

Mort loosened his tie and said it was wonderful the way
the film had become a hit even though Warners had aban-
doned it. Well, in my opinion, *Greystoke* was a pretty meat-
less kind of movie. John Alcott shot it, a terrific cameraman
when he works for Kubrick, but the studio printed his negative "up," so his work came across as Sabu illustrations for
kids.

No Nestor yet. I worked the wallflower vote for a while. I
ate almonds and olives and a triple helping of sushi. Nibbled
martini lemon rinds. Sipped sake. In my habit-forming days,
when I came home with cowboy hats on, booze used to firm
up my fantasies of being captured by something affectionate. Now I was smoking too much, trying to digest fun and
death at the same time. What was I supposed to do? Re-
pierce my ears? Move to an irrelevant city like St. Louis and
shoot Hard News? Maybe it was time to hit the road again.
I hankered to be anyplace but this party—preferably in a
place without sidewalks, where the graphics were puzzling
and beautiful, where the poor were primitive, wise, and re-
signed, where wretchedness was a hallowed tradition, where
the women were broad-hipped and slo-eyed, where the air
was redolent with peat and jasmine. Like Bali. Saigon, even.
I knew this was only a movie version of the world—gauzy
calendar pictures wafting above the inexorable grid of days

that eroded their prettiness—but it kept me going. It seemed that I aged only at home, where my work and my cameras and my cronies and my perfectly meshed environment—sixteen years in the same loft—conspired to deliver that most neighborly lie: nothing changes.

I noticed a woman with blue hair and an uncontemporary dress, standing under a dull red lamp that swung like an injured eye. She was carrying on a brisk dispute with Zazi, who'd flung a Day-glo boa across her shoulders, topping off her trash-from-Mars look. The issue was what cassette to play next: which was dirtiest for dancing?

In the middle of three-way polite remarks, I searched the woman's eyes. She didn't enjoy being scrutinized, but she sure could dish it out. I waited for her to blink. She didn't. Her glasses caught the light from all directions. They were not ornamental. She strolled away like a Brazilian to get a refill and supplies. (There were no hors d'oeuvres forks for the snails; a shrill claque of Rock intellectuals was hogging the baked Alaska, served flambé.) Zazi went off to make kissy-face with an eighty-year-old swami who'd been hawking his videotape about ecstasy. The woman came back right away with an armful of beer and cheese and crackers and the insinuation—where was it, in her blinkless violet eyes?—that there was something bawdy about these ingredients.

"Instead of real food, oysters," I said. "Instead of real music, this Yuppie tom-tom shit. Instead of real drugs, champagne."

"I know exactly what you mean. Instead of real people, stars." She picked up a nutshell and admired it. From her topknot to her toes her body formed a bow, a grace of line not exactly human, more like something drawn. "The first time I went to the jungle, I went with four Colombians. The men made a big fuss about being sure I had a room by myself. While I was sleeping, a vampire bat landed on my stomach. The men gave me a hard time for screaming."

Polly was a photojournalist. Raised in Grosse Pointe, she'd spent most of the past ten years in one version or another of the Third World—Appalachia, Africa, and Colombia—where she had learned the power of uncomplicating things, or so, at the moment, I was prepared to believe. She did not know who the Boss was.

But I had to admit I wasn't so interested in doing her sort of work anymore (expedition photography), risking my neck for somebody's conscience-stricken home movie. Fuck it, my theory was . . . Ray Charles for President. Still, there was such transmission in her face, I felt like a lonely fan.

"You want to know how Mrs. Gandhi mowed her lawn?"

"I'd love to," she said with warm precision.

"There are no power mowers in India, there are no lawnmowers of any kind. There wasn't even an electric typewriter in Mrs. Gandhi's office. There are these people, the Sweeper caste, they're the poorest people in Delhi. They kneel, you know, in that flat-heeled Third World way, plucking the grass, blade by blade, with their fingers."

"You're kidding."

"It's a living."

She drifted toward the window. She warmed her hands over a candle and looked out at the bridge.

"Well, it couldn't be much clearer," she said.

"What couldn't?"

"The sky. I just saw a moving star. A satellite."

It had swept across the stars with the first breeze of early spring. The stars didn't look exactly still, either.

Polly slipped her arm in mine and steered me to the next window. "It looks like I'll be spending this summer in New York. I'd like someone to go to a drive-in with once in a while. Do you have a car?"

"Drive-in projection is notoriously crummy, just let me warn you. Some nights in July they'll start the movie before it's totally dark. So when they tell you in the Industry, shoot for the drive-ins, that means watch your shadows, go easy on the low-key stuff. I never go to the movies, anyway."

Then I heard myself explain, despite the body-wide thrill and the sudden runup of my pulse, that this was an essential feature of my politics.

"Of course. I know what you mean. That's just like Latin men and their broken hearts." She nipped my neck, cupped my face and kissed me brackishly. "Anyway my dear, I am in the market for a drive-in summer."

It couldn't be much clearer. I suggested we go home early to watch a Kirk Douglas commando movie. I love those lock-jawed commando movies.

I poked my sneaker toe in the slush to test how frozen it was. Not much, considering the bite there was in the wind. Polly walked with her eyes up at the sky and wondered matter-of-factly where in the Milky Way we were.

At my loft, she was silent for a long while, bending her nose with a wineglass. The movie was *Heroes of Telemark* and it featured lots of stupendous cross-country skiing, which Polly said she'd done just once, on a golf course, with one of her friends from a high-class Louisville horse family.

There was a lot of stealthy sneaking around corners, and low-angle shots of cartoon-nasty Nazis.

"I hate shooting in the snow," I said expertly. "Nothing works. The film gets brittle, the batteries get sluggish."

"How come this movie looks funny?"

"Movies fade. This was made in Sixty-six.

"Should I get contact lenses?"

"You should get different frames."

"Like what?"

"Nestor has those thin red frames."

"Yes. Contacts are trouble in the jungle."

I suggested we go to bed now, before the climatic raid on the heavy water factory, which was bound to be a gory success. She responded with encouraging nips. I fingered her curls on the pillow. She blushed down to her breastbone. "I went through a phase of photographing people's faces on pillows," she said. "I haven't had that many lovers." Tongue mid-lips, laughing.

She also didn't know any good Spanish sex slang. Like *culo*, which means the bottom of a bottle, for buns. This was a clue, I thought, in a strangely shrewd-hearted torpor . . . her Latin lovers must have been very literal-minded.

"But there was a lot of fascination. The first one was a fourteen-year-old Indian boy." She fondled her necklace superstitiously.

I bit my lip. I was out of fantasies, I was exhausted from hankering, but she had me wanting to be her Indian boy. We gentled down. A blue curl looped through one of her earrings. I fell asleep listening to the scuff of her eyelashes on the pillow.

Fat Chance Films Ltd. flew me out to L.A. to shoot a Subaru commercial that demonstrated the advantages of four-wheel-drive in Beverly Hills. We spent most of the first day getting measured for custom-embroidered satin jackets, checking the drug inventory, negotiating permits to shoot on a rugged stretch of Rodeo Drive, and listening to Legendary Rooney's ragtime tapes. Rooney's theory is that music quiets the racketing of crosstalk and carpentry; helps the crew see better. Legendary Rooney is the soundman who talks to his plants. He shouts at his cactus because it's deaf. Weekends he works as a bartender in Bay Ridge; he wears breakaway bowties so the drunks can't yank him across the bar. But the significant thing about Legendary Rooney is that he is bald *and* beardless, an uncommon combination these days. Hair is not important to him. Technology is. He wrote the first telecommunications program for portable computers. Life might take Legendary Rooney's hair, but not his intelligence, nor his ability to install it in a machine.

I drove to the Sunset Marquis, ate room-service fried oysters and went for a dunk in the pool just as the lifeguard was turning out the purple underwater lights. I went back to my room, bare soles slapping on the chilly tiles, and brushed the battery chargers off my bed and tried to sleep in order to revise the day, which had been a damp dream of more things than I could make sense of.

Headlights washed my window and spilled through the venetian blinds. This is a lighting effect associated with certain B films of the forties and fifties. Most cameramen don't pay much attention to it anymore: usually they just pan a light from one side of the window to the other, but that wasn't what really went on. The light source in this case was a traveling pivot, something rather tricky to reproduce on film, but far from impossible, and quite telling in the way it expressed the complete experience—something about a motel's posed emotions, high-strung and commonplace, like a movie.

Some years ago, not far from this very motel, I'd watched Alfred Hitchcock enter a room. The room was in Beverly Hills and it was full of rich and handsome people. Hitchcock was a short man, five-six maybe. He was in his late sixties at the time, very round. He moved slowly and smoothly, propelled by an effortless inner force, a Buddha on casters. His hair and shirt were white, his suit and tie black, his skin pink. He was a high-contrast rainbow, dazzling and mysterious. It was clear that there was no better way for Hitchcock to be than to be pictures of himself. The room beheld him in suitable silence. What more was there to say?

Anyway, when I'm alone at night and headlights pass my motel window, I pay attention, analyze things. In these solitary moments, reflexively scanning the world with the bribed eyes of a cameraman, I say to myself: Duke, what's it all about? It's the freest of American jobs, this mechanical exercise of fantasy. Maybe we live in our own world, but movies, for those of us who make them, are seldom an escape. The thing about making pictures, as opposed to looking at them, is you have to be there. Movie crews, even more than civilians, get sick of being pestered by what *is*.

I was standing with my father at a bus stop in Rockaway when I found a little turtle with *Duke, New Orleans* painted on its back. That little turtle was infinitely alive and suggestive in a decorative, indifferent way. It was art on the hoof, just like the movies, I imagined. On the dust of its shell, with the tip of my finger, I traced *Duke*.

For a while I kept Duke in the bathtub, but one day my mother pitched him out the window. He tucked in his head and tumbled toward the garbage like a chubby coin. "Made too much noise," she explained.

My father rented a bungalow upstate, in Monroe, a resort for cops and firemen. We lived near a lake necklaced with bars. My father commuted on weekends. Tuesday nights, five miles down the road, the Monroe theater showed double features of Lash LaRue or Cisco Kid westerns. Ma didn't drive (despite lessons and epic excuses, she'd failed her test three times), so every Tuesday, after supper, we hitched into town. One time a motorcycle stopped for us. I got on behind the biker and Ma got on behind me. Sandwiched, excited by the roar of the bike and the whoosh of the wind and the deliciousness of our destination, we zipped away to the movies.

I put another quarter in the Magic Fingers and shimmied off to sleep. The next day I created for the director, a young

Japanese guy who chewed gum and affected a groovy American manner, the effect of Subaru headlights whooshing authentically past venetian blinds. He flipped out, called me a genius. A lot of us guys are geniuses in the Industry.

"Some cowboy doctor is talking about putting Roni in a high-tech hospice," Barry said over the phone. "Sounds like a contradiction to me. Would you pick up the *Times* on your way over?"

I videotaped Barry and Roni and Jonah at home. The scene was Barry getting Jonah dressed for a trip to the aircraft carrier *Intrepid*.

Thorazined, Roni stared irritably, bricked in behind the drug. When Barry and Jonah left, I put the camera down. I asked Roni if when she slept, which she'd been doing twenty hours of her days, she dreamed.

"They're not hopeful dreams. I need two animals to wake up. A lizard . . . and an eagle." The Thorazine caused her to speak in sluggish non-sequiturs; her words were a slow tolling. "It's roulette. I'm tired of being on the losing end. It's drugs and injections and wake up and take a pill and get a shot. You have no . . . idea . . . how . . . tedious it is."

How much work it was to die this way. "Your face looks good, Roni."

"Thanks. People say nice things about my face."

I was still boy enough to consider death an implausible goodbye. "You'll always sparkle."

A thunderstorm lashed through the bedroom skylight, staining my mint-condition *Tales from the Crypt* and spoiling Mr. Honda's ceiling in the loft below. He phoned at 4 A.M. to complain that it was leaking on his shy young cousins from Kyoto. I rummaged in the moonless dark for a garbage pail to catch the water with. I slipped back into bed, brushing cookie crumbs and other amorous debris overboard.

Three hours later the garbage pail was too heavy to carry away. Also, the water heater had been extinguished by a spanking draft. When I tried to light it, the gas went *bloof*! and flamed around my face, singeing my right arm and crisping the hairs to a prickly stubble, tender when my bathrobe rubbed the wrong way.

Polly of the Jungle's glistening blue hair showed the waves of a morning combing. She made pancakes with honey. I buttered my knuckles first.

"How do you want me to slice the oranges?" she asked.

"Thusly." I made four wedges of each half. It was pleasant to blurt out advice over breakfast.

"Oh, let me see your knuckles." She kissed the crisp ones. "Oh, your poor knuckles."

"What's knuckles in Spanish?"

"Uh, *nudillos*. I got very sick once in Bogotá. I had a fever. I wanted to get to Ráquira, in the Andes. I thought, I'll get on the bus for five hours, get off and I'll be home and get into bed. But it was the rainy season, the road was washed out. It was night and the road went up and down the mountain, like all the roads do. I walked for hours. . . ."

Suddenly, in the middle of her story, as she spoke of walking the Andes at night, I began hearing her like baseball on the radio, and I woke to something besides the predictable photography of breakfast, was flooded with sense impressions of Colombia, though I'd never been there, imagining the vapory jungle night thick and dark and private and humid as a human body—Polly of the Jungle's body, for example— and these things clustered in my heart to form an ikon of her bravery.

"You think I'm brave? I don't want to be."

Polly's simplicity was so complete it struck me as a kind

of clairvoyance. Or maybe she was just spiritually neat, like her mother, who kept a tidy house and ordered her daughter around.

"My mother and my grandmother used to worry that my arms were too hairy. 'What will happen when you grow up?' my mother used to say. Mrs. Payson, who owned the Mets, used to pick my grandmother up in a private plane and fly to the Elizabeth Arden health spa; they roomed with Eva Gabor. My grandmother wanted to take me to have my hair straightened and something done about my ass, which she said was too big or something. I haven't shaved my legs since I was eighteen. I tried it once in the dorm at Andover but it stung. Would you like to shave my legs?"

I scampered down West Broadway and bought two white and yellow Bics, feeling a vandal's exhilaration and murmuring thanks to her mother and grandmother and Mrs. Payson and Elizabeth Arden and Eva Gabor for their part in making Polly of the Jungle a little insecure about invisible things. Her real hair was blond. She was weedlessly fair-skinned, a faint dusting of golden down, like pollen, on her shins.

She drew a bath. "Is it too hot?"

"I like it hot; I like it hot."

I sat at the faucet end, she sat with her back to the window, soft morning light spilling on her hair and shoulders. The razor floated.

"I hope you don't cut yourself," she said, watching it, feeling absolutely no menace to herself. Much married, I was accustomed to a certain amount of skepticism in the foreplay.

She lifted her right leg over mine. I lathered it and stroked downward from the knee. She leaned forward to look, blinking. The razor was so sharp it was impossible to feel it cut, but soon we began to see hairs floating around us. The

blade made a zipping sound in the water when I cleaned it.
She leaned back. Once, when the razor turned on its edge, I
thought I'd cut her, but no. "Well, I guess that's it," I said.

"That's it? What about the other leg?"

Just out of the tub, she teetered on tiptoes. She moved
with a twang, her right shoulder drooping from carrying a
camera bag. Wrinkles on her kneecaps! The smallest things
about her were becoming vivid to me. But I don't want to
leave out some immortal part: she was of English stock—
fascinated, the way the English are, by primitives, herself a
practicing Presbyterian primitive, smolderingly stoical, determined, shy, and in moments of passion wildly accepting.
She kept stashes of clothes and photo equipment in Washington, Chicago, Cambridge, Kentucky, Paris, London,
Kenya, Grosse Pointe, and Colombia, not to mention Park
Slope and SoHo. She'd seen *Body Heat (Cuerpos Ardientes)*
and *A Clockwork Orange (Naranja Mecánica)* in Bogotá. In
the tenth grade she'd played Joan of Arc in linoleum armor.
Her English grandfather had a wooden leg named Alfie. One
of her boyfriends in Montana made chairs; chair making
was a mountain thing inspired by high-altitude dreaming.
This boyfriend had made a chair from grapevines shaped
like snakes, brought it to Washington and had his picture
taken with President Nixon. He gradually went blind drinking moonshine. Last time Polly saw him, he'd put his hand
on the window to feel if the sun was shining.

A door slammed downstairs and snow slid with a wash-
board noise off one of the skylight panels. There was a new
and impressively steady leak.

"I left my spike heels in Kentucky. I had a good time at
Christmas."

"Spike heels? Christmas? Kentucky?"

Despite her provocatively tinted hair, it was hard to imagine she'd ever partied that way. Her photos of Appalachia

were very WPA: wrinkled faces, wrinkled landscapes. My cinematic bias insisted there was something Middlewestern about still photography, landlocked. Boring. Required a gardener's patient ardor to appreciate. Though Steichen— wasn't he the most soulful of image makers? And what about Maneul Alvarez Bravo? *Ay, caramba!*

Drained, the tub was sprinkled with soft hairs. It didn't occur to me to clean them out. During the day and into the evening, I returned to the bathroom to look at them. True love has a reputation for clearing things up.

Except, of course, in one's own case. A week-and-a-half later, Polly went wild again. Over her dark red softball shirt, she put on a white sleeveless blouse—inside-out, blue Sears label peeking through her lovable unkempt curls. And over that, her *ruana*, a Colombian cape. Then she flew away to the Andes to make a movie about her best friend Ava, the witch.

"They want us to go to Bali, Duke. Bali! What's it *like*? Gorgeosity. The only thing is, the woman in the tourist office, she's talking cholera."

For the past couple of years, I'd been shooting most of Yvonne Hannemann's commercials for Citicorp. The bank was expanding its operations in the technological crescent stretching from Tokyo to Hong Kong to Singapore to Jakarta, and now they wanted some pictures of it.

Balancing a cup of tea on her knee to warm a bruise, Yvonne went over our smuggling procedures: the zoom lens would be buried under brassieres on the theory that Indonesian customs inspectors, being Muslim, wouldn't go near the dainties.

"But before we pack, Duke, I'd love to record some snarling traffic. I love the word 'snarl.' "

I advised her to bring boots; the guidebook spoke

glowingly of the Temple of the Snakes, which lay partially underwater.

"Here come the Hollywood!" said Johannes, our Jakarta driver, flinging away his cheroot, which made a darting red trail like a toy rocket through the bougainvillea. "Have you see *The Day After*? They say is too much talking. We are expecting more actions."

On the way to the hotel, Johannes pointed out "Sukarno's last erection," a two-hundred foot marble column tipped with forty kilos of gold. I was contemplating a side trip to Borneo to augment my legend and aggravate my ex-wife. No problem, Johannes said. It was only an hour by plane to the coastal cities of Borneo or Sumatra. But these coastal cities were surly places, and traveling to the interior meant taking one's chances on packet boats, an expedition of a month or more.

Yvonne and I took a weekend break in Bali. A Qantas jet touched down right behind us, disgorging hundreds of Australians, eager and frolicsome, their surfboards revolving on the luggage carousel in surfboard cozies.

We dined by the pool of the Bali Hyatt, the beaches tapering to a turquoise smudge. In the slowly trembling shadow of a palm, sipping a piña colada served in a coconut shell with a gladiola jutting out of it, I pinked. This was a movie mission indistinguishable from tourism.

The morning after returning to unfragrant, nostril-puckering Jakarta, I woke at 2 A.M. with a retching that wanted to split my gorge. I was sweating and I couldn't get warm and I said hello again to the malaria I'd picked up in India.

At the peak of my fever, I was inspired to phone Polly of the Jungle in Bogotá. She was depressed. Last Sunday, right in front of her apartment, the national police had pulled an architect friend of hers from his truck and emptied their pistols into him.

Why was this woman a photographer? I wondered, yanking my hair to keep my scalp warm, and why did she wander, forever a captive of the Oedipal west? Polly of the Jungle took pictures that made the jungle look quiet. But silence in the jungle is an ominous deformity. I swallowed a handful of Chloroquins and fell asleep in soggy sheets.

Dissolve to RÁQUIRA, a village in the Colombian Andes. POLLY OF THE JUNGLE writes by candlelight:

> *I got up this morning when the priest started playing music over the church loudspeaker. I found my little silver pot and made coffee on my hot plate and ate breakfast in front of the window. I washed my hair in the waterfall but the water was so cold that my head ached from it. My body felt great. I saw my friend Ava the witch, who said she had been dreaming about you and me flying over the mountains together. She bought me granadillas and scolded me for missing her birthday. Eight bombs went off yesterday in Bogotá. This afternoon I called Larry, my friend the cultural attaché who is being fired because he doesn't agree with the ambassador's drug-busting program. He wanted to know if I knew anyone who wanted to buy his Mercedes because he couldn't bring it back to the States. Tomorrow I'm going back to Bogotá on an early bus so I can watch the sun rise.*

I woke at dawn, hungry, and amazed by how fast my second chances kept coming. I ate breakfast with some Secret Service men anticipating the arrival of Vice President Bush, who was due tomorrow.

On the way home, Yvonne and I found ourselves with three hours to kill in Hong Kong. Because we were flying east across the international date line, this was a stretched May 19—thirty-five hours from Jakarta to San Francisco. It was also the tenth anniversary of our car crash outside Bombay. I bought her a ring with a starry stone.

"Kiss me," she said. She bought perfume and daubed some behind her ear. "Now kiss me again."

We grazed in the duty-free shops, pricing jade baubles and dreaming synchronously of the flames around the car and the sweetness of still having a history.

Good old right-angular North America.

Dressed in a resounding tie, I had lunch with Sunny, my third ex-wife, the one who'd run off with Dr. Victor Jory. Sunny always had the knack of looking especially good in restaurants, and today she was sporting a tan from her ski trip in Utah. Her coat was a husky garment that seemed made of coonskins. She was carrying a cone of low-budget flowers. Dinner tonight with a friend? My shredded understanding of women informed me that she must be fond of Dr. Victor Jory, as of an accomplice. She'd made her escape with him, made a thrilling escape into romance. She started to smile, then seemed to postpone it. She gave me a dry enemy kiss.

"That outfit you're wearing is quite incredible and sort of amazing, Sunny."

"Yes, thank you. You know what's wrong with this restaurant? The bar is too far from the stove." She talked on her toes, unsentimentally distracted.

"You still complaining?"

"Anyone who doesn't complain isn't alert." She adjusted her glasses and peeled the subscription label off her *Scientific American*. I asked if she'd mind holding my umbrella while I unbuttoned my jacket.

"I'll hold anything of yours that isn't wet, darling."

We sidestepped two Greeks drunkenly installing an air-conditioning duct. Our table was so tightly squeezed against the adjoining one that it was a stunt to get into the chairs. Wheel, a conceptual artist of my acquaintance, walked in, nodded hello, sat at a corner and opened his conceptual art magazine. Wheel carried himself with the otherworldliness of a Werner Herzog movie.

Sunny and I talked about Roni, who'd been feeling livelier as a side effect of the steroids she was taking to shrink the tumor that had metastasized to her brain. Then we discussed the sexual, geographical, and fiscal limits of our marriage. My foot brushed hers.

"Don't worry," she said. "It's asleep."

There is a pride lacking in lunching with your ex, and an indecisiveness about what to touch.

"Reminds me. How's your friend what's-her-name—name begins with an O. The one who's always committing suicide."

"You want me to fix you up with Ophelia?"

"She's very feminine."

"You know my opinion of you. You're the second worst husband I ever had."

"You want to hear a Polish joke?" I'm terrible at telling jokes, but I thought that telling one might take my mind off feeling like a drippy, umbrella-toting Polish joke myself.

"The police department has to hire a new detective. They interview a Jewish guy, an Italian guy, and a Polish guy. The Jewish guy comes in first. They ask him, 'Who killed Jesus?' The Jewish guy says, 'Well, the Romans did it . . . Pontius Pilate.' Okay. The Italian guy comes in. They ask him 'Who killed Jesus?' 'The Jews,' he says. 'Everybody knows that.' 'That's swell,' they say, 'we'll let you know tomorrow.'"

Sunny snickered. Wheel cocked his head like a bird listening to his breakfast.

"Now the Polish guy. They asked him, 'Who killed Jesus?' The Polish guy stands there. They say, 'C'mon, who do you think killed Jesus? Just give us a hint. We have to make up our minds by tomorrow.' The Polish guy doesn't say anything.

"He goes home and his wife says, 'So how'd it go? You get the job or what? He says, 'Yeah, I think so. They already got me working on a murder case.'"

Sunny sat there. Wheel cackled.

While she went to the ladies' room, I scanned an article on distant spiral galaxies in her magazine. The pages shone like something was really happening, but for the first time in my life I failed to get a lift out of the notion of light years.

Meryl Streep sat down at the next table and opened her mail.

"You seeing the doctor today?" her sculptor-husband asked.

"Just the film doctor. They look at you and they say, you feel okay? It's for the insurance."

Sunny had left her address book under the napkin. Shamelessly, without a warrant, I slipped the three-by-five cards out of it. They were numbered consecutively and here's what they said:

1. affair, reservations, Rhoda, Debra, idiot, negative, gynecologist, arthritis, quandary, furniture, superficial, liar, really, activities, accident, so many Australias.

2. surmised, happening, half plane, future, reservations, coronary, Winnie, Isles Drive, superb, lovely, improving, deceased, prescription, federal employee, fondly, appreciated, tapestries, Rhoda.

3. hiatus hernia, finally, apprehensive, hysterectomy, wreck, certificate, marriages, envelopes, summer, nineteen, Bahamas, envy, Dotty, embassy, emergency, Arthur, sincerely, ordeal, bronchitis, *jahrzeit,* cousin, daily spares,

interesting, Biscayne Blvd., detect, electrocardiogram, symptoms, equipment, newlyweds, analyzed, dynamic, function, cyclops, usual, itch, hopefully, bodice.

Daily spares? What *did* they want? New furniture? Justice for their bodies? Sovereignty? *So many Australias?*

I replaced the cards and consoled myself with Bogartisms: she got me pretty imperfected, Sunny did. Yeah. Got her fingerprints all over my insides. She was my self-inflicted wound, that woman. Yeah. Kept accusing me of things I had to look up. Yeah. Kept trying to get me to pronounce the *h* in "human."

The new English waitress was overpouring my second beer. Streep paid her bill with a twenty. The waiter returned with a single, which she autographed on the eagle side.

"I missed you last week." My voice was half its size. "I dream about you all the time."

"We tried for eight years."

Streep and her husband left. That was pretty quick.

"I tried for eight and a half," I said. "I miss your alertness. We should've had a baby."

Her eyes melted. She got a strange soft look—sad, it was—as if she'd come to accept our status as weary guests in each other's lives. This was a new, measured approach. Not shyness, exactly. Just no imagination. She looked into my eyes when I was feeling nothing and when I couldn't imagine what she was feeling. Just fashion a lens to look at a lifetime—how simple it seems when you start.

I kicked her foot again. "Why didn't it work? What did we do wrong?"

"Stupidity," she said.

"Stupidity?"

"We were working on a murder case." She sighed and said she wanted to see a movie. I recommended the new

Truffaut, *Confidentially Yours*. I neglected to mention that she reminded me of Fanny Ardant, specifically of the new gracefulness I saw in her, nor did I say that I considered the movie a merry *conte morale* about our combats, betrayals, and true love.

She applied some Caesar's Palace lip balm, patted me twice on the arm, and hurried away like spring weather, leaving me with the check. That was pretty quick too.

Maybe it was my habit of cartographic speculation on her face ("Here's looking at you, kid."), or maybe it was just my old cameraless photo-tic, heckling again. I sat there, numbly remembering the times we'd romped from one exaltation to the next.

I opened my dripping umbrella and came to a deeper understanding of Eisenstadt's snapshots of DiMaggio and Monroe in their sunnier days.

"Lookit this mob, Duke. There's only two things like it in New York—that's making a movie and somebody getting shot."

I was eating a hotdog and hanging out with Teddy Churchill while he shot a trailer for *Ghostbusters*. Laurie, the still photographer, tripped on the tailgate of the camera truck.

"Step right up, ladies and gentlemen!" Teddy said. "The game of life! Everybody gets injured! Make big bucks!"

I slumped in the shade of an awning. I'd come home from Indonesia and immediately started eating too much America—movies, errands, magazines—and I was feeling like slush. Sauerkraut plopped on my new sneakers.

During lunch hour Teddy and I stopped by the city film commission's exhibit. Hebrew National's stall contained an enormous map of the five boroughs fashioned from hors d'oeuvres; Jamaica Bay was hard-boiled eggs garnished with parsley. Teddy attempted to eat Coney Island but was restrained by a flabbergasted guard who said he'd have to wait till the mayor made his appearance and a publicity photo was taken.

"By the way, Duke, how's your friend who's dying?"

Roni's hospital phone wasn't answering.

I walked home in the drizzle, enjoying the mess. Taped to the front door of my lobby was a note: *Dear Habib, Raoul is at Sylvette's. XXX, Zazi.*

Not one normal name in the whole note. Plus another Chinese restaurant takeout menu in the mailbox. Number forty was *Squid in Love*. And a cassette letter from Colombia, with a decal of a bluebird on the back.

Dissolve to RÁQUIRA, a village in the Colombian Andes. POLLY OF THE JUNGLE records by candlelight. Her voice is breathy. A TV chirps in the background. POLLY sings:

Happy birthday, dear Duke. Happy birthday to you.

I was startled by the sound of my name, enameled to a science fiction strangeness by time, distance, and the cassette. The stinging mechanical insect had injected it with surprising insect joy.

Click, stop. POLLY starts again, a different show in the background, the tinny obvious music of a *film noir*.

> *I am picking up my life in Colombia where I left it six months ago. The people here are surprised to see me. They say, Y este milagro?—just another miracle. When I got here my stomach tightened because I remembered how hard it was to live here alone. To comfort me my friend Ezequiel gave me fried ants, a delicacy. They are an inch long. You have to crush the shell with your teeth and hold it against your bottom teeth while you suck the insides out. I couldn't do it right.*
>
> *To begin research for my film on popular magic, I went to*

the Templo de lo Indio de las Amazonas to have a con-
sultation. It was filled with trashy occult memorabilia and
potions and herbs. They even had a smiling inflatable bat
hanging from the ceiling. Ava read the tarot cards for me.
The last medium I found went crazy and died because dis-
respectful people made fun of her while she was under a
trance.

I rewound the answering machine. "Duke, this is Tillie of
LFS Productions. Do you have any food shots on your sample reel?" That was it, plus two hangups.

I sat on the washer-drier to see if that would improve my
concentration. I sat in a classically pensive pose, but I could
not think. The washer-drier went *chickee-chickee-chickee*
across the floor. I remembered few of Polly's words, none of
her silences. I remembered her eyes, her fingers and the beat
of her heart, louder now in her absence. Her silences were
ordering me to think about her.

I took a shower with my sunglasses on, a little too Jack
Nicholson maybe.

The customs inspector was too amused by the spider in my
passport to pay attention to my film equipment.

Polly of the Jungle stood at the sink looking soft and
pretty, a ribbon around her waist. She'd taped religious pictures on the kitchen walls, one a portrait of Santa Clara,
who, because of her talent for "bi-location"—her ability to
appear in several places at the same time—is revered in Colombia as the patron saint of TV. Polly's apartment was
over a hardware store in a run-down section of Bogotá, directly across the street from a pink two-story building that
housed the Partido Comunista Colombiano Comite Central.

"The wiring's a mess," she warned. "Be careful when you
open the refrigerator door, you have to wear shoes."

I peeled a piece of fruit. It had the skin of a snake, the

texture of grizzled meat, the flavor of crystallized candy, and the scent of a woman.

Polly brewed tea and poured it without a strainer, creating floating gardens in our cups.

She divided her time between Bogotá and Pan de Azucar, the hometown of her friend Ava the witch, across the *cordillera*, the spine of the Andes, in Cauca, Colombia's principal coca-growing region. She was teaching Ava how to take pictures and compiling a book of her oddly titled self-portraits *(Sleepyhead's Ghost and His Dog, The Saint Called Sunday Falling From Fright)*, and she was making progress on her film about Latin witchcraft. I'd come down to shoot some scenes for fund-raising.

Bogotá was cool, overcast, and melancholy. We got into a scarlet-interiored taxi and drove to the left-wing salsa joint near the bull ring. "Most of Ava lives astrally," Polly said. "But she's a *tipa fresca*—she's cool."

Ava stared at the guitarist's fingers. She was sitting at a table next to a poster from New York's School of Visual Arts and a relief map of South America. She cradled three-year-old Carlos Andres, her son by a Korean missionary unaware that he had a son. Carlos Andres was named after Queen Elizabeth's two sons.

I'd been expecting a wizened, secretive woman who humored men and cultivated superstitions about herself. Ava Ramirez was twenty-nine, sturdy and voluptuous, and a political leader in her barrio. She spoke hotly orchestrated Spanish.

She touched her hometown on the map over the table. To the northwest, she said, there are beautiful opaline pools where children pan gold.

Polly wanted to know where the volcanoes are.

"Yes, north," Ava said in English, with an athletic Yanqui nod. "Really big explode." She had mastered that serenely idle Latin way of stirring coffee. There were patches of white on her wrists and ankles, ringworm probably.

The conversation bubbled into hilarity on the topic of a *narcotraficante* who'd approached a friend of hers to buy some paintings.

"The dealer pulled up with two Mercedes and four jeeps full of bodyguards. He selected a slide and asked how much. '$40,000.' He said, 'I'll take twenty.'"

As a down payment, the dealer advanced Ava's friend a *finca* with four tennis courts and a swimming pool. He would spend the next two years painting twenty identical canvases.

She fanned the bugs away with a dreaming motion. Her face took on a sincere, sculpted look. "Of course, in the coca trade, you have to be willing to take risks. Risks that might last your whole life. Coca has become the oil of the eighties. Coca is the true coin of international exchange. In Colombia, it is a crop. In *gringolandia,* it is a status symbol, the numbness needed by colonialists. North Americans may not acknowledge this in their frontal lobes, but it becomes clear, does it not, as soon as you set foot in the Third World, that you are the enemy of the rest of the world. Not just because of your bombs and guns and planes. You eat too much, you drive too much, you spend too much, you are too intensely safe. You are more Yanqui than human."

She closed her eyes and slowly stroked her forehead. She sneezed, giggled, sang *la-la-la* and stared while I tied my shoelaces. She stuck a badminton racket down the back of her blouse, between her shoulder blades, and drove off on her motorbike.

The next day, at dawn, Polly, Ava, Carlos Andres, and I entered the Spike and Indiana Jones environment of an Andean bus: backfires, drooling gaskets, burst oil lines, deafening *salsa* cassettes, campesinos snoring like trombones, dust, wheezing brakes, incessantly smoking Indians toothlessly demanding to be transported at half fare.

"Did you see the morning paper?" Polly asked. The front page of *El Bogotano* displayed a color picture of six crisp corpses, victims of yesterday's bus crash, under a headline that hollered HUELEN DE CARNE ASADA!—THEY SMELLED LIKE FRIED MEAT!

Just short of the helicopter base outside Popoyán, the police presented themselves in a dense mist. Two soldiers with shotguns ran up the aisle, kicking seats.

The frisk was languid, without suspense. Everyone out of the bus, men lined up against the bridge, searched by boy soldiers, teenagers with shiny Uzis, stocks folded, toylike. There was nothing to do in the gray, wet-faced void but relax and appreciate the power of little things—the twiddling of trigger fingers, the icy agelessness of the soldiers' eyes—and keep glancing at Polly, who was standing to one side with Ava and the other women and who, if I'd allowed myself to think about it, looked ready to mourn. I spent the eternal seconds wondering why only the men were required to remove their shoes.

One of the soldiers, a blue-eyed black man, pinched my shirt. "What is this, my friend?"

"Cigarettes. From New York."

"I was a student there." He fired a burst across the field where a DC-3 was rotting. "Now every Tuesday I get to shoot the niggers."

No one laughed. We had all bought a ticket to silence. I ignored the instinct to look around for the escaping soul of what might have been murdered. The fluttering of a single engine plane gave dimension to the mist. Then a whistle. This evidence, I mistakenly concluded, made our location a beach.

"Every Tuesday." Another burst. The noise hung rancidly in the air.

The soldiers nodded. The shotgunners clambered out of the bus, smiling, and the men put their shoes on. The women straightened their blouses in unison, restoring the world to its feminine parallax. Polly kissed me through my shirt and pulled away. She was a girl with cozy dreams of old age.

"Get inside, stupid," said the trigger-happy soldier.

A wind came up from the north, very fresh. The mist burned away. Popoyán was a city in splints, nothing over two stories left standing after last year's lethal *temblor*. A billboard advertised *Six Antiseismic Apartments*.

For the next few hours, Carlos Andres sat on my lap. Fatherly and proud, reflecting on the way kids own your body, I talked baby Spanish with him. "God is taking pictures," he said when it lightninged in the west. I fell in love with Polly again.

Don Leonides, Ava's grandfather, stepped gracefully through the smoke of a coconut-husk trash fire. "Welcome. We live like pigs." Pan de Azucar was a settlement of thirty families in a pocket-ledge softened by burro trails and centuries of acrobatically steep cultivation. Next month, Don Leonides announced, there was going to be a festival featuring a ferris wheel in which the women of the village would be spun till dizzy.

At ninety-five, he still walked with a farmer's firmly planted spine. Abuelita Pepita, his wife, was eighty-eight. She had just been circled by a bee who was yellow on one side and blue on the other. By this sign she knew that visitors were on the way.

She served rice and sardines and hard-boiled eggs—very fancy fare. And coffee, bowls of it, coffee as nourishment. The walls of their shack had absorbed its aroma.

Don Leonides, the first to be served, lowered his head reverently. "Our marriage has been good, thank God." There were hard times, of course. Some years ago, when Abuelita Pepita slapped his eldest daughter with a tortilla she'd overcooked, he'd gone for his gun and shot her kitchen to smithereens.

He conducted a tour of his yard, insisting we sample the verbena—one variety to mend broken bones, another for bad dreams. Most nights he dreamed of walking, walking for days to Popoyán before there were roads. Popoyán had been destroyed because its citizens offended God by drug dealing. "Since coca, the people are like bees after their nest has been crushed. Now all we can do is wander."

He sat and, gazing uphill, rocked Carlos Andres in his arms. In other days, there used to be tigers in these mountains; now they were pretty much confined to the coastal jungles. Once he ate a tiger that had been killed by a bus. It tasted *no maluco*—not too awful. Something like rodent.

Baby chicks cheeped behind his chair, terrified of a jealous rooster. He fended him off with a bamboo pole. When the rooster got past him, he grabbed its tail and tossed it in the direction of the kitchen. Abuelita Pepita caught it by the wing and, in a kind of domestic tag-team move, flung it into the backyard.

There was a terrific storm at dusk. In an instant the world smelled musty. At the peak of splitting thunder and clatters of hail, Don Leonides's monkey bounded for a safe high place and puckered up as if looking for another monkey. Half an hour later the wind subsided; frogs burbled louder than the remains of the storm. The rain left. It became a gracious and agreeably cool evening.

Don Leonides led us to a room where we'd be able to sleep without being troubled by fleas. He chuckled at our sleeping bags, the first he'd ever seen. Ava hoisted Carlos

Andres on her shoulders, arching her cramped back. "Oh
my son," she groaned, "you weigh more than poverty."

"Carlos Andres was born on a mountain," Don Leonides
said, grinning and twisting his magical measuring thongs.
"He should know how to walk."

He agreed to cure Ava's back if we'd meet him tomorrow
at his coffee plantation further up the mountain. He disap-
peared into the banana grove, thumbing an almanac he
couldn't read and wielding a machete with his three-fingered
hand. Behind him, a white horse and two sorrels dragged
bamboo logs, stooping to graze in the yard.

Grimy and exhausted, Polly and I fell asleep to the aroma
of roasting coffee and the patter of light rain and the sound
of Abuelita Pepita kneading *suspiro* dough, *flup-flup,* in her
lap. I dreamed so vividly—something about the blue keys of
a cloud piano—I couldn't tell if I actually slept.

At first light, a radio went on and Carlos Andres started
playing marbles with Don Leonides.

We climbed through stalky purple orchids and citrusy-
smelling lantana. Stopping at every stream, I soaked my cap
and flopped it on my head so the water would air-condition
my neck.

At noon, after a three-hour climb, by the coffee grinder
on the plantation's porch, I found a tattered comic book
about a *jazzista* who sacrilegiously ripped off ritual black
music, became famous, then had to pay for his success by
dying at the hands of avenging demons. Which could have
been avoided if only he'd worn the amulets owned by his
wife, who had the Evil Eye.

Campesino culture ascribes the Evil Eye to blue-eyed,
light-skinned people. When Ava was a little girl, her Evil Eye
had destroyed notebooks, pencils, and finally an alarm clock
she'd coveted. Now, as an adult, she merely touched things
she wanted, like her home town on a map, making them

harmlessly hers. She still respected the Evil Eye's power of telepathic petty theft.

Ava opened the copy of *One Hundred Years of Solitude* she'd been carrying since the start of the trip. Carlos Andres stared at it, astonished by this crazy new ornament his mother seemed to be wearing lately. She recited the passage about Padre Nicanor levitating every time he drank chocolate milk. Carlos Andres smiled and came closer, enchanted.

It was a swollen effect, as of a national anthem. But here, scanning a seventy-mile view of the magical Andes, in the heartland of the richest drug economy on the planet, holding hands with Polly of the Jungle and waiting for the sly witch doctor to cure his granddaughter the beautiful witch, it did not seem out of place.

I remembered seeing, on the road into Bogotá from the airport, the usual billboards for Avianca and Sony. Among them, standing alone, gaudily lit, was a billboard advertising the *obras maravillosas*—the wondrous works—of Gabriel García Márquez, conveniently available in a cardboard six-pack with carrying handle.

Of all the quaint indulgences once allowed American writers, the sweetest was the grandiosity of thinking your prose might save the country. But this fever cools the first time you watch TV: literary careers—not to mention life itself—have become inescapably cinematic. American writers *dream* about America; Spielberg plays. This is better, perhaps, than the Latin American use of the electrical arts, which often tends to be Inquisitional. Still, the scale of things, for writers, seemed saner in Colombia.

Ava came to the last line: *It was foreseen that the city of mirrors (or mirages) would be wiped out by the wind and exiled from the memory of men at the precise moment when Aureliano Babilonia . . .*

A strange little wind whipped over from the west. Don

Leonides packed 150 pounds of coffee down the mountain on his burro. He was brightened by the good day's work he'd done. There'd been a frost, he said, scratching a neck bumpy with flea bites; the coffee harvest had been halved. But he'd never farm coca, no. "People kill for it. Leave it to the whites." He was chewing something.

I perceived a continuity problem. How had he arrived so soon? How had he arrived at all? How had this ninety-five-year-old farmer climbed the mountain above us and come back down with all that coffee? Very quickly, winking, Don Leonides aimed a Lazarus grin at me, admitting no memories, omitting no futures.

Smiling nervously, Ava described her symptoms. He measured her wrists with grass thongs, tied a rooster high on a post, and jiggled a coin in a vial of purplish paste.

"I know there is something strange about my eyes," she said into her skirt. "It scares me. Please God, forgive me. I'm a good person, God. I've heard stories about people who make pacts with the devil and about witches who fly. Dear God, why do I have to be a witch? Just because my eyes happen to be a certain way? It's not my fault I have the Evil Eye. But it's true—I do want to know the devil."

She felt something leave her body. She was frightened because now, in a way more eternal than blood ties, she was bound to Don Leonides, her *curandero*.

"Food," said Don Leonides. "Coffee and bananas and chickens. Food to eat . . . everything else is fantasy."

The next day we went for a swim in a fast river called *Culebra*—Snake. Nineteen people swarmed in and on the peach-colored jeep: ten children and seven adults inside, two young men clinging to the tire mount on the back door. Plus two chickens, live, in a sack, for lunch. Pots, pans, and a plastic skeleton rattled over the dashboard. Everything, everyone jounced. "Mules are more affectionate than jeeps," said Ava.

The river rushed in the gorge, a freshness ascending from the brown water. We traversed down a steep slope, sheltered by trees from the razoring sun. The men cast fish nets and collected firewood, the women drew water and suffocated the chickens by stretching their necks. Ava gathered orchids while Carlos Andres shoveled pebbles to divert a sidestream in hopes of trapping the trout whose flashing fascinated him.

"I like to take my glasses off sometimes," Polly said. "Sometimes . . . never mind. Do you ever go blank?"

I crouched closer, under a branch, to hear her over the waterfall.

She lay back and closed her eyes. "I like it the way people go off in separate pockets."

I took this as a suggestion to look for a shady spot where we could make love, but it was a prelude to serious negotiation.

"Pictures are fine," she said, "but everyone wants a real life."

"Meaning babies?"

"Yes."

She talked about stumbling into marriage when she was nineteen, after a tour of doping, promiscuity, and perilous hitchhiking. For a while she'd been interested in "this bisexual Hawaiian," who was in training to be an astronaut. "Once he phoned me from mission control. I used to think if I could just make it from one episode to another, I'd be all right. But you cut yourself short."

A low, distant thump. Upstream, the men were dynamiting pools to stun the trout.

In a reversal of seduction, in a more precise kind of lurking, I reconsidered Polly as a stranger with a separate life, separate enthusiasms. Like Don Leonides, she'd wandered in the Andes and learned to discriminate, how to be strong in desire. The midday moon was staring. It was a moment of love alignment that would not last. Polly of the Jungle was a picture, which made me want her too much. So much I felt unsafe, bewitched. Our conversation under the trees and the sun and the midday moon was so calm as to be almost a tease: a civilized discussion, it seemed, between separating lovers pretending to plan but really only assessing. In Pan de Azucar, I'd watched her emerge from Abuelita Pepita's kitchen, skin aglow with photographic exaltation, caressing Ava's braid and showing her the image on the Hasselblad's ground glass. My imagination, like the viewfinder, flipped everything from left to right, and wobbled when I thought of a life that was together and independent. She became not Polly of the Jungle but simply Polly, a woman I'd not be able merely to imagine but might have to live with.

The men splashed downstream to gather the trout. Polly said, "Wow."

We looked at the mountains and their companion clouds, generalizing all difficulties, then walked on. We skidded downhill toward deeper shade. We rolled into a pasture and slipped her rings on our toes and held our feet under the green water of a pool to see how they looked.

I saw a snake, diamond-backed, the soft white spike of an immature rattle at the tip of its tail. It glided to an attentive halt and lay perfectly still on a log, head up, like a mosquito coil. I threw a stone and missed. The snake reacted not a bit, stayed coiled in suspension. The second stone clipped it in the back of the head and it limped away, rolled over, and collapsed. With a twig I flipped it down the gorge. We napped under eucalyptus trees, the red-and-white blossoms floating down on us.

*   *   *

During our farewell dinner, stove smoke twisted from the kitchen chimney, chasing raindrops. Dim candles swayed from small horseshoes. The squeak of guinea pigs under the table was homey and entertaining, like a TV chatting in the next room. Abuelita Pepita served a stew of potatoes, yucca, yams, and a few slices of chicken. Don Leonides snored contentedly in his hammock, the bonfire glittering in his unclosable eye as in the eye of his tasty tiger. The fire flared and jerked, bringing light to one part of the hut at a time, so that from one flare to the next I saw fish swimming on the ceiling, following rivers described by the smoke, which in the flicker might have passed for waves. I fretted about how to light this scene for Polly's film. So much slippage between literal-minded emulsion and the inner life. . . .

Ava told a joke about the *bogotano* baby who, because he knew from the moment of conception that he could survive only by selling contraband cigarettes, popped from his mother's womb squawling, "Marlboros! Marlboros!"

We told jokes about coffee, babies, disease, men and women, death. Chuckles all the time. Things stopped being merely beautiful. What had happened? A small dream? The influence of the last movie I'd seen? A blush rose and heated my ears.

"Yes, first it's beautiful," Polly said, trimming the candles, "then it's boring, then after a while it's more beautiful. I remember, after about nine months here, walking the hills and thinking this is the most beautiful picture I'd ever seen. Because by that time I knew Ava and Carlos Andres."

Carlos Andres flung himself between his mother's thighs and asked her to put him to bed. She giggled. "That's the first time he's ask me to put him to bed." He jammed his hand in her blouse. "Do you want me to cut off your arm?"

she asked, realizing that before long her baby would become another miniature man.

Polly had another month of work before her visa expired. The night before my flight left Bogotá, we partied at the salsa joint. I spun and watched her sing; her white skirt, her substance, was lit by spinning lights. I moved, she moved and the others moved, dancing, and then, like sparks we hopped away, instantly distant. We ended the evening staring into ice cubes illuminated by candlelight.

It stayed with me until Miami—the music, the flavor of rebellion, and the heat of Polly's mouth—testifying, as John Berger says of good photography, to the always slightly surprising range of the possible.

"Roni could do with a quality visit, Duke," Barry's voice said on my answering machine. She was in St. Vincent's because St. Vincent's was the best at pain management. It was a matter of weeks now, days maybe.

She gazed across her knees at the picture of Colette on the wall. Her eyes were very big. "What's Colette doing coming out of the laundry basket? Oh, I'm in terrible shape. My nights are named. I mean . . . you know . . . my days are numbered."

With deliberation, she turned her head toward the window, calibrating the pain this caused. The throbbing in her neck artery quickened. Her chest and shoulders were tattooed with purple radiation grids, like a construction site. "Did you see pain in Colombia?"

"No pain. No, Roni."

She glanced delightedly at her pink socks hanging on the back of a chair. I slipped them on her swollen feet.

Winnie, the nurse, fed her methadone pills. The pain was in her legs, which were soft sticks. It was in her lower back and all along her spine.

"Is this going to make me feel better?"

"Yes." Winnie wanted to believe it too.

"You always say that. Oh God, oh God."

Twenty minutes later the methadone kicked in. She lay back and fell asleep, lips loosening. She wasn't Roni anymore. To be awake, to be alive, to be Roni, was to experience intolerable pain.

Kettle, Ky.

I have been thinking about what you said in Colombia about feeling better at high altitudes. Even Kentucky isn't high enough for me now. I can't think straight. I feel like a tree that's been covered up by kudzu. I can only hear human voices in the distance.

I went up to Luveena's tonight and I feel much better. She said I'd gotten old looking in the last three months, but that was all right because she'd gotten fat. I saw her new baby and heard the news of the creek. They've been doing some shooting over a right of way at the head of the holler. The "hoodlums" live up there. They're from Detroit and no one gets along with them. Luveena's sure they're devil worshipers. They're feuding with her grandmother over the right of way. One night she thought she heard some shots behind her grandmother's house, so she got out there with a rifle in one hand and a shotgun in the other. Her uncle came out with a high-powered rifle and they blasted away for a half hour and there never was anyone up there. Luveena says I need me a baby so I'll stay home and not run around so much.

Where are you? I hate to wait.

I'm sorry this isn't a very cheery letter. I do love you, and wish you were lying here on my cedar bed.

Un beso,
Polly

Kettle, Kentucky was eight miles down the road from Pot. A cricket kept chirping in Polly's kitchen. She'd brought home a Colombian devil mask and a picture of Pancho Villa smoking a cigarette, wearing bandilleros and high boots, lounging with his compadres under a tree that for a posed second provided shade from the revolution.

There were muddy paw prints on the porch, deck paint pimpled with stuck bugs, a fountain with dead bees floating in it, a bird dog licking the barbecue grid, and pigs so tame they let me scratch their snouts. I came here to be touched, to find a woman's forgiveness. I sipped moonshine—clear, expensive, and paralyzing. Twenty dollars a bottle from the manufacturer.

Polly burned her fingers when she lost control of the pan she was heating lasagna in. She asked me what to put on her thumb. Butter, I said, but first hold it under cold water. This she didn't want to do because it would only hurt when she took it out. When after several minutes she did take it out, I buttered her thumb and two fingers.

"Hot buttered thumb," she said. "How long is it going to go on hurting?"

An hour maybe, I said, and put on Ray Charles's "You Are My Sunshine" to distract her.

We spread the blankets on the lawn and ate our dinner on them. We had huckleberry pie with Redi-Whip for dessert. It darkened and thundered and lightninged and began to rain. I'd never seen wind blow like that. It got blue-black and lovely and the rain thrashed so thick that the trees looked dim and spiderwebby. A blast of wind bent the trees and turned up the pale underside of the leaves and then a gust set the branches to tossing their arms wildly and next, when it was bluest and blackest—*fst!*—it was bright as day and I got a glimpse of the treetops plunging hundreds of yards further than I could see before. Dark as sin again in a second and now I heard the thunder let go with a crash and go grumbling down the sky like empty barrels rolling downstairs—long stairs, bouncing.

"Duke, this is nice. I wouldn't want to be anyplace else but here."

Polly knitted the hem of her housecoat and ran off to the chicken coop. The dogs had a big romp and a good sleep.

Luveena lived down the road in a mobile home with wall-to-wall shag carpeting and a $1,000-color TV hooked up to a $2,000-dish antenna. Polly took a picture of her and her boyfriend Weed and their son next to the dish. "Not too many people have one of these growing in their garden," Luveena crowed.

Weed used to be the poorest boy in the holler. One night when two boys wouldn't stop teasing him, he gutted one of them. After he got out of jail, he raised a little boy with Luveena, the loose woman of the creek. He was getting rich growing marijuana in a greenhouse built over his old root cellar, had it all tented with plastic. The plants were spindly, very tall, like him. He had no fear of state troopers because he kept two shotguns on the bed under the quilt. I ate a top from one of his plants but I didn't get buzzed, not a bit.

We had Cokes and pretzels and watched a memorably bad Peter Bogdanovich movie about a guy who ran through a lot of women and money.

"There's no forgiveness in this movie," Weed complained.

What Luveena said was, "Maybe there just isn't any."

Polly's old Subaru had been sideswiped; did Weed know anything about it? He looked soddenly puzzled. There was dirt along the dent, maybe a backhoe did it.

So Polly's Subaru went to Whitesburg and waited for Weed to drive it to Arkansas for body work, electrical work, and a new muffler. We borrowed a little old Fiat from a film coop couple who'd gone to Portugal to show their movie about the history of the hillbilly image at a film festival. The Fiat had an eight-track stereo and a stack of tapes, but the only ones that worked were a Jesse Winchester and a Papa John Creach.

Weed phoned to say the engine had to be rebuilt, it throwed a rod in Arkansas. He'd have to find some guys to tow it home, two hundred miles, for a dollar a loaded mile. Luveena was worried because Weed would be driving through feud-and strike-ridden hollers, and he didn't have a CB in his truck, didn't even have a gun.

Friday morning, after we'd paid a visit to Luveena, who was drying beans, I noticed the front right tire on the Fiat was nearly flat. We limped to a shed labeled GARAJ. It was run by the young man who'd shot up Weed's pickup, wounding him in the stomach. Not only was the Fiat's tire torn, it was the wrong size. The spare was flat and it was the wrong size, too. We bought a retread for $14.

Saturday morning, the Fiat wouldn't start. I jumped the battery from Weed's pickup. We drove to Sears, figuring we needed a new battery (Polly's good battery was in her Subaru). At Sears the battery tested okay. The mechanic had been born in Brooklyn but he had a hillbilly accent from twelve years in the mountains. The problem wasn't the battery, it was the fan belt, which was loose because it was the wrong size. Sears didn't deal in fan belts. So the Brooklyn hillbilly jump-started us again and we drove a couple of miles to a parts shop, parked, and kept the engine running. Four men were watching the air conditioner dribble on the front door. I bought a fan belt and we drove another couple of miles to a service station. The mechanic didn't have the right metric wrenches. He jump-started us and we drove four miles to a Texaco station and made an appointment to bring it in at nine Monday morning, when the mechanics could look at it up on the rack, since they couldn't get at the fan belt from above. We parked the Fiat in the lot and transferred the battery to Polly's Subaru, which started. Weed would pick the Fiat up first thing Monday. Polly and I, appreciating the leaves on the trees and feeling American, drove home in the Subaru.

I went to a Fourth of July barbecue at Susan Meiselas's apartment in little Italy. The sidewalk was ankle-deep with spent firework cartridges.

Susan was a friend of Polly's. Last week she missed her own birthday party because she'd been in Paris for the annual Magnum meeting. Everyone at Magnum was gloomy about the dwindling market for photojournalism in the States. "They just don't want to know what's going on," Susan said. Her German shepherd, deranged by the fireworks, kept running around the apartment, humping his mistress's pillow, shaking it in his teeth, tossing it away and running around some more.

Two years ago, in El Salvador, Susan had been in a jeep when it ran over a mine. The reporter sitting next to her was killed. Tomorrow she was going back to shoot a film there with Haskell Wexler.

She had small fiery features on a large face and a quick way of disappearing and reappearing during the party. She wasn't flitting. El Salvador had taught her to get a clear look at things while taking evasive action. She was an agile veteran, the most celebrated combat photographer in the States. Her right forearm was tattooed with medical measurements, the result of a series of inoculations for a tropical parasite which had been causing her skin to lump.

We had a brief discussion about the kind of equipment she was going to use in El Salvador. She preferred film over tape. "There's something unreal about tape. Or too real. But in the end, it always seems you just have to close your eyes and do it."

Back home, I climbed the water tower on my roof, where

I could watch the fireworks tinting the night for miles around. The city sky was crazy as a screen.

The summer I worked at Radio City Music Hall, they were showing *The Prince and the Showgirl,* which I never actually got to see, because in those days, Music Hall ushers had to stand with their backs to the screen. So the only movie I saw was in the projector rays twitching through smoke trapped over the first mezzanine, and on the faces of the audiences—pale washes of light: blues and greens and pinks that bounced off the screen and flickered across the audience like spots on the wings of an enormous moth, slowly metamorphosing. Which may have something to do with why the Irish make great natural ushers, or why I turned out to be a cameraman: someone who's neither in the audience nor on the screen.

Tonight, for some reason, or for reasons which seemed too simple, because they synchronized so plainly with a personal and national sadness—like French horns or rain telegraphing Deep Feelings in a movie—the fireworks looked feeble, a celebration of bellicose imbecility. But from her window, if she were still conscious, Roni might be able to see them. And, though forever blind to one another, we would all be sparkling and changing in the same show.

Dem Ol' Talkin' Cinematography Blues

> When Daguerre announced his great invention to the public in the summer of 1839, he explained how it worked but not really what it was for.
>
> —John Szarkowski, *Looking at Photographs*

Years from now, when cultural historians have sorted it all out, most of today's cinematography will be seen to have the charm of Etruscan statuary. Charming, but stiff. Inhibited by its ritual purposes. Whether cinematography will ever achieve a humanism as monumental and loving as Greek sculpture or Renaissance painting, well . . . these are not questions one gets paid to ponder on the set.

215

There is, nevertheless, a fine-art tradition which seeks to justify photography for its painterly qualities: such-and-such a photograph is like a Vermeer, like a Rembrandt, like a Georges de la Tour. Or, in *films noirs,* like a frame from *Dick Tracy* in the days when the strip was drawn by Chester Gould, whose command of grotesquerie rivaled Hitchcock's.

There is another tradition subversive of photography's connections to industrialism. It threads through Paul Strand, Robert Frank, Albert Maysles. It thrives on the snapshot ethic—an offhand approach, deceptively simple—and nurtures visionary "accidents." It derives from and runs roughly parallel to the ironic naturalism defined by Thackeray, Stendhal and Flaubert. *The Sentimental Education,* composed in shards of photographic observation, is the definitive *cinéma vérité* novel. Though William Gaddis continues to attempt the ultimate talkie, only James Joyce, in *Ulysses,* wrote as if he really thought he could beat photography, as if words could still do more. Joyce won. So much of the movies, in comparison, seems naive exploration.

Comparisons between photography and writing or painting, in which photography generally takes a flogging, are a search for photography's soul. We are satisfied that the older arts have a soul; we are stirred by their recognition of spirit. But photography, like slaves for the slaveholder or women for St. Thomas Aquinas, may be only marginally endowed with humanity. Pictures are just *there,* illiterately happening, bless their woggy little heads.

The trouble with talking about photography is that there is a big difference between looking at pictures and making them, something Susan Sontag and Roland Barthes are unsteady about. Photography, when discussed by Sontag or Barthes, is a melancholy, even morbid art. It reminds us, they point out, too literally of moments in the past. Pictures, like mummies, tease us about the continuation of life in a sweeter world. They are in fact mummified, extinguished, fringed by hieroglyphs which remain poignantly untranslated. In this vein, considered as a language which ought to be saying something, photography teaches us little more than to be befuddled by the way dead people peek cryogenically out of the past.

Meanwhile, everyone is merrily remembering favorite movies and looking for the soul of America. Bruce Springsteen, Steven Spielberg, Elvis Costello, Albert Brooks, Lily Tomlin, David Byrne, Sylvester Stallone, Lee Iacocca, Willie Nelson, Pee-wee Herman, Gary Hart, John Cougar Mellencamp, Jackson Browne—everybody's doing it. Even Rubén Blades, the Panamanian salsa king, is *buscando America.*

This may be a natural occurrence at the end of a century, when we get an urge to add things up. But a haunted nostalgia, sometimes sentimental, sometimes irritable, accompanies most quests for America. Perhaps memory, the genuine article—myth-piercing memory on the order of Marguerite Duras's or Gabriel García Márquez's—is a more strenuous enterprise than spinning stools in the old soda shoppe. Perhaps the problem is that we don't really feel nostalgic anymore; we just feel empty. Maybe America's memory is MIA. Movies, under these conditions, may simply be our most direct way of talking.

Whatever their essential alchemy, movies remain our national conscience, like the novel in Latin America. Movies, North America's Magic Realism, are mostly about dreams and expensive machines. In the Latin American model, Magic Realism requires a bloody history, a magically inclined readership and dense family foliage. As a literary style, it has come, since Faulkner's passing and Pynchon's silence, to feel foreign, and has been replaced by plainsong, *nouvelle* prose bordering on the anorectic. Or displaced by the movies.

Magic Realists foster memory in the European manner, by pursuing a nature-centered theory of history. Leaving movies, the organized religion of technology, to deal with the problem that has haunted the world since *The Sun Also Rises,* since Stendhal: how to behave when, wounded by the machine, you can't love.

"Every day has a different light," wrote Billy Bitzer, D. W. Griffith's cameraman. Agreed: photography is first of all a record of light. You are alone behind the camera, doubling as artist and scientist, hoping that your light—and it is *your* light—will bring it all to life. But cameramen, like everyone except poets and astrophysicists, have a documentary experience of life and love. Thus far, movies have seldom been a record of privacy, not in the way that Van Gogh's canvases resonate with the shriek of his missionary soul escaping nature.

The plots of today's movies, however, will one day seem as quaint as the theological underpinnings of medieval paintings. If you think cinematography is window dressing or a complicated nuisance, you have only to consider the shadows cast by Ava Gardner's eyelashes.

If theatrical cinematography *is* an art, then it most resembles the manufacture of equestrian statuary. The vision is monumental, bordering on vaingloriousness; the process is at once industrial and delicate. You have to know a lot about engineering and the expectations of your patron and the public. There are certain specialists you must turn to if you require the seamlessness of, say, lost-wax casting. You do the job, you display it in a public place, and you await the reaction of critics and pigeons. So cameramen tend to be material guys.

The art history of movies is disorderly dates and the stories of the artisans who worked on the great cathedrals, as much as it is the chronicles of kings and grand campaigns.

1894: the Eagle Scout era of cinematography, guessing at exposures, shooting by the seat of your pants, hand-

cranking to instinctive tempos. 1916: Billy Bitzer, noticing
the way the sun bounces off California pavement and
brightens Lillian Gish's face, discovers backlighting. Hence-
forth, most movie stars will wear haloes. 1927: James Wong
Howe gets promoted to a first cameraman when he hits on a
way to darken the eyes of blue-eyed performers. (The
orthomatic emulsion used through the end of the twenties
was insensitive to blue, causing skies to wash out and blue
eyes to go blank.) 1929: camera movement, immobilized by
sound, acquires a stammer. 1941: in *Citizen Kane*, Gregg
Toland perfects deep focus and includes ceilings in his shots.
One feels there is nothing more to see. Ca. 1951: TV, that
uncontrollable American child, demands that things look
clear and simple and frequently in closeup. 1959: Al Maysles's *cinéma vérité* cave paintings, along with Godard's
jump cuts and Jack Kennedy's sex life, reinvigorate mass
media. 1968: Gordon Willis shoots *Klute*. Stars go dark
without being extinguished. 1983: *Flashdance*. Slam-dunk
cinematography. High energy compositions, sweaty closeups, steam, backlight, very low angles, very high angles,
quick cuts, go-go-go, proto-MTV—American Capitalist Romanticism's response to Soviet Socialist Realism.

January 1987 (barely a century since Van Gogh's skies began to twitch and swirl): strolling in the aluminum winter
light of lower Manhattan, passing 841 Broadway. Here, on
the roof of this dumpy building, nearly a century ago, the
Biograph Company built its first studio. Its most advanced
feature was a platform which revolved to take advantage of
the sun's arc.

Ed Lachman's loft, a few blocks uptown, is laid out like a
cross between a flea market and an ad for 47th Street Photo:
14' ceilings, cathedral acoustics, stacks of film cans, cables,
light stands, funky furniture leftover from films he's shot and a
pair of the most enormous stereo speakers in the world.

Lachman is a cinematographer who takes chances and makes decisions. Very few cameramen have worked on so many different kinds of movies for such various sensibilities. He has shot for Bertolucci, Herzog, Godard, Wenders. He learned to be loose and resourceful. At the moment, small-eyed over morning coffee, he projects a fumbly Clark Kent demeanor.

"My father owned a movie theater in New Jersey. I grew up with pictures but I never took them seriously. I was interested in painting. I left Harvard after a year and went to France. I learned about American films in Europe."

After the success of *Desperately Seeking Susan,* Lachman had his pick of trendy scripts: Yuppie Meets Money, Yuppie Loses Money, Yuppie Gets Soul. "I got worried about selling out, so I took an assignment in Colombia. It cost me $20,000." Since then he's shot David Byrne's *True Stories,* Susan Seidelman's *Making Mr. Right* and Volker Schlöndorff's first American TV movie.

At first glance, *True Stories's* snapshoty, frontal photography looks lame. "But who's to say it's not beautiful?" Byrne asks as he drives past a row of tract homes in the tackiest process shot since *Marnie.* Byrne's goggle-eyed innocence—and Lachman's shooting—is a new kind of concentration. Its *faux naiveté* is the opposite side of coin from *One From the Heart,* another self-conscious attempt at the Great American Graphic.

Lachman's movies are not egregiously well lit, nor are his moves as suave as John Bailey's in *Cat People.* But his pictures are *different.* There's something a little "off" about them, like a farmer carrying a watering can. They are in fact sophisticated photographs, tricked out with a knowledge of art and photo history and a cavalier sense of humor about the literal-mindedness of conventional shooting. Now that the glamor has gone from simply being slick, we relax into a comfortable kind of irony: cinematography as ukelele (Byrne's first instrument).

Lachman hikes half a block to the other end of his loft to take a phone call, then returns, suddenly alert as a winged creature. "In Europe, cameramen are hired for their style. In America you're supposed to be a chameleon; you're hired because you're a cameraman. I mean, if it's a visual art, why does it have to have this kind of conformity? We don't trust images here. When MTV hit big, you felt it could liberate movie language. But now there's a conformity of ikons and clichés. Now it's selling things. In *True Stories,* we used selling as a metaphor in reverse. In *Making Mr. Right* I tried to capture, almost, bad lighting—fifties' false optimism lighting: you see everything."

One reaches, in this centerless esthetic, for labels like "eclectic" and "postmodern." Cameramen don't go around brooding about Roland Barthes, but they are finely tuned to styles and trends. The postmodern sensibility is two-dimensional, indifferent to the pathetic fallacy of the proscenium. If there is only the screen up there, if all we're actually seeing is light cunningly impersonating people, let's put aside traditional taxidermy. Let's make things yellow, or blue, or red or whatever. Why not?

Why? Think sideways: what if movies were not invented until today? What if no one had thought to make a movie until the technology of sight and recording had time to detach itself from the theatrical apparatus towed from the nineteenth century? Maybe we'd all be shooting movies that look like *True Stories* or *Aguirre, Wrath of God* or *Mean Streets.*

Cinematographers of Lachman's generation came of age watching TV, where pictures are a collection of pixels—colored electronic dots. The film process, with layers of color embedded in the emulsion, is closer to painting, or at least to what painting was when movies were invented. The result is that much of contemporary cinematography, with its quirky use of color, amounts to tuning a TV screen. This is postmodernism's scariest message: meaning is arbitrary, fictional. Which may explain the prevalence of creatures rather than human characters in American movies. The postmodern Tattoo Theory of Cinematography affirms that movies are mostly skin; if it's sensuality-with-wisdom you want, watch a Satyajit Ray movie or read Proust.

The Technicolor process peaked in the forties and fifties, along with American automotive design, and shared much of its bulbous grandiosity. Americans have the disposition to go for technical perfection and the machinery to accomplish it—libraries of filters, battalions of technicians. Postwar Europeans started with only the emulsion and, typically, a minivan or two of spluttery, antiquated lights. But with these crumbs from the table of American technology, they did, from De Sica through Fassbinder, what the Japanese did with electronics and García Máquez did with Faulkner. They made a magic that cross-pollinated and often surpassed the original.

The original Technicolor process exposed, by means of a prism system, three separate strips of film, one for each of the primary colors. In the printing process, a fourth matrix—black—was added. It was this black matrix that gave Technicolor shadows their liquid, nacreous glow. *Captain from Castile* (1947) is a primo example. *The Godfather I* was the last American film shot in Technicolor. In 1976, our Bicentennial year, the Technicolor Corporation sold its four-color machines to the People's Republic of China. There hasn't been a true black on the American screen since.

The Europeans have always considered the question of color vs. black-and-white more gravely than Americans—as an art-historical rather than simply a technical-cosmetic problem. Fellini, for example, was so self-conscious about making his first color film, *Juliet of the Spirits,* that he re-painted lawns until he got a satisfactory green.

Most of Fassbinder's films were made with low budgets, small crews, primitive laboratories and equipment con-sidered laughably inadequate by Hollywood standards. Nev-ertheless, or therefore, Michael Ballhaus and Robby Müller, who shot for Wim Wenders, have gone a long way toward redefining color cinematography.

A piece of film, rather like life itself, has two sides—the shiny and the dull. The problem is that this piece of film, the emulsion, has a few fixed ideas of its own. For example, the emulsion thinks that sunlight, most of the time, is blue. It thinks that incandescent light—the light of ordinary bulbs—is white. It thinks fluorescents are blue-green. Mercury-vapor lamps, the kind you see on highways, go yellow-green. Technically, by the standards of color temperature meter, the emulsion is correct. Most human eyes, unless they're bobbing in a disco or deranged by drugs, don't quib-ble about color temperature; it's enough to know the light is either bright or dark.

One way to shoot movies, an increasingly voguish way, is to play with the accidents inherent in the material: let the fluorescents go green, let the windows go blue. Rock video photography, or the photography of "Miami Vice" (except when it's shot by the brilliant Oliver Wood), says it's okay for things to look the way the mix of lights in the world today makes them look to the emulsion. Which is an en-hancement of the idea that it's more fun to see the world the way machines see it.

Off-screen, however, the world keeps happening. Cam-erawork keeps you close to it but leaves you too numb to think about it. It seems that only the happening—the jerky processional—is real. Most daunting, perhaps, is the realization that of all the things that kaleidoscopically happen to us, movies make the most sense. Without pictures, the anxious world would go completely crazy. We may hanker for the old blindnesses, but it's too late to rebuild them, and too early to utter. . . .

So why, all of a sudden, are cinematographers talking? One reason is that *these* are the good ol' days, and cameramen are the last cowboys. We may look back on the seventies and the eighties as the time when cinematography, a chemical-mechanical craft with roots in nineteenth-century lanternism, peaked.

Because the future is robotics and video. Stubbornly, few cinematographers take video seriously because, on a large screen, the video image still looks like cheap rotogravure. To evaluate the film image, you have to wait overnight for the lab to soup it. In video, what you see is what you get; the cinematographer, on the other hand, holds the image in his eyes till the lab delivers it. These days of expensive risk are numbered. A few years from now, when digital video and read/write laser discs are in place, the making of moving images will be a lot like playing with MacPaint.

The rather grandly titled *Masters of Light* is a collection of fifteen interviews with cinematographers alphabetically arranged from Almendros to Zsigmond. The non-professional may have to read the results with a sieve. Repetitive answers to questions such as "Do you enjoy using the 5247 film stock?" sound like fifteen shortstops telling you one after another what it's like going to their left for a double-play ball. And when the conversation turns to footcandles, the layman may feel he's blundered into a convention of kinky podiatrists.

Most cameramen are not used to talking without a tool in their hands. Which may be a good thing. Their adopted tongue, cinematography, is a gaudy dialect much given to histrionics and melodrama, like Brooklynese or Brazilian Portuguese or Homeric Greek.

Michael *(Taxi Driver, Raging Bull)* Chapman tries to explain why he selects one angle over another:

There's no sense pretending that the mystery isn't there.

Are there other people who think the same way you do?

I have no idea.

Do you ever discuss this with anyone? With Scorsese?

Everything's unconscious to Marty; everything's mysterious to Marty. No, I've never talked about it to other cameramen much. I don't think that cameramen have a lot to say to each other, in a funny way. I mean, Gordy [Willis] and I were the only two I knew who did talk to each other. But then I was his operator and we spent night after night on location with nothing else to do but drink and talk. So we talked. Other than that, I've never had a successful conversation about cameras, about cinematography with a cameraman.

For those of you perversely fascinated by the ethics of cinematography (and you know who you are), *Masters of Light* offers some startling words from Haskell Wexler, Conrad Hall and Vittorio Storaro, Bertolucci's cameraman. Frame-for-fame, Storaro is probably the most talented, if sometimes the most overwrought cameraman in the business. His interview is impassioned, semi-mystical; you can smell the steam rising from his neglected plate of pasta.

The film is so sensitive that it can register the emotion of the people present. When you see a movie, you can feel if it was done with joy, anger or passion . . . I really think that a picture is not just a picture and that we put all of ourselves into it as human beings.

For the past several years, Conrad Hall, a *wunderkind* cameraman of the sixties *(Butch Cassidy and the Sundance Kid)*, has been writing, looking for a film to direct and paying the rent by shooting commercials in partnership with Haskell Wexler. Hall's interview is refreshingly raw:

> To me, despair is a wonderful subject for motion pictures because it's such a common plight of man . . . I just want to be able to go to a movie, pay five dollars, despair for two hours and not go out and shoot myself afterwards. I want to have a good despair.

August 1985: the seventy-sixth day of shooting *The Money Pit* starts at a Mercedes showroom on Park Avenue. The walls and ceiling are mirrored. Everything sparkles: the expensive cars sparkle, the expensive lighting equipment sparkles. And between takes, wheat-blond Alexander Godunov outsparkles them all by utilizing the sun-kicks off the mirrors to perfect his tan.

The set is eerily civilized. Though the quarters are tight, there is none of the poolroom ambience of the average production. No cross-talk, very little clubhouse chatter. Everyone enunciates. Lots of "thank yous" and "you're welcomes" and "excuse mes." Many people are chewing gum—a cool substitute, one assumes, for molar-grinding.

Gordon Willis is wearing a navy-blue safari shirt that hangs creaselessly outside his pants. His thick, curly hair is gray. There is an air of abstraction about him. His face is friendly, but it is not made for laughter; it's a watcher's face.

"Money Pit," he says, "is kind of a new experience for me. It's a very high profile comedy; it's full of sight gags. It's a Spielberg movie all right: it's Pyrotechnics Incorporated. Walls collapsing, stairways falling down, rain inside the house, kind of infinitely circus. . . ."

Frank Marshall is one of Steven Spielberg's partners and the executive producer of *The Money Pit*. Instead of the customary embroidered jackets, Marshall says, each crew member will be given a Mercedes. Considering the resources of Amblin, Spielberg's production company, the jest comes alarmingly close to possibility.

While the crew copes with the mirrors (it will be a long wait: the shot involves an intricate camera move, so reflections have to be dealt with), Richard Benjamin, the director, takes a seat in one of the sales offices and discusses his director of photography.

"Gordon doesn't talk about what things ought to look *like*—like this painting, or that movie. He wants to know what the motivation of the scene is. If somebody did it a certain way in another movie, he'll say, 'Well, that movie had its motivation. What's ours?' Working with Gordon is like working with an actor."

"Look, my philosophy simply is this: I like to shoot and go home, you know what I mean?" Thus speaks the Great Gordy in *Masters of Light*. Gordon Willis is, by the testimony of his peers, in a class by himself.

Though he insists that cinematography—and filmmaking, for that matter—is a craft rather than an art, Willis is *serious*. Part of his legend is a tale about him heaving a troublesome tripod into the surf off Easthampton. One way or another, he has tamed his tools. In fact he talks, when he talks at all, like a lion tamer—eyes wary, whip in hand, always sensing the animal sensing him. "One of the secrets of doing anything is to see what you're looking at. It's knowing what's black and what's not really black. You know what I mean?"

Well, uh, yeah. . . .

If cinematography had a Hall of Fame, Gordon Willis would be one of the first ones in it. Certainly fellow cameramen would like to see him get an Academy Award, if only because the Oscar for cinematography will be worth more once he gets one. Until he does, it will be a something of a bowling trophy intent on trivializing itself.

It probably hasn't enhanced Willis's Oscar chances to have shot so many films for a director who prefers tootling a clarinet to collecting *his* Oscar. When *Zelig* was nominated for Best Cinematography, there was a certain amount of PR: an article in *People,* trade journal testimonials to the effect that Willis was a regular guy. But *Zelig* was not an upbeat film, and the Academy was not happy with the director who made it. It's survival of the cutest out there.

The problem is not really politics, nor personality. The problem is Willis's work. There's something unsettling about it, it stands to one side of the Hollywood community.

The standard of excellence that runs through cameramen's testimony about their craft is *indetectibility*—submission of style to narrative: how to achieve clarity, how to be in the right place, how to get there gracefully or wittily, how to show what's essential without bullying the viewer's eye. This shy ideal, understated technique, is what cameramen promote in the pages of *The American Cinematographer.* It is pleasant for producers and peers to hear. Beyond a certain level of expertise, most cameramen get hired for their speed and affability.

Willis's style reached the ideal vanishing point very early on. "Style" isn't exactly the word with Willis. What he has is total technical command and an attitude about what's right and wrong. One hesitates to trash everyone else's hard work by using the word integrity. In Hollywood, the all-time banana republic, it simply won't do to say and mean, as Willis does, exactly what one sees.

The difference between video and film is the difference between formica and wood. When Willis, the great puritan illustrator of pandemonium, shoots your movie, you're getting polished mahogany. The trouble is that it's hard to tell the difference with Rodeo Drive sunglasses on.

How to Tell What Kind of Camerawork You've Been Looking At

(Instructions: look at the movie, then close your eyes and turn up some music to blot out the plot. Louder. Remember that styles of cinematography can be compared to automotive styling or gate fold photography or to any "styling" that aims to romance the consumer. Most cinematography has fur dice dangling from the dashboard. Take your time, think carefully.)

You feel as if you've

(a) been flipping through back issues of *Vogue* or *Interview*

(b) spent the weekend on the beach reading old *Archie* comics

(c) been mugged by Norman Rockwell

(d) been watching Luciano Pavarotti lose fifty pounds while climbing the Washington Monument in a space suit, hitting high C's and swashbuckling all the way

(e) been to the Whitney Museum for an important retrospective of a painter whose work you should have appreciated (it was an elegant party, but everyone was tense)

(f) been looking for ninety minutes into the eyes of a pleasant but intense stranger who returned your gaze and never blinked.

If you checked *f,* you've just seen a film shot by Gordon Willis.

He is the only cinematographer ever to have been profiled

in *The New Yorker,* but he is not the hippest cameraman in the world. Alan Daviau *(E.T. The Color Purple),* Phillipe Rousselot *(Diva),* John Bailey *(Cat People, Mishima),* and Robby Müller *(To Live and Die in L.A.),* are the hippest. Storaro is hip, too. Barry Sonnenfeld *(Blood Simple)* and Joanna Heer *(Sugarbaby)* are so hip they can hardly shoot straight.

Nor is Willis always the "best" cameraman; it would not be cost-efficient to hire him to shoot a frivolous film. But what Willis has done, by the quality and consistency of his work, is to lend dignity and weight to the craft of cinematography. He is one of the very few American craftsmen in recent decades to have turned out first-class work, job after job.

The director of photography's major task is to mortise the light so scenes fit together, to preside over the hypnotic seamlessness we've come to expect of movies. This is easier to do in southern California or Sweden, where the light is consistent. Elsewhere, if there's enough light, it's often the wrong color or not in the right place. Reviewing the body of Willis's work, what you see is a technical mastery as miraculous as weather control.

Fellow cameramen look at Willis's movies and know that he is getting something extraordinary out of every frame. It's not that other cameramen don't know how to do these things, no more than composers don't know the same notes Mozart knew. It's just that Willis manages to do it frame after frame, movie after movie, while most other cameramen, for one reason or another, settle for "effects." Willis produces continuity in a discontinuous craft. He is the cameraman's cameraman.

You also see that with few exceptions he has photographed good movies, and that these movies have dealt with major American themes of recent times: paranoia, alienation, mordant romanticism, urban frenzy, the violence of the system toward the individual. He has mounted these themes with an elegance and emotional logic deeper than photo tricks.

If movies are camp followers of industrialism, then Willis is a *sui generis* corporate artist: resourceful, buttoned-up, patient, compassionate. The only Hollywood precedent for his vision is in the work of George Stevens, himself a cameraman before he became a director: Willis, like Stevens, looks at Americana with precision and middle-class steadfastness. But Willis is perhaps more accurately understood as an illustrator in the tradition of the sensual, almost sullen naturalism of Eakins and Rothko. He shares their passionately clinical probing of the medium, and—what is most astonishing in commercial photography—their respect for the point beyond which you'd rather see no more.

He is a classicist, a proportionist. He favors lenses of medium focal length, eschewing distortion and conveying an "ordinary" feel. His is a proscenium sensibility, as opposed, say, to Phillipe Rousselot's swooping eye in *Diva*. He likes to compose frames within the frame: many of his shots look through doorways or windows. His doorways or trees or telephone poles are always plumb, reinforcing the verticals. Horizons tend to be high and straight as shelves. The effect is two-dimensional composure, solidity, strength. The third dimension—depth—he adds with light. Typically, actors walk through shadows into light, and into shadow again, often stalling there. In crowd scenes, he likes to pick out the principal actor in medium closeup and follow him through the crowd, letting you feel the crowd without ever seeing it all at once. He has an almost Oriental reticence about moving the camera, increasingly so. These are his ABC's, the stylistic leitmotifs that stood out in the weeks I spent reviewing his films on cassette.

Hard to appreciate, so many years after its release in 1971, what a revolutionary film *Klute* was. Astoundingly dark for its time. A revamping of *film noir* photography. One feels *inside* the shadows.

"I'm afraid of the dark," Bree (Jane Fonda) says. This is a scary film to watch, even in the daytime. A movie that cancels daytime. But there's a richness to the shadows, and the serene, Cartesian tracking shots calm things down a bit.

Klute was shot in CinemaScope, a very wide screen format that has been giving cameramen headaches since the fifties, particularly in the framing of closeups. The human face and figure tend to take a vertical rather than horizontal configuration. CinemaScope, on the other hand, has a diorama bias; it's a flounder of a format. Willis's ingenious framing and his chiaroscuro—he paints vast swaths of shadow across the screen, as Eakins might have done—render the closeups at once romantic and paranoid. Comparison: in *Still of the Night,* another film whose subtext is psychoanalysis and its exploration of human nature's damp closets, Almendros's version of sinister is merely bilious.

In *The Drowning Pool* (1974), Paul Newman is a clean-cut private eye, and the lighting is clean-cut. The moves are graceful, almost stately. Very little is done on a diagonal.

Comes a Horseman (1978): exterior compositions feel almost vertical. No fill light in barn and cabin interiors. Most colossal nose shadow ever allowed by a major star. But *Horseman* is a sluggish movie, very down. Gratuitous Oedipal conflict. More Pakula paranoia. It comes to life only once, in Willis's 360-degree tracking shot of Caan and Fonda at the square dance.

The Parallax View (1974): conspiracy film. Long-lens, surveillance-photography look. Pakula's coldest, baddest, most loveless film. The late sixties and early seventies were a time of the paranoid epistemology of Pynchon (and Pakula). Hitchcock in despair. The investigator is trapped in a grid. No verve, too *maudit.* Warren Beatty is annihilated by light.

All the President's Men (1976): another Pakula movie

about investigation. Willis's most fluent film. It looks no more lit than a Fred Wiseman documentary. Red desks under absolutely flat, shadowless light. The nervousness of this film is ignited by sudden, high-speed tracking shots of Dustin Hoffman through office. Pretentious overhead shot in the Library of Congress, more or less disowned by Willis in interviews. Overhead is the most unnatural angle, God's point of view. Only Hitchcock pulls it off. Underground parking garage geometry: Deep Throat in blue light, Redford in warm light.

The Paper Chase (1973, directed by James Bridges): Willis's cleanest, most clinical film, though the modulations of light and dark are not severe. The compositions have a Mondrianlike geometry. Willis takes the measure of each scene, creating a stately academic environment. For Bridges, Willis also shot *9-30-55*(1978) and *Perfect* (1984), inarticulate movies about young people and their hormonal obsessions. Bridges is straining to "say something." His screenplays are spare as Robert Towne's, but often empty. Wrong-headed. With Bridges, as with Woody Allen in *Interiors,* Willis seems to be on his own. Forget the plot and just enjoy the way he leads you from light to dark to light, often in the same frame.

Pennies from Heaven (1981): a most peculiar picture. Overripe British camp by way of Beverly Hills. Steeped in forced show-biz guilt and self-contempt. Like *The Purple Rose of Cairo,* a movie hypocritically critical of movie escapism. Why was this movie made? The idea is really less complicated than the production. This should have been a smaller film, a review. It feels instead like a "big musical" staged on the dark side of the moon. Hellish, grottolike interiors. Static tableaux. We're looking at a Hopper painting of a musical rather than the musical itself. It's about as lovely as Steve Martin's dancing—an impeccably rehearsed stunt.

What is real? Steve Martin: "I'll tell you what real life

is—a bowl of dog biscuits." How movies, tinkering with our credulity, contaminate our imaginations. The lethal romanticism of the naive imagination. Compare *King of Comedy*. What if Caleb Deschanel *(The Natural, The Right Stuff,* and a pal of Willis's) had shot this movie? It would have been cheery. Willis was hired because he had the most extensive cinematographic vocabulary, and he used every word in the book.

What does Willis do best? Dis-ease. Campfire magic. Outside the circle of warmth and light and conversation, there are monsters, natural and unnatural, as in Hawthorne's forest. Willis guides our gaze at the fire and its infinite species of smoke. But the story is more in the flame and the smoke than in the words.

Willis has shot seven films for Woody Allen. Directing: perhaps no craft this side of surgery requires its practitioners to remain students, to keep up with the state of the art. Allen learned to be a wise guy in Brooklyn and Greenwich Village; he learned about great ideas and sex from Hegel, Kierkegaard, and Bergman; he fuses his firecracker genius with psychoanalysis; he learned film editing from Ralph Rosenblum; he learned *mise en scéne* from Gordon Willis. He prays every night to Charlie and Groucho: how can I make a movie—a life—that's more than just a collection of gags?

Annie Hall (1977) and *Manhattan* (1979): the warmest in Allen's continuing saga of the civil war between the sexes. The autobiography of a city that composes itself into photographs but is only occasionally picturesque. Lush, almost levitated effects. Engaging confusion of fashion and passion. A marriage of emulsion and the charms of incandescent flesh.

A Midsummer Night's Sex Comedy (1982): Laura Ashley interiors, spritely imagery. The most beautifully blocked of the Allen/Willis films.

Zelig (1982): The wedding of Leonard Zelig, the chameleon man, and his analyst, Eudora Fletcher, is "a simple ceremony captured on home movies." For the "White Room sessions," the narrator adds, "clumsy photographic lights are nailed to the walls for sufficient illumination." The interviews with Susan Sontag, Saul Bellow, Irving Howe and others are as lamely lit as the interviews on the average PBS talking-head documentary. Willis threw up a coupla lights and let it go at that. No attempt to sculpt the light. In contrast to the "witnesses" in *Reds*, where Storaro went to a lot of trouble making imposing portraits. Sometimes the wrong pictures do the right work.

Broadway Danny Rose (1983): the most succesful Allen/Willis collaboration, a perfect novella. No pretense in the photography. No superficial complexities. Allen at his least coy. How to make a movie that's more than just a collection of gags.

The *Godfather* films (1972 and 1975): one of the supreme moments in American storytelling. A saga about families, animal cunning, and seeing in the dark. Also about the Napoleonism of directing. The sheer number of setups and the seamlessness of them is astounding. The Sistine Chapel of cinematography. Willis's problem on movies so sumptuously mounted was to simplify. Otherwise, they'd look overstuffed, like *Ragtime* or *Amadeus*. Though "*Godfather* lighting" made Willis famous, he'd been lighting this way since his first feature, *End of the Road*. Ordinary light made artful. Photography's morbidity is voluptuously fleshed out. The darkness of the interiors is really an attempt to modulate Coppola's operatic tendencies. When Coppola started hiring Storaro, he may have found a *simpático* temperament, but his epic ambitions became heavy-handed, obvious.

November 1986: Elite Films, the Manhattan offices of a commercial production company, designer gray decor, glass bricks, 38D receptionist.

Jordan Cronenweth stands at the end of a darkened room twiddling the knobs on a bank of monitors. Satisfied at last with the color balance, he smiles the wry smile of an old-fashioned aviator and rolls his commercial sample reel. Watching the impeccable products whizz by, one feels a kind of aesthetic greed: this is an art of Islamic surfaces, miraculously lacquered.

Cronenweth is a second-generation Hollywood cameraman. His father, a studio portrait photographer, belonged to the same country club as Johnny Weismuller, who promised young Jordan a role in one of his Tarzan movies. For months he practiced swinging from trees, but he didn't get the part. After working with Conrad Hall (who'd worked with James Wong Howe), Cronenweth set out on his own. His first job was shooting a dog food commercial. "But I couldn't figure out how to get rid of a shadow on the cans."

He learned fast. Along with Steve Burum, Vilmos Zsigmond and Caleb Deschanel, Cronenweth has perfected the burnished, chrome-plated commercial look. You feel, watching Deschanel's heroic silhouettes in *The Right Stuff,* that you're being sold rather than shown something. But the intention is not merely hucksterish; the motivation is pride of ownership, pride in technique. It's as earnest as the lofty mechanics of a duel. Besides, Vermeer made an immortal career of it.

Jordan Cronenweth came to international prominence with *Blade Runner,* a dazzlingly, not to say dizzingly, stylish film directed by Ridley Scott, an English director-cameraman of commercials. *Blade Runner,* with its lyrical smog and shafts of backlight borrowed from *Citizen Kane,* is a hymn to the beauty of toxicity, a retro-future prophecy of digital sensuality.

Cronenweth is heir to the high Hollywood tradition. But he also shot the lovely, low-budget *Cutter's Way* and *Stop*

Making Sense, a movie whose modest visual style goes against the prevailing wisdom of music shooting. "I didn't want to use the camera as a musical instrument," Cronenweth explains simply.

We have a moment of communion on the subject of a long hand-held take in *Peggy Sue Gets Married* (when Peggy Sue meets her kid sister). This is the simplest kind of camerawork, technically no different from a home movie. Cronenweth's fondness for this scene is a somewhat wistful acknowledgment that, though he is the fancy man of cinematography, he is not wedded to fanciness.

"Why did Coppola hire you?"

"I guess he wanted some good photography."

Francis Coppola, our most operatic *auteur,* has a conductor-to-soloist relationship with his cameramen, so it's instructive to review his choices: Haskell Wexler for *The Conversation,* Gordon Willis for *The Godfather I & II,* Vittorio Storaro for *Apocalypse Now* and *One From the Heart,* Steve Burum for *Rumble Fish,* Stephen Goldblatt for *Cotton Club*—an honor roll of the very brightest and best in big-time cinematography.

Jordan Cronenweth, the mild master of special effects, is a trickster with a whim of iron. Which makes him a good choice for Coppola, who has long been trying to achieve escape velocity from conventional narrative but is not always in control of his instruments. Since *The Conversation,* he has been obsessed with and trapped in the medium itself. Is stylishness lethal to the soul of the story? Coppola's response is the impresario syndrome.

The impresario syndrome is fetishized on technique. It gives each film component—beautiful bodies, lighting, special fx, movement, sound—equal weight, and all at once. By comparison, the mundane concerns of humanity look dim. But the principle moviemaking tool is not lenses or lights or stars or words or even Winnebagos. The principle moviemaking tool is money—the dispersal of expensive materials in a manner so grand as to be matched only by the military. As with the military, so much runamuck money is often a violent thing.

The star of *One From the Heart,* the high-water mark in film design, is Vittorio Storaro, whose contract—a cameraman's dream—stipulated absolute control over the visual aspects of the movie: he could call for another take, even after Coppola was satisfied. The result is an epic spaghetti sauce, the *Brazilo-garmento* look. It's tasty and it's fun, but we are left with the metallic aftertaste of artificial intelligence.

Now and then a great shoestring movie like *Stranger Than Paradise* or *She's Gotta Have It* comes along and blows the game. Tom Dicillo, a raw beginner, shot all of *Stranger Than Paradise* with one wide-angle lens, very much in keeping with the freaky, monomaniacal spirit of the movie. Jarmusch's next feature, *Down by Law,* photographed by the celebrated Robby Müller, suffers from its cinematographic sophistication; it's long on precisely posed attitudes, short on soul.

Topheavy tech notwithstanding, Coppola is making personal films. He still seems to want the things his innocence wanted. It's painful to watch his struggle between globalism and ethnic intensity. What comes through are the mutterings of Napoleon exiled on Elba: lighting products, lighting people—what's the difference? If history wins, must love always lose? Was it worth so many costly campaigns to ask such questions?

"Nothing is absolute except exposure," Cronenweth reminds me. "The screen is like a piece of paper in a typewriter." Maybe. After sending the last chapter of *Finnegans Wake* to the printer, Joyce fretted that his writing may have become too "suburban," by which he meant detached, so concerned with display that it had lost its emotional bite.

*   *   *

Willis is touching up the trim on the picture window of his suburban New Jersey home where he lives with Helen, his wife of thirty years. The paint is pale-toast color—the color of the filters he used on the *Godfather* films. It is roughly the color of sun-faded newsprint, the shade of the Labor Day weekend before last. He wipes his fingers, stoops to inspect a bald spot in the lawn, then walks toward his meticulously tended tomato patch. We are trailed by a brace of miniature poodles: Louie, the black one, is sixteen years old, blind, and wobbly on his legs. The white one, Henry, is younger, but the hair over his eyes makes a mystery of how he sees. Willis shakes his head and smiles when Louie collides with a tomato stake.

Art is a preposterous word to use around working film people. It will get you looked at weirdly. "Creativity" is the euphemism of choice; it litters the trade journals. A TV biography of Elizabeth Taylor was canceled, according to a network spokesman, for "creative reasons." "Creativity" describes a state of grace in which commerce, ego and, lastly, taste, are all sufficiently served.

"Yeah, art is a tricky word. I have a lot of respect for what I do, and I try to get it right—what I think is right. My range is fairly wide. I've worked with, I guess, intelligent people. But I'm not an intellectual. God forbid that should ever happen to me. I have a lot of common sense and a lot of logic, I suppose. I'm a humanist.

"Generally the discussion boils down to lenses, f-stops, my new dolly—that kind of thing. But it's not about your dolly and your crane and your lenses and your meters. The mechanics . . . it's not there."

He palps a tomato and quizzes me on how the video cassette transfers of his movies looked. The wedding scene in *Godfather I*, which he'd intentionally overexposed, was "corrected," and the exquisite wine cellar scene in *Godfather II*

looked like it had been shot in a men's room on the 7th Avenue
IRT.

"Oh yeah, they'll fix it for you. Here—you like
tomatoes?"

He calls for a 9-light, a small fill unit, each of whose bulbs
can be triggered independently.

"Put a lot of lights on." Click. "More." Click-click.

"Let's have the background Yuppies!" the assistant director commands. "Yo! Yuppies! Yuppies in one second!"

"How long, Gordon?" Richard Benjamin asks.

"Fifteen minutes."

I clock this one. Such ETA's are cameramen's equivalent
of "The check's in the mail."

To mask the reflections, the prop guys rearrange some
ficus and philodendrons, whose silvery tubs create more reflections. "Fun house," Willis says flatly.

Thirteen minutes later, the first rehearsal starts. The shot is
a 180-degree pan that looks first through the showroom window, frames a Yuppie couple ogling a Mercedes, refocuses
across the street to pick up Alexander Godunov and Shelley
Long advancing rapidly through traffic; dollies back and
pans with them as they enter the revolving door (more reflections), and pans further as they stand next to a Mercedes.

Clustered around the camera are the camera operator, the
assistant cameraman, the dolly grip, the director, and the
assistant director. As the camera turns, they pivot, squirm-
ing to follow the action and keep their own reflection out of
the mirrors. One is reminded of Bugs Bunny corkscrewing
five Elmer Fudds into the floor. Godunov, the dancer, must
be amused.

Willis sits in the reception area, eying the balance of the
light, which changes as the sun arcs over 5th Avenue. He
becomes invisible, letting the machines and the director do
their job.

There is the screech and thump of a fender-bender on the uptown corner, just out of the shot. "Stand by to take it again!" the assistant director barks. "Life is real!" The tempo of the gum-chewing accelerates.

His living room is fresh, simple, spacious. He seems uneasy in the role of a talking head, at least when the subject is himself. He conveys the wariness of a man who builds the best custom fly rods in the world, but knows that most fishermen are fools.

"You know what a dump truck director is? He shoots the movie, he doesn't shoot the story. He shoots the long shot, the medium shot, the closeup, the over-the-shoulder closeups, the closeup of the closeup. Any idiot can run around with a camera and shoot a hundred setups of Indians throwing rocks at each other.

"I think simply. I'm an eliminator, not an adder. If the audience is defining it visually, you've probably made a mistake. People say, 'Gee, that's so real.' But the truth of the matter is, as soon as you photograph something, it's not real anymore. One of the things that's magical about a movie is that it's not quite real. The idea is to take something that's sophisticated and reduce it to a very simple form so that it's accessible to everybody. You have to start by saying, 'This is a movie about . . . whatever: the attack on the film should be *this*.' And so forth and so on until you finally push the idea of the movie to the surface.

"I try to fit the punishment to the crime. Every movie that I shoot has some principle in the back of my mind. There was a film I did with Jimmy Bridges called *The Paper Chase*. You had a student and you had a teacher—a teacher who, we decided, was a bigger-than-life character. When you watch the movie, you'll see that John Houseman, at the very beginning of the movie and towards the center of it, we always dealt with him in closeup, as a large head—relative to

Tim Bottoms, who we dealt with as a small, insignificant student. As the movie progressed, we peeled that back: we made Houseman start to get normal—or smaller—and Timmy started to get bigger. It's a principle of shot structure that's been applied in a few movies that I've done. We did it in *Klute* and in *All the President's Men.*

"Finally all of it is emotional. People make a fetish out of certain techniques: fog filters, smoke, on and on. The problem is, how do you do change something so that you still have a coat cut out of the same cloth? That's always tricky. See, there has to be a change, but it has to be a change that does something without doing something."

I was persuaded, despite Willis's fortune-cookie tone, that he was talking about, or working from, an unsunny feeling for human nature. His darkness, after all, raises the question of obscurity, of a complexity that may be out of place in popular entertainment. We don't go to the movies for introspection. Does he enforce his muted aurora borealis on a director's material? Is he, like Georges de la Tour, a one-joke painter? He gets sarcastically hot about such observations.

"I've never been dark; I've been emotionally structured for the moment. Bruce Surtees does things that I would never do on the screen. But as I understand it, that's what Mr. Eastwood prefers. *Escape From Alcatraz*—I saw it. I didn't see it, actually; I listened to that movie for an hour or so. If you're going to do low-key work, you can't run leader through the camera. I mean, you have to either light the set and not light the actors, or you have to light the actors and not light the set. But if you don't light both of them, the specifics of what's going on are totally lost. What I've been accused of doing was total nonsense compared to misappropriated low-key lighting. Whatever I did, there was always an idea behind it, and also relativity built into those scenes, against other scenes."

"The French gave Eastwood a medal. And Jerry Lewis."
"Jerry Lewis! God, the French!"

The crew has moved to the sidewalk in front of the Apthorp, a rococo apartment building on the Upper West Side.
Passersby, veteran UFO watchers, begin to gather. A
skinhead citizen hoots. The all-time nerd with earlaps grips
the cuffs of his raincoat sleeves.

Willis and Benjamin stand by themselves at the entrance.
Fingers forking, they mime setups. Chin-scratching, lip-
gnawing. Sum up the scene with a closeup of Willis's fingers
tracing lines on the script.

Tom Hanks and Shelley Long do a run-through of a brief
dialogue scene layered with action: dozens of pedestrian extras, a scurrying doorman, clots of cars accelerated by hotdog stuntmen. Hanks and Long stroll out of the Apthorp;
she dashes through traffic to catch a cab. "How're my curls
doing?" she inquires after three rehearsals. The stylist re-
stores their flounce.

Willis points at the sun, as if commanding it to descend
properly. His eyes turn hawkish. He calls for the viewfinder,
tape measure and chalk. Gremlins disperse. Hieroglyphics
are chalked on the pavement signifiying lens height and
dolly position. Willis sits in a camp chair savoring a straw-
berry popsicle. It's ninety-two in the shade, the air is soupy.

"How's the sun treating you today?"

He grunts. What I really want to know is why he is
shooting a Spielberg film. Spielberg may be the wittiest
industrialist in the world, but his slapstick pursuit of hi-
tech excitement has not been a Willis specialty. However
fetching Spielberg's characters may be, they are creatures,
not people.

1982: Life makes little sense, says rock video, but anyway
there's dancing. There *is* lots of dancing, the movies agree,

somewhat defensively, and in the end there is some sense, maybe even justice.

For the past few years, the School of Spielberg and its branch campus, MTV, have been posing the Big Question (big, that is, for the generation to whom World War II is a grainy newsreel and World War III a video game): is the new world—i.e., technology—malignant or benign?

The Spielbergian answer is at once ingenious, scary, reassuring, and cute: Even Suburbia Has a Subconscious; or lately, All God's Chillun Are Toys. The MTV response is easier to dance to: Somewhere in Every Yuppie Soul There Lurks a Little Richard.

Other variations are acceptable: after the sexual revolution, Pee-wee Herman's full-frontal infantilism is okay—a soothing diversion, at least, from Rambo's rage. It's not that these visions are simple-minded; nothing is that simple-minded, even in a world bemused by media. They are becoming predictable, not to say evasive.

No one is instinctively fond of the future except kids and Californians. Spielberg assures us that the future—being "grown up"—however scary, is essentially suburban, safe.

So movies continue to make a perfect world—perfect love, perfect heroism, perfect pain. And money, so much money. And Gordon Willis is currently living in this world.

He walks fifty feet to dispose of his popsicle stick by the trunk of a long-suffering city tree. "Steven's wonderful because he's got a very fine sense of now, of what you have to deliver as a moviemaker. He's got a wonderful grip on the mental age of the country, he's got it by the throat. It's going to be very interesting to see Steven step out into a different kind of moviemaking. You get in trouble if you think too old. I'm not sure Steven will ever grow up. It might be to his detriment to grow up.

"It's very hard to find directors who understand and appreciate the totality of good moviemaking. Coppola—he has a good sense of opera. I got Francis at the right time. But I don't know what Francis thinks he's up to these days. He asked me to shoot *The Cotton Club,* but I knew it was going to be a shitbath. I don't believe in sitting in trailers and talking to people over loudspeakers. Removing yourself from the actors, removing yourself from the floor, removing yourself from the smell of what's going on . . . not good."

February 1986: lunch on Melrose Avenue with Teddy Churchill and Allen Daviau, who's just been nominated for an Oscar for his work on Spielberg's *The Color Purple.*

Spielberg shares with Disney, Hitchcock and Truffaut a genius for camera placement, for composition and juxtaposition. Their intuitions of childhood are different. Truffaut's is a survivor's tenderness. Hitchcock's is terrified and vengeful. Disney's is Michelangelo without Greece or the Church. Spielberg's is a sunny skylight installed in the suburban subconscious. The vivacity of Allen Daviau's cinematography promises the gleeful unwrapping of endless presents, and is perfectly suited to Spielberg's childlike wonder.

Daviau sends back a bottle of so-so wine. He pulls it off with aplomb because he is a regular and he knows what he's talking about. He is a precisionist, a connoisseur with a cause: the imminent introduction of hi-resolution video, he insists throughout four sumptuous courses, will only smudge the cameraman's palette. If we want something really sharp, why not wait three years for a practical digital system? The trouble is that Japanese manufacturers want to cash in by rewiring the world with the European system, an "improvement" that won't significantly improve anything. If this happens, we'll have to wait another twenty years before the market's ready for digital TV and we can start making the pictures the medium is capable of. More wine? Dessert? Some coffee?

Allen conducts Teddy and me to a store specializing in movies on video disks. He is a regular here too. He scoops up an armful of disks, inquires about others on order and, despite my demurral, presses the manager for a discount on video disk players for his benighted pals from New York.

Teddy scans the many unanswering machines and scratches himself. "Growing up in the Industry, you want to be the most efficient art tool that ever lived. But we're dealing in the realm of garbage here, Duke. 'Our computers are down; it's only a cold sore; Audi, the art of engineering.' You need something to keep you real. You know that feeling, Duke? That's a famous feeling."

The assistant director squeezes his walkie-talkie and asks one of his production assistants how the traffic control is coming along. "Just tell me as soon as you're in some sort of quasi-human shape there, Jimmy."

"Wonderful, piece of cake," Jimmy squawks invisibly. "It's just a pain in the ass, that's all."

The traffic's getting surly: sirens, bells, ambulance whoops, squad car gobbles, stuck-record shrieks of teeny boppers who've spotted Tom Hanks: "*Eeee,* I don't be*lieve* it! *Eeee,* I don't *believe* it! *Eeee,* I don't be*lieve* it!" No one seems to be able to locate the Dairy Queen bell, which jingles unsilenceably. The din increases: fire engines hoot. A four-alarmer has developed just around the corner. Willis stares, alert as a deaf detective.

"Woody—if there's any failing there, it's that he reflects too much on other people's work. It's part of his charm, but sometimes it gets in his way. I've looked at a great deal of Bergman's material, but I'm not that much of a fan of his later stuff. It's a little northern and heavy and he's too preoccupied with death. His early films were so full of life; I loved them. But he got unhappy. So Scandanavian. It's dark up there. Nothing to do but brood about God.

"But of course Woody loves that all that. He's a very unique man. He's got a good mind, a good imagination. You're not wrangling with pedestrian ideas. Which makes it easy for me to shoot well. It was heaven, I had a lot of freedom. I loved *Broadway Danny Rose*. It was so New York. I thought a lot of people are going to like this movie, but . . .

"If every director was a Woody, this would be a wonderful business. But then he wouldn't be unique, would he? Now he's working with somebody else, heh-heh. I got crossed up on scheduling, had to stay in California for *Perfect*.

"More and more, it's a simplistic time. A studio wants to make as much junk food as quickly as possible and get the biggest return in five minutes. That's the thinking, right? So what happens is, it becomes impossible to make a range of movies.

"That doesn't mean I don't like violence on the screen. I mean there's romance in killing, if it's done the right way on the screen. But just blowing holes in people's heads, it's a kind of commercial poisoning. With the coming of *Rambo*, I expect pretty soon to see them linking five hundred bridges together and blowing them up one after the other for an hour-and-a-half and that will be it. It's scary because it's what everybody's been reduced to."

February, 1986: A top-down winter day in L.A. Assistant director Harvey Waldman is working on a breakdown of special effects for a low-budget movie, numbering each shot.

    147 set Pontiac afire
    149 Pontiac explodes
    149 window shatters

155 smash door
159 spear Fenton
161 gunshot to head
162 stabbing vamps
163 gunshot deputy
164 crumbling vamps

"Hey Duke, I got this script maybe you could help me on."

"Sure. What's it about?"

"Well it's not so much a script yet as a concept. . . ."

"So what's the concept?"

"Well it's not so much a concept as it is a title. See, the whole thing is in the title."

"So what's the title?"

"Attack of the Killer Nuns."

Right. I flick the fast-forward switch on *Rambo, First Blood.* Uh-oh—bla-*DOOM!*—Rambo's been dynamited in a cave by the bad cops, who are determined to hunt him down and kill him for sport. I've been counting his dialogue word-for-word, and so far, halfway through the movie, I still have six fingers to go. This is not very inventive violence. This is the holy pain of a child, just a maze of very ordinary troubles, hyperventilated by cameras and gunpowder. Lumpen problem solving. Don't we have anything to sell anymore but bombs and bad dreams? Who's minding the store? Fie on thee, wax apple of American movie Eden! This guy is a infantile fascist given to tantrums.

"Yeah, but so was Jack Kerouac," says Harvey.

It's pretty dark in the cave (it should be, there's no electricity there). *Rambo, First Blood* was shot by Andrew Laszlo, a veteran, very fast and adaptable. Laszlo works rather like Bruce Surtees, who shoots most of Eastwood's films. There's never been a movie darker than *Escape From Alcatraz;* Eastwood spends a reel or two crawling through air-conditioning ducts. Looks like Surtees lit it with a flash-light. Works brilliantly.

Okay, that's better now: Rambo's got a torch, made out of rags still incredibly dry. The things some guys learned in Nam! Okay, now he's stumbling and spinning and splashing around in the water and okay now the light is sparkling in his sweat and glistening on his slobber and gleaming on the slimy walls and now—whoops—it looks like maybe the rat-infested water is going to extinguish his last hope, the only light illuminating this scene . . .

Wait a minute. Why is this so beautiful? There's no deny-ing it: this shot—the trickle-down savagery of it—says more about us than a million more polite pictures. Not that it makes much sense. Just a lot of money. But compared to what is to come, the coarseness of today's image industry is warm and humanly wonderful. At least we are still able to dance around our graves. Rambo evokes an unendurable hideousness, an apocalypse, a holocaust forever brewing, that cannot be articulated, or if uttered, can barely be heard. Stallone is our Ayatollah, our fundamentalist soldier-saint railing against the new. And this is perfect Reagan-era moviemaking: it lies to us but for the most part we like it. Because movies are realer than most politics.

Harvey rolls his shoulders and goes on typing.

169 steel trap on foot
186 kick in window
186 set coffins afire
189 shatter gym window
192 set cellar afire
197 smoke & fire
201 stab Axel
 77 eat Sherry
 97 suck blood of cow
121 Joe spears Abner
144 gunshot

December, 1986: in a loft in Woodstock, New York, Danny
Lyon is screening *Willie,* his feature-length documentary
about Chicanos doing hard time in New Mexico jails.
Danny Lyon is the kind of Daniel you call Danny right
away; his belt is missing a loop in his jeans. He is a confron-
tational, political-personal photographer, a Guggenheim fellow, best known for *Conversations with the Dead,* his book
about Texas prisons that changed the state's penal laws.
He's made many films, but PBS won't show them. Tonight's
crowd is comprised of serious students respectful of funless
evenings.

The reason for his unsuccess Danny attributes to his dis-
interest in narrative. He is being disingenuous, or he hasn't
thought this through. The shagginess of his camerawork is
as distracting as the fender-polishing of commercial style.
Danny never troubled himself to master the professional
lingua franca. He barely wears a belt; he'd certainly never
wear suspenders.

But *Willie* is not a video game. This is dangerous stuff.
This is sloppy life, pornographically fascinating and re-
pellent.

So you root for Danny Lyon. Remembering the shock you
felt on hearing Dylan for the first time, you want to believe
that the only thing that matters is authenticity of feeling.
Danny delivers the primordial photographic thrill: transub-
stantiation, a conviction that the people and things on the
screen are really *there.* His photographic fundamentalism is
more than a simple record, the sort of thing amateurs expect
of cameras. "The best thing about his work is the contact he
makes," someone remarks, touching on how hard it is for
photography, and especially cinematography, to see *inside.*
Think of the marmoreal surfaces of *Scarface,* the frenzy *sans*
insight.

Willie stuns us out of the trance induced by the big-time
image industry. But its naturalism is as *au courant* as Jimmy

Carter's cardigans or the sixties' *cinéma vérité* credo: care for the ordinary, put things in proportion, be alert, be kind. We want feelings bigger than ourselves. We want the Movies—part fluorescent dazzle, part honesty—the light belonging to this time and no other. Prettiness is aspired to. We've lost our taste for being told that we're on the wrong side.

The Saddle River soda shop is a cute time capsule from the forties. The waitress nods maternally; Willis is a regular. He orders a black-and-white shake. We are not in the Polo Lounge.

"Right now, at this point in life, I'd like to shoot a good period piece. That's what I'd love to do. They're becoming more and more expensive to shoot, however. But I enjoy making them. I just enjoy making movies. Some people would ask why—you know, after being through it so much. But it is an interesting life. I don't mind the marathon aspect of it. There's a continuity about telling a story that I enjoy. I like having that."

"I've been trying to decide, looking at all your films, where the real Gordon Willis is—which film has the most of you in it."

"What did you decide?"

"*Klute*—in the role of John Klute, the dedicated investigator, the quiet, caring watcher."

"Pretty good guess." He blinks, makes a move to leave, settles back. "Remaining an individual in this business is not easy. But I'm not *trying* to be an individual. It's a matter of conviction and doing your job. Human beings are strange. We're all kind of strange. I mean, we can't wait to invent the thing that'll snuff everybody out. We can't wait to invent the thing that will remove the responsibility of what we do in our everyday lives.

"I've learned a lot about actors and I've learned a lot

about, oh, other things. I've waded through the bog of the motion picture industry and I would do it again if the story was wonderful. I've played around. I'll play around again, but better. I guess there's a certain reality to what I put on the screen, but in my own mind, I can pretend to be a romantic. I see romance in a lot of things that some people don't see it in."

It is futile, finally, to think of Willis as a painter. For all the similarities—composition, tonality—a picture is simply not a painting, however artfully arranged. The plausible comparison, if anything is plausible here, is that Gordon Willis is the Gerard Manley Hopkins of cameramen.

Hopkins, the most technical of poets, so concerned with the mechanics of words, with geometrizing their relationship to the physical world, is like no other poet. He was a painter who became a priest (Van Gogh was a failed priest who became a painter). Deprived of paint and canvas, Hopkins developed an idiosyncratic stubbornness about observation. With him, technique and the forces of nature become one.

Willis's work is an exercise in "instress" and "inscape," Hopkins' code words for a magical rightness in seeing. He suggests firmly that there is something precious, sacred about seeing.

> I was looking at high waves [Hopkins writes in his journal in August of 1872]. The breakers always are parallel. . . . They are rolled out by the shallowing shore just as a piece of putty between the palms. . . . The slant, ruck, or crease one sees in them shows the way of the wind. The edge between the comb or crest was as smooth and bright as glass. The silver white in front marks where the air begins, the pure white is foam, the green/solid water. It is pretty to see the hollow of the barrel disappearing as the white comb on each side runs along the wave gaining ground til the two meet at a pitch and crush and overlap each other.

One of the secrets of doing anything is to see what you're looking at.

November 1986: the set of *The Glass Menagerie* is an atoll of imagination on twelve-foot stilts. Elsewhere, in the darkness of the studio, there is a silence so acute it amounts to a slight deafness, like fog. Michael Ballhaus, fresh from his success on *The Color of Money,* is watching the take on a TV monitor set on top of a stove.

John Malkovich delivers his line, exits and settles next to Ballhaus, waiting for the director, Paul Newman, to call cut. Malkovich twists a towel around his fist, searching for something to punch. "Tell me what you think of my performance."

"It's good." Ballhaus reflects. His parents were theater people; he pays attention to actors. "It depends on the energy off her [Joanne Woodward]." In subsequent takes, Malkovich dials his intensity downward.

Like Ballhaus. He has not really had a chance to strut his stuff since he came to the States. He has assimilated by becoming the ultimate user-friendly cameraman. "I think there's a line from Fassbinder to Scorsese," he says during a lull. "But I'm not too optimistic. In a country as big as this, though, there might always be a couple of directors with integrity and a couple of good stories. I would never shoot a film like *Top Gun*. Never. That's the kind of movie Goebbels made."

Paul Newman is shoveling popcorn into his mouth like a kid at a cartoon show. "Michael's got a great sense of moving the camera. We talked about warm light for the past; a cool, wasted look for the present." Newman stops chomping, thinks about what he really wants to say. "Look, what it is, he's a nifty guy."

Later, in the off-set dimness, Ballhaus says, "The most interesting thing is that you could shoot right now, here, in

this room." He is a cinematographer to whom the present—
any shot—seems vividly possible. He's placed no more than
five lights on today's set, and small ones at that.

"They kid him about it," says Drew Rosenberg, a prin-
cess masquerading as a production assistant. "Michael just
smiles. He's quick, he's quiet." Drew is having a problem
with her diet Coke: the poptop has broken off without
opening the can. "Does anybody have a hard tool?" she im-
plores.

December 1986: Harry Matthias and Pierre Mignot, Robert
Altman's cameraman, are fending off the despondency of
listening to Christmas carols in the lobby of the Montreal
Sheraton. Ed Lachman joins us, then Jean-François Robin,
the disarmingly mild Frenchman who shot *Betty Blue*.
Johanna *(Sugarbaby)* Heer is expected.

We're here to take part in a Canadian Film Board panel
discussion about, uh . . . gee, what *are* we going to talk
about? The conversation stumbles off in search of the best
16mm lab in L.A., the most practical spot meter.

Jean-Jacques Beineix, the director of *Diva* and *Betty Blue*,
takes his seat on the dias. His eyes are black and hard and
bright. One feels registered as an image. He speed-reads
people. "The imperialism of hardware over software . . ."
he begins, and sets off on a lengthy explication of his work,
utterly charming and elegantly devoid of any conceivable
meaning.

Beineix's movies are semiologically sly atonements for
scopophilia, the "sin" of voyeurism all filmmakers, and
cameraman in particular, *de facto* commit. *Betty Blue* starts
with steamy lovemaking under a print of the Mona Lisa, *the*
painting that looks back at you. After that, life unravels
tragically. Beineix's movies, like *One From the Heart* or
Rumble Fish, are about the felicity of images vs. the unhap-
piness of the humans who inhabit them. Where's the crime?

Is this an original sin? What's wrong with this picture? Maybe even impresarios feel there is something offensive about spending so much money merely to peep.

The panelists' talking heads are projected on a mammoth proto-Maoist TV screen behind us. In the vivisectionist spirit of the modern m.c., I inquire about the meaning of our work. Are cameramen accountable? Are artists accountable? Are bankers accountable? This is beginning to feel like a demented experiment to prove the existence of the soul by weighing the body immediately before and after death.

"I think it has peaked already, the kind of commercialism we've been seeing," Johanna Heer observes. "Eighty-six was a turnaround year, don't you think?" Her eyes are intense as a silent movie heroine's. "I am a visual artist," she announces. Insufferably arty as it sounds in this arena, Heer is right.

Once in a great while, you see something that changes the way you feel. *Sugarbaby*'s shimmying dolly shots are a wonder out of nowhere, something no cinematographer has thought to do so far. It's as if a Navajo suddenly started weaving circles into her blanket. In *Sugarbaby,* the camerawork works *with* the people; it is witty but not depersonalizing. Heer's moves—the sympathy of her camera for the pulse of emotion—are the first radically new ideas in cinematography since *Klute*'s chiaroscuro colors. But unlike Willis's, her style is uncopyable; where it will lead, I have no idea.

Later, there is a party at a fancy lodge on a hill overlooking Montreal. The Sony Corporation has provided a laser light show with tom-toms and dancers from a colorful, faraway land. Harry Matthias's girlfriend, a painter, stands coatless on the frigid patio and points out Orion, the constellation, not the film company.

Checkout before dawn to make an early flight home. The snow is falling in plump, stagy flakes. Ed Lachman slithers back from a night on the town. Now, in the lobby, he is taking snapshots of a landscape painting next to a lamp, leaning into it. Snapclicksnap.

In the beginning, before things got Bergmanesque, the job of the cameraman was to perforate the film, load it in the camera, crank it, develop it in a bathtub and project it.

Joseph Walker, a relative latecomer, started shooting in 1916. With his wife Juanita, he wrote *The Light on Her Face,* a memoir of a career that included many of Frank Capra's finest films. Walker learned to shoot movies before "movies" was a respectable name for them, when a radio was a wireless, when a driver was an automobilist, actresses were named Nell, and leading men named Ronald. Want to know why cameramen used to wear puttees and caps turned backward? Read *The Light on Her Face.*

In jaunty Tom Swift prose, Walker writes a careening, gee-whiz, one-thing-after-another narrative. He warms to the story of his 1919 expedition to the wilds of northern Canada: "Nell and her business-manager husband, Ernest Shipman, along with self-assured James Oliver Curwood, the noted author of adventure novels, held the center of attention in this deluxe Pullman. . . ." Though nearly frozen by the end of the chapter, Walker remains indefatigably Californian, daunted only by the prospect of unemployment. "How many miles to Hollywood?" he cries from the tundra. "How many miles to civilization? How many miles to a lab?"

The studio cameraman, in Walker's time, was regarded as a fashion photographer with a sensual eye for industrialized flesh. He showed up for work wearing a suit and tie and advanced his career by glamorizing aging actresses and tacky sets. One of Walker's best stories recounts a meeting called by the ineffable Harry Cohn to determine the cheapest way to visualize heaven for *Here Comes Mr. Jordan* (later remade by Warren Beatty as *Heaven Can Wait*). Walker's suggestion—a budget-conscious carpet of dry ice fog—prevailed.

The Hollywood autobiography follows a form as rigid as a sonnet, and *The Light on Her Face* concludes with the classic valediction, awarding its author a merit badge for Beauty. "Had the glamorous days slipped by? We sold beauty in our time. Idealism. But *now* what were we selling? What did the future hold?"

Corny as these remarks may be, they are a *geschrei* for the perfect shot—the eloquent shot, as Conrad Hall says—the shot that satisfies the craftsman's own standards, pleases the crowd and illuminates the soul of the picture. But Hollywood is very far from heaven; one grows sick of theoretical uncertainties, and we soothe ourselves by becoming day-to-day data dolts. Still, there's got to be more to it than gamma toes, one-quarter double-fog filters . . .

In some dimly lit recess of our cartoon hearts, brooding on ancestral memories of the days when the cinematographer was pretty much the whole show, cameramen know that implicit in movies is a promise to replicate the experience of the complete sensorium. This may account for dodo devices like Smellovision and 3-D, but behind the impulse is also the stumbling fervor of the true explorer, the mapper of belief in the world beyond—magically foreseen and ritually accessible, something like the afterlife. This is the yearning behind *Lost Horizon* (filmed by Walker), *Close Encounters* (Zsigmond) or *The Purple Rose of Cairo* (Willis).

So don't fret about faded beauty, Joe Walker. Vittorio, lighten up. Teddy, stop snarling. And Conrad, don't despair. Anyway, don't sell despair to yourself. Because in heaven, my friends, in the perfect future, all images will be utterly beautiful and true and real. Sure, we'll still have to watch Harry Cohn's tacky sets on TV, but this will be strictly ceremonial. Old movies will be monuments to the primitive earthbound past, warmly regarded in the big movie show in the sky. Old timers will reminisce about them, recall personal experiences with them, mostly exaggerated, and sigh. So picture yourselves up in heaven not as martyrs or prophets or scholars—not high up there with the fully illuminated or superlatively holy saints or anything—but just regular nice guy cameramen saints, all dues paid.

Yes, my friends, there is life after rock video. It may be, at best, a Thurmon Munson sort of immortality, but it's all we've got. Saint Gordy, pray for us sinners.